FOLLOW LOVE

A DIAMOND CREEK, ALASKA NOVEL

J.H. CROIX

This is a work of fiction. Names, characters, businesses, places, events and incidents are either the products of the author's imagination or used in a fictitious manner. Any resemblance to actual persons, living or dead, or actual events is purely coincidental.

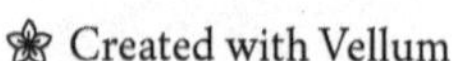 Created with Vellum

DEDICATION

To my Mom, always there for me in every possible way. To my Dad who cheers on my dreams. And to my husband - the drum-beat in my heart.

Sign up for my newsletter for information on new releases & get a FREE copy of one of my books!

http://jhcroixauthor.com/subscribe/

Follow me!
jhcroix@jhcroix.com
https://amazon.com/author/jhcroix
https://www.bookbub.com/authors/j-h-croix
https://www.facebook.com/jhcroix

CHAPTER 1

Nathan leaned over the side of the guide boat and tugged on the fishing line. While he didn't know what was on the other end, it was definitely live because he could feel the sense of vibration. Still tugging on the line, he looked over his shoulder to call to his oldest brother, Jared. Just as Nathan turned away, water splashed his shoulder. Turning back, he glimpsed a king salmon, now fighting madly against his grip on the line. King salmon were called king for a reason; even average ones weighed in at fifty plus pounds with some topping one hundred and more. He guessed this one to be medium sized, roughly two feet long and had to wrestle to keep hold of the line.

"Damn!" he said as the salmon bumped against the side of the boat. "Could use a little help here," he called. Wrestling a slippery salmon wasn't easy.

Michael, the man who caught the king salmon, started to move towards Nathan, fishing pole in hand.

"Stay put, I don't want the line to loosen at this point," Nathan directed. His other older brother, Luke was coming his way from the front of the boat.

Nathan and his brothers ran a commercial fish and guiding business, The One That Didn't Get Away, in Diamond Creek, Alaska, a small town on the shores of Kachemak Bay. Kachemak Bay was one of Alaska's coastal jewels, straight out of a postcard. A large bay off of Cook Inlet in South central Alaska, Kachemak Bay was home to several tourist hubs in Alaska. Though small, Diamond Creek was busy and catered to its tourists with world-class restaurants, shops and art galleries. Mountains encircled Kachemak Bay, eerie translucent blue glaciers were tucked between a few mountains, and Mount Augustine, a lone volcano, sat sentry in the bay. Along with the natural beauty, the bay was famous for its salmon and halibut fishing, drawing hordes of tourists from spring until the snow fell.

Today, they were hosting a family - Michael, Tess, Simon and Jordan - for a full day of fishing. Michael was father to Tess and Michael, both adults, and grandfather to Jordan. Nathan had to tamp the impulse to flirt with Tess. He couldn't keep his eyes off of her. She had short honey-colored hair that curled in a tousled bob around her face. She had a soft, rounded figure, curves in all the right places. Her ginger colored eyes and luscious mouth, bow shaped and bright pink, kept drawing Nathan's gaze. Though quiet, she had a sly sense of humor in the company of her family.

"So Dad, I thought the plan was to catch a record size halibut," Tess commented sardonically.

"I'll take a king salmon," Michael replied with a wide grin.

Nathan looked to Tess. "Oh don't worry, we'll make sure he gets that halibut," he said with a wink. For a flash, he saw a spark of interest, a tease, in her eyes and he almost lost his hold on the fishing line. *Focus on the fish, stupid.* He had to force his eyes away from her—she was distractingly delectable.

Luke reached Nathan's side and leaned over with a net as the king salmon continued to thrash against the side of the boat. With Nathan maneuvering the feisty salmon into the net, he and Luke lifted it over the side together. Just as they set the net down, Luke lost his grip, and the salmon flung itself free from the net and slapped Nathan in the face with a slimy tail. He lost his footing and slipped onto the boat deck, landing just beside the salmon.

"Really?!" he said, looking to the salmon who ignored him and gave another flick of its tail.

Luke shook his head, trying and failing to hold back a grin. "Sorry about that, couldn't keep a hold of the net."

Nathan rolled his eyes. "Noticed that. Only wish you'd been the one whacked in the face."

A towel landed in his lap. He turned to see Jared grinning at the wheel of the boat. "Thought you could use that."

Nathan snatched the towel up and wiped the slime off his cheek. Standing, he tucked the towel over his belt and looked to Michael. "Your call on whether you keep this one or release it. You have a king tag, so you can keep it if you want."

Michael came to stand at his side. He looked admiringly down at the salmon. "Let's release it. My goal is halibut and if I'm gonna keep a king, I want it to be record size. Let me get a picture though." He quickly snapped a photo with his phone.

Nathan nodded and turned back to Luke. "Let's get this back in the water. Think you can manage to keep me from getting knocked down again?" he asked Luke.

"Oh I'll do my best. Salmon love a fight though. He seems to have settled down now," Luke replied.

Nathan looked down at the king salmon, which lay still on the deck, its gills laboring. "Good size one, at least fifty pounds," he said. With efficiency, he and Luke went into motion. Luke held the salmon's mouth open while Nathan grabbed the hook and carefully worked it out. In short order, he picked the salmon up and lifted it over the side of the boat, holding it steady in the water for a moment before gently letting go.

* * *

THE SILVER of the salmon flashed briefly in the water before disappearing under the waves. Tess stared out over the water for a moment to see if it would reappear, but all she saw was the sun's reflection against the water. She lifted her gaze to look at the volcano sitting in the distance. She'd read plenty of tourist materials on the flight to Alaska from North Carolina and learned that she was looking at Mount Augustine, which sat alone in this area of Kachemak Bay. It rose starkly from the water, wispy clouds floating around the top. It had erupted twice in recent decades, once spewing ash for days at a time. The latest eruption had been subtler, if there was such a thing as a subtle volcanic eruption, but ash had still disrupted flights in and out of Alaska. The volcano seemed lonely to her, but then she wondered if she thought practically everything seemed lonely since most of the time she felt that way. With a mental shake, she turned to look towards her father.

He was getting ready to drop his line back in the water, listening patiently to one of the guides about the best way to prep his line. His smile was wide. This fishing trip to Diamond Creek, Alaska was a dream for him. He'd planned to go for years. Her mother, Celine, had come on the trip with them, but was prone to seasickness, so she'd stayed ashore to visit the many tourist shops in town. Tess had joined them for this trip in addition to her brother, Simon, and his son, nine-year old Jordan. While Tess might not be the fishing connoisseur that her father was, she loved the outdoors and enjoyed fishing.

Tess shifted her gaze to Nathan who was talking to her father. The three Winters brothers ran the guiding business, The One that Didn't Get Away. Tess guessed Nathan to be the youngest. All three had almost identical black wavy hair. The only difference in how unruly it was. Nathan's was the shaggiest, his black curls almost touching his shoulders. He had dark blue eyes while the other two brothers had green eyes. Tess had to keep dragging her eyes away from Nathan, which annoyed the hell out of her. He was the quintessential outdoorsman—handsome with a rugged, sexy edge—so sexy that a mere glance sent her pulse wild.

He and his brothers had been nothing but kind and funny. They happily regaled her father with fishing stories and earnestly shared his love of all things fish. She could tell they'd let him talk all day and that earned major points with her. They were also kind to Jordan who was so excited about this trip he was practically vibrating. He was a relentless font of questions, filled with a sense of curiosity and wonder.

Her father caught her absentminded stare and waved her over. She stepped around a cooler and dodged a fishing pole with the few steps it took to get to him.

"Tess, honey, I was just telling Nathan here that I used to take you and Simon fishing when we went out to Cape Hatteras in the summers. It made me remember that time you caught a giant grouper," her father said, curling an arm across her shoulders.

Her father looked towards Nathan again. "She was around Jordan's age, eight or nine, and had a blast tugging that fish into the boat. Grouper's good to eat. Not quite as famous as Alaskan salmon and halibut, but cooked right, it's delicious."

Nathan turned his bright blue eyes to her. They crinkled at the corners when he smiled. "So have you inherited your father's love of fishing? Or you're just a good sport and tag along because you know he loves it?" he asked with a wink.

Tess felt her lips curling in a smile, almost in spite of herself. Butterflies swirled in her center, rattling her composure. Nathan's smile was sparks to tinder—hers, that is. She forced her attention to the moment, tilting her head to the side and glancing to her father. "It's a bit of both. I almost always go fishing with my dad, so you could say I tag along. But then, I love it whenever I go. Hoping to take my turn at a halibut in a bit here. I was just waiting to give dad a chance to be the first to catch one."

Her father smiled even wider, if that was possible. He was so damn happy since they'd stepped off the plane here, just about everything elicited a smile.

Nathan glanced back and forth between them. "That makes your dad happy," he said with a chuckle. "Whenever you're ready, let me know. May not have known your dad long, but I doubt he cares who catches the first halibut."

Tess didn't try to avoid smiling this time. "You're right about my dad, which is why I want him to catch the first halibut. As much as he loves to fish, this is his to take." She looked to her father again. "Get that line back in the water before Jordan or Simon beats you to it. You love talking about fishing as much as actually fishing, but you can talk and fish at the same time." She leaned her shoulder into him with a soft push. "I'll sit with you." She turned back to Nathan. "If he doesn't bring a halibut up in the next half hour, how about helping me get going?"

Nathan nodded. "Of course. That's my job."

"How about you help me get set up this time?" her father asked Nathan. "I thought I knew how far to let the line go, but I'm not sure."

Her father's arm slid off her shoulders as he turned to step to the side of the boat. Nathan gave her a long look before he followed her father. Her heart fluttered and she felt a flash of heat in her core. It had been so long since she'd felt that way towards any man, it was unsettling. She distracted herself by looking around the boat. Jared appeared to be the assigned boat driver. He stood at the helm, holding the steering wheel in a relaxed grip. Of the three brothers, he was the most reserved, but still friendly with a wry sense of humor. Luke, the other brother, was busy talking with Jordan. He knelt beside Jordan and appeared to be explaining something related to nautical knots as he held a length of boat line in his hands and gestured to one of the knots. Jordan nodded along. While Tess couldn't hear what they were saying over the wind on the water, she could hear the tone of their voices, Jordan's lilting in the way it did when he was asking question upon question. The fluttering in her heart had stopped and the heat subsided inside. She shook her head. The last thing she needed was to get worked up over some fishing guide from Alaska.

The pace of the day picked up with her father catching the first halibut of the day, Jordan following with another catch and finally her brother. With Nathan's help, Tess got a line in and felt a tug on the line within minutes. Luke was nearby with Nathan, both helping get fish situated in the cooler. Luke looked over when Tess exclaimed, "That was fast!"

"Sometimes it's all timing—seems to be on your side. Hold steady and reel in at a slow, even speed," Luke said.

Before she knew it, Tess was looking at the flat eye on one side of the halibut. A few fish later, Jared had turned the boat towards Otter Cove, the boat harbor for Diamond Creek. Tess sat on a bench at the back of the boat. The salty wind blew through her curls as the boat bounced in a rocking rhythm on the waves. Turning back towards the ocean, she took a long look at Mount Augustine. The cushion shifted under her legs. She turned forward again to find Nathan sitting down beside her.

"So how was your first day on the water here? In love with Alaska yet?" he asked.

Despite her usual reserve, Tess felt herself smiling without thinking. She was disconcerted by how easily charmed she was by Nathan. His nearness flushed her, just *melted* her reserve. Nathan waited patiently for her to respond. Little did he know she was just trying to get her bearings. His presence was potent, her body humming while her mind reminded her not to be silly.

"My first day on the water here was pretty good. Dad has wanted to fish in Alaska forever. I'm glad he's finally here," Tess said politely.

Nathan's eyes took on a mischievous glimmer. "Your dad was an easy mark to love it. But...I meant how was *your* day?" Nathan asked.

Tess looked back at Nathan, his dark blue eyes crinkled at the corners, his shaggy curls in disarray. Paired with those amazing eyes, Nathan had chiseled features with a perfectly proportioned nose sitting between sculpted cheekbones and a strong chin. Much as she resisted it, just looking at him raised the heat inside her. She looked away, not comfortable with how much she wanted to keep looking into the deep blue of his eyes. That inconvenient melting sensation flared.

"Didn't realize you'd need to think so hard to answer," Nathan commented wryly, his words bringing her attention back.

Tess looked back into his eyes for just a moment, giving in to the temptation to tumble into that mesmerizing blue. Since the way her last relationship had splintered about a year ago, she rarely let herself think much about how she felt. It was easier. But she was in Alaska for a three-week stay. Allowing herself to indulge the intense yearning Nathan elicited wouldn't matter in the long run. After they left, she'd likely never see or hear from Nathan or anyone in Alaska again.

"Okay, how was my day? My day was good. It's beautiful here, no doubt about that. I love being on the ocean anywhere and Alaska's no different. Except for getting a view of mountains, glaciers and a volcano. That's an amazing sight to witness. Plus, catching a halibut in under fifteen minutes was fun," she finally said.

Nathan's quick grin only raised the heat inside. "I'd like to take the credit for how fast you hooked that halibut, but it's clear you've had some experience with fishing. And the view here is pretty phenomenal. We love it. That's one of the reasons we moved here."

Her heart racing—dear god she practically needed to fan herself—Tess found herself asking a question before she had a chance to stop herself. "Where did you move from?"

"Seattle. Like your dad, our dad loves to fish, so we grew up fishing in Washington waters. We decided to start a commercial fishing business down there together and eventually came up here to fish a few times. Liked it so much that we relocated the business and ourselves up here. Can't imagine living anywhere else now."

"Diamond Creek is a bit of a change from Seattle," she said.

"Up here, we live somewhere we love instead of planning to travel here. Kind of like your dad really. Sounds like he spends a lot of time visiting places he might rather live."

"You can say that," Tess said, relieved that polite conversation seemed to slow her heart rate. "Where he lives in North Carolina, he's right on a river, so he gets to fish pretty often. But he likes to try different places. Alaska's been on his fishing bucket list for years."

The wind had started to pick up. The boat rode into a

large swell, followed by a smaller choppy wave that threw Tess against Nathan's side. He reflexively put his arm around her waist. Just when Tess thought she'd gotten a hold of herself, her heart was off to the races, her stomach fluttering. His arm was warm and strong against her back. She wanted to lean into him and stay that way. She glanced up at Nathan and found him looking down toward her intently. Her heart gave a quiver and the simmering heat in her center turned up a notch. Nathan's hand rested just against her hip. He flexed against the soft curve, a subtle caress. She gasped and tore her eyes away, the water a blur of whitecaps in her muddled gaze. Nathan's loosened his grip and let go, his hand curling the bottom of the bench again. Her body immediately missed his touch, sighing at its absence.

Whether he meant it or not, Tess wondered if he was reacting to her confusion. His gaze had been direct...ardent. Yet she'd looked away...the moment passed. Relief and disappointment tinged with sadness clashed. If she imagined herself to be someone else, someone that could just let go and enjoy this attraction, it would be so much simpler.

Nathan called out to Jared. "Looks like the wind is kicking in. Want me to take over steering for a bit? You've been at it all day."

Jared called back without turning. "No worry. Be to the harbor inside of a half hour."

Nathan shook his head. "That's Jared. Can hardly stand it if we offer to help for something he thinks is his job."

Curiosity rose in Tess. She wanted to know more about his family. While Nathan could have sounded critical, his comment had a loving tone to it.

"So I guess he usually drives?" she asked.

"Almost always. But it's okay. We may be brothers, but we get along better than most. Luke and I take care of whatever Jared doesn't," he said. 'Speaking of that, nice chatting for a few, but I have to take care of a few things before we get to the harbor." He stood from the bench and looked down at her, another easy grin gracing his face. "Don't suppose I could persuade you to go to dinner with me sometime in the few weeks you're here?"

Tess flushed head to toe, her heart danced and those magnetic eyes of his stoked the smoldering heat in her center. She wanted to jump up and say yes, and *that* annoyed the hell out of her. Her cautious side was dominant, oh-so-practical. She could recite by heart all the reasons any romantic entanglement wasn't worth it. Though practical and safe, it was a lonely place to be. A tattered corner of her heart wanted more. Before she knew it, she was answering honestly. "I'm not sure. I don't know what our plans are for the next few days."

His grin didn't waver. "Think about it. Diamond Creek may seem like it's the middle of nowhere, but we have some good restaurants here. You'll be seeing me again either way. Your dad booked us for four more trips."

Tess nodded. "Okay, maybe. I'll think about it." As soon as the words slipped out, Tess couldn't believe she'd said them. The last thing she needed was this way too handsome Alaskan fishing guide to take her on a date.

Nathan winked and turned away, striding to the boat's small cabin. His back muscles flexed as his arms swung. She could only imagine what kind of shape he was in, given the active life he and his brothers led. He was tall, easily over six feet, with broad, strong shoulders and a rangy build. He seemed far too handsome to consider her worthy of a date. While Tess didn't consider herself unattractive, her last boyfriend had often made passive comments about her being a little too curvy. Her breasts were prone to spilling out of blouses. She was on the short side and could rarely find tops that fit right as they seemed to be designed for thinner women. She absentmindedly tucked her hair behind her ears, her honey-colored curls getting wild in the wind.

She spent the remainder of the ride watching the shore get closer, trying and failing to keep her mind and eyes off of Nathan. The shoreline here was nothing like the ocean shore in North Carolina, which was bright sand, patches of tall grass and swaths of flat beaches with the occasional sand dune. In Alaska, the ocean splashed against glaciers, mountainsides and rocky beaches. The shore in Diamond Creek included steep cliffs, leveling off into lush green spruce forests, and beaches of gray sand covered in colorful rocks. Otter Cove was the name of the tiny cove in which the boat harbor was tucked, protected somewhat from winds and cold. Jared deftly steered the boat into its slip at the harbor docks. Nathan and Luke were ready the minute they pulled in, tossing lines over the dock pilings. Tess's eyes were glued to Nathan. He was tall and lanky, his sinewy muscles rippling under his cotton shirt. Jared cut the engine and quickly went into motion, getting the two full coolers ready to pass over to Nathan and Luke on the docks.

After stepping off the boat, Tess, her father, brother and nephew entered a whirl of activity. Within an hour, she was waving goodbye to Nathan and his brothers as Simon drove their car rental way from the Fish Factory, the local business that would be flash freezing and mailing their halibut back to North Carolina on overnight delivery. A friend of her father's would be picking up the packages and depositing them in the chest freezer in her parents' garage.

Tess looked out the car window and saw Nathan give a wave. Her hand lifted in return. He flashed a wide grin. She couldn't believe he had her even considering a date with him. Just as she started to turn away, Nathan turned to look towards Jared and stepped into one of the small boulders lining the parking lot. He stumbled into Luke who was beside him and then onto the ground. Before she looked away, she saw him look in their direction again and couldn't help but laugh. As handsome as he was, he seemed to have a knack for falling, at least today.

CHAPTER 2

*T*ossing her rain jacket onto the hotel bed, Tess headed for the bathroom. She turned on the shower, stepping in when steam filled the room. They had gone out to dinner after fishing, meeting her mother at a local seafood restaurant. The day had gone from sunny and bright to gray, rainy and cool while they were eating. The dash from the car into the hotel had left her dripping wet. Stepping out of the shower, she grabbed a towel and toweled her hair off. With a shake of her hair, she set the towel on the edge of the sink and looked in the mirror, scanning herself. Her dark honey-colored curls were damp, hanging just to the tops of her shoulders. Her eyes just about matched her hair. She never knew what color to call them, although her mother always said she had ginger eyes.

Tess didn't look for long but wondered what Nathan saw when he looked at her. Self-doubt had burrowed in her heart and held on during and after her relationship with Chad. She often wondered if she'd only ended up with him because she was too trusting. She'd met Chad through work. She ran her own fundraising business and handled contracts almost exclusively for non-profits. Chad handled accounts for various businesses, mostly those in the medical field. They'd met at one of the functions she hosted. He was handsome and charming, if a tad too sleek for her taste.

After the fact, she wished she'd listened to that small voice inside that pointed out that Chad worried a bit too much about appearances. While he'd been nothing but compliments and charm when they first dated, he gradually began to make small comments about her curves, that loose clothes made her look dumpy and more fitted clothes made her look like she was trying to get the attention of other men. Instead of realizing that Chad was a jerk, she kept trying to find ways to make herself look different so he wouldn't comment. About two years into their relationship, Tess found out she was pregnant. It had come as a surprise because she'd been on the pill. The next month was nothing but a blur. Adjusting to the unexpected pregnancy had been…well…unexpected and emotionally disorienting. The loneliness of her relationship became blatant when she balked at telling Chad, not out of a desire to hide something, but because she didn't trust that he'd be supportive. Cocooned in confusion, unsure of what to do, a miscarriage took any choice out of her hands. She was thrown into facing a loss that echoed through her heart. The tumult of emotions had exhausted her.

The only good that came out of the miscarriage in Tess's opinion was that she'd finally seen Chad for who he was. While still reeling from the emotional aftermath of her miscarriage, he'd made one of his passing comments about her weight. A voice that had been quiet inside of her came roaring out. She immediately broke up with him and moved out the same day. It was the most sensible thing she'd done in the two years she'd dated him. She learned later that he'd been quite busy with other women during the time they were together, likely why he worried so much that other men noticed her. He'd also offered minimal support during the weeks she tried to adjust to the news of her pregnancy and subsequent miscarriage. Since the end of their relationship, she spent too much time questioning herself and wondering what had led her to stay in a relationship that she'd known deep down wasn't good for her.

Tess gave her head a hard shake. She didn't want to think about Chad. It had been a mistake, but she had found the courage to walk away. That had been a year ago. The hard part was trying to find the woman she wanted to be—strong and smart. She couldn't believe someone as handsome as Nathan would be interested in her. Her thoughts flicked back to the moment that Nathan's hand gave her hip the barest squeeze. Her breath caught, her pulse leapt and a flush rose—her body craved that tiny moment. She couldn't fight the small smile that bloomed inside.

Shoving those thoughts away, Tess stalked out of the bathroom and dug through her suitcase, slipping on a pair of leggings and a tank top. She grabbed the remote, scrolled through the channels and settled on HGTV, one of her favorites. With the rain coming in sheets against the hotel window, she settled in for a few hours of mindless television.

* * *

A FEW DAYS LATER, Tess carried a cooler in one hand and a cup of coffee in the other as she walked down the dock in the harbor. Her nephew, Jordan, walked alongside, carrying his new fishing gear to the Winters brothers' boat. Tess held her breath in awe when she saw an eagle seated on one of the dock pilings—its size magnificent, its bright, fierce eyes fixed on the water. She'd started to accept that eagles were pretty much everywhere in Alaska, but being this close to them on the docks was startling. The one just ahead of them spread its wings and took off in flight. The wings cast a shadow so broad it encompassed her and Jordan. She'd read their wingspan was as much as seven feet.

"Did you see that eagle, Jordan?" she asked.

"Yeah! I was trying to be quiet. Granddad said it's better to try not to startle them. They're so cool!" Jordan said. With the eagle flying off, he commenced to chatter about how many fish they might catch today. Between Simon and her father, he was well on his way to being a third generation fishing addict.

Tess was glad for Jordan's excitement. It took her mind off the anticipation she felt about seeing Nathan again, which was just short of ridiculous. Her mind careened from visions of his blue eyes and dimples to steamy fantasies, which she kept swatting away. She hadn't seen him in the two days since their first trip. Not that she'd expected to, but Diamond Creek was small enough that it was definitely possible. They'd spent the last two days checking out the local art galleries. There were far more than Tess would have expected in this tiny seacoast town in Alaska. They'd also taken a drive up to Seward, another coastal town on the Kenai Peninsula. Seward was north of Diamond Creek and sat tucked close into the mountains. While it had been lovely, she found she liked the more open view from Diamond Creek better. Diamond Creek was on the western side of the peninsula and had a wide-open view of the mountains across Kachemak Bay.

Tess looked out from the harbor into Kachemak Bay. The water was a deep navy in the bright sun today.

"Tess!"

She turned and saw Nathan waving to her from a larger boat beside the guide boat they'd taken the other day.

"Hey Nathan!" she called in return, trying to ignore the way her heart leapt at seeing him.

"Nathan, Nathan I got a new fishing pole!" Jordan hollered as he started to run. He promptly tripped and stumbled. Not missing a beat, he surged back up and kept running towards the boat.

"Hey Jordan, slow down buddy," Nathan called. He stepped over the side of the boat and started to climb down a ladder.

Tess looked ahead at Jordan. "Jordan, listen to Nathan. Take it easy on the dock."

Jordan stopped running and turned back. "Okay, but only because Nathan asked," he said with a grin.

"Oh really? Just because Nathan asked, huh? You better watch out."

Jordan just kept grinning. "I know Aunt Tess, just teasing." He waited for her to catch up and then politely walked alongside.

Nathan met them on the dock. "Can I help carry some of that?" he asked, glancing at the jumble of fishing pole, windbreaker and tackle bag that Jordan held haphazardly.

Jordan shook his head emphatically, his straight brown hair swinging. "Nope, a guy has to carry his gear."

Nathan lifted an eyebrow. "I'd say a guy has to have enough sense to accept help when he needs it."

Jordan appeared to mull this over. With an emphatic nod, he attempted to hand Nathan some of what he was carrying, only to lose his grip on most of it. Nathan moved quickly and caught it all with both arms.

Tess couldn't hold back her laugh. "Close call, buddy. Maybe, just maybe, we needed some help."

"Yup, we did. But it's okay," he said. He looked toward Nathan who was carefully trying to organize the handful he'd scooped from Jordan. "Aunt Tess already had her hands full. I was doing okay until I started to run."

Nathan glanced at Tess before turning his gaze to Jordan. "That's why you shouldn't run on the docks. Can we make a deal that you won't try that again?" he asked with a serious tone. "Not joking on that one. The docks aren't a safe place to run. Even I don't try that."

Jordan took his request in and looked serious. "We can make a deal. I just got excited."

"Of course you did. I'm excited every day I get to go fishing. Just got to remember there are places to walk and places to run. We made our deal, so let's keep it."

Jordan nodded, his grin returning in force. "We have a deal! Now can we walk to the boat?"

"Where else would we be going?" Nathan glanced to Tess and winked.

Tess looked away, flushed inside and out. How it was possible, she didn't know, but Nathan appeared more handsome than he'd been the other day. His hair was only slightly mussed so far, his black curls tumbling across his forehead. She could look into his deep blue eyes all day. He wore heavy brown rubber boots with the label Xtratuf on them. She'd never seen Xtratufs before and so many people wore them here, they could have been confused as part of a uniform. Over his boots, his jeans were worn and frayed and paired with a T-shirt and a bright blue windbreaker. He had a clean, sharp scent to him this morning.

She wondered if Nathan would ask her out to dinner again and chided herself for wrestling with her attraction to him. She needed to either let it go, or get over herself and say yes.

Oblivious to her predicament, Nathan was casually talking with Jordan who had question upon question about fishing in Alaska. Since their trip the other day, Jordan had persuaded Simon to buy him a book on fishing in Alaska and proceeded to regale the rest of them with facts and photos. He was determined to catch another Alaskan king salmon. Tess was accustomed only to Atlantic salmon and wasn't sure what could be so different about the types of Pacific salmon, but had quickly noticed that locals made clear distinctions with king salmon considered the most prized.

Nathan patiently answered Jordan's questions. Despite her misgivings about dinner with him, she had to admit that they were more about herself and not him. His patience with Jordan was a good recommendation for him. They had arrived at the guide boat and stepped onto the dock between it and the larger boat Nathan had been on when he waved.

"Is that another boat of yours?" Tess asked Nathan.

Nathan glanced up at the boat. "Yup. That's Iris—our commercial fishing boat. Named after our mom. Iris is for the big trips. We used to come up here from Seattle on her to fish. That's when we fell in love with Alaska and Diamond Creek," he said with a quick smile, a dimple flashing on one side.

Her return smile came in automatic response. She shook her head at herself.

Nathan tilted his head. "What's that for?"

She felt caught and blushed.

Jordan looked between them. "Aunt Tess doesn't have fun much," he announced. "You should come to dinner with us and make her smile more."

Tess hadn't thought she could blush even more. "Jordan, really?! I have fun sometimes. And you have to check with your dad before asking someone else to dinner with everyone."

Nathan appeared unperturbed with Tess's discomfort and humored with Jordan's comments. "No worries. Of course, we'd clear it with the grownups. But Jordan may be right. A little fun doesn't hurt anyone," he said.

Tess held her embarrassment in check and hoped her

blush was subsiding. "Perhaps he is. That's why we're on vacation, to have a little fun. And I'm sure my family will be happy to have you join us for dinner. I just didn't want you to feel put on the spot."

"As I said, no worries," he replied. "Let's get you two and this gear into the boat. When will your dad and brother be here?"

"They dropped us off and headed back to get some sandwiches for the day. My mom told us about a place she had lunch the other day, Misty Mountain Café."

"Misty Mountain is a local favorite—great sandwiches. How come your mom doesn't come fishing with the rest of you?" he asked.

"Oh, she gets seasick pretty quick. She's happy to fish from shore, but she rarely goes out on the water."

Nathan nodded as he grabbed one of the mooring lines and tugged the boat flush against the dock. "Makes sense. There's some shore fishing here, but you have to head out for a better chance at halibut and king salmon."

He carefully set Jordan's fishing gear on the dock and held his hand out for Jordan while he gave him a small lift to get him into the boat. He turned to Tess next, his hand extended. Tess set the cooler down on the dock. Nathan reached over and took the cup of coffee from her with his other hand. "I got this."

Tess nodded and placed her hand in his. His touch sent a warm buzz coursing through her, sparking a quiver of heat in her center. His hand was large and warm, his grip firm and strong. She looked up, straight into his blue, blue eyes—that small quiver of heat flickered and spread through her, a simmering pulse of desire. The flush that had finally faded from a few minutes ago blazed to life. Nathan held her gaze and with a lift, helped her up and over the side of the boat. Her hand felt cool and empty when he released her. Stepping back from the side of the boat, she turned to see him waiting with her coffee held aloft.

She found it hard to look at him, disconcerted. She carefully took the coffee from him. "Thanks," she said, the only word she could manage.

"Anytime," he said. Lowering his voice, he continued, "I'll take dinner with just you too, in case you were wondering if I forgot."

Tess was aflame from the blush that just wouldn't fade. She looked in Jordan's direction. He was busy examining the fishing poles lined up in a rack. Returning her gaze to Nathan, her eyes ran smack into his. She smiled, in spite of herself. "You mentioned that the other day. Is that something you ask many of the women you take out for fishing trips?" The question slipped out, and she promptly regretted it.

Nathan was unruffled, but he didn't seem the kind of man that let much ruffle him. "Actually, no. You're the only one. Make what you will of that," he said. For a flicker, Tess saw uncertainty in his eyes.

She waited a beat before responding. "I'm sorry I said that. The thing about whether you asked other women out like this. It just came out."

Nathan shrugged. "It's okay. Can't say I blame you. But the offer stands. I'd love to take you out to dinner," he said, his dimple making its appearance.

For the first time in a while, Tess just let herself do something without thinking it to death. She allowed the smile she'd been trying to suppress to bloom instead. "Well then...yes. I'll go to dinner with you. I just don't know when. Let me check with my family on what our plans are for the next few evenings."

"Awesome! Your dad seems to have planned this trip out pretty well. Much as I want to take you to dinner, I don't want to interfere with your trip."

"Dad did plan this trip well in advance, but the parts that matter to him aren't dinner. Just anything to do with fishing."

Just as Nathan opened his mouth to respond, she heard someone call his name. They turned in unison to see Jared walking down the dock towards them. Luke was further behind with a tall woman walking alongside him. Nathan waved to Jared as he stepped back onto the dock. The quick grin he threw in her direction ratcheted up the heat that crackled between them.

Before Jared and Nathan made it to the boat, Michael and Simon walked onto the dock. She watched curiously as Luke approached with the woman she assumed to be his wife. She'd noticed he wore a wedding band the other day. They were holding hands in a loose grip. They held cups of coffee from the same coffee truck where her father had stopped this morning. Nathan and Jared were waiting beside the boat.

"Good morning lovebirds," Nathan said with a wink. "Starting to wonder where Luke was. Ever since you two got married last year, I'm the early bird."

Luke rolled his eyes. "It's not like I'm late—just not the first one here."

"Exactly the problem. Can't be sure you'll have coffee for me," Nathan said with a weak attempt at feigning annoyance.

Jared stayed out of the teasing and shook his head. He looked over to Tess. "Tess, this is Hannah, Luke's lovely wife," he said, gesturing towards Hannah.

Tess nodded. "I'm Tess. I guess there's no point in me explaining that I'm here on a fishing trip," she said.

"Nice to meet you Tess," Hannah said. "And it's excellent that you're here on a fishing trip with your family. That's what these boys do." She looked up at Luke, her eyes warm and soft.

Tess felt a flash of envy at the comfort she saw between Luke and Hannah. Jared's description of Hannah was apt; she was lovely in a casual way. Her build was tall and willowy. She stood almost shoulder to shoulder with Luke, and Tess would have guessed him to be a few good inches over six feet tall. Hannah had sky blue eyes and long, dark hair that fell in loose waves around her shoulders. She was dressed in the uniform Xtratufs, jeans and a long-sleeved t-shirt. Luke basically matched Hannah with the exception of a flannel shirt over his t-shirt. Jared, along with everyone else, wore Xtratufs and jeans. She looked down at her own rubber boots, which were multicolored with stripes.

As the brothers bantered, Hannah looked over to her again. "They'd do this all day if life didn't interrupt them," she said ruefully. "Boys, hop in the boat and let's get going."

Luke, Jared and Nathan kept up their banter as they loaded a few more coolers on the boat and helped her father and Simon get their gear up. The brothers included Jordan by having him carry the smaller items, which Jordan loved. Hannah invited Tess to sit with her on one of the benches. Tess shivered when a small gust of wind came off the water.

"It's chilly here in the mornings on the water," Hannah said.

"I noticed that the other day. I have a jacket in my bag but I'm doing okay except for the wind."

Hannah took a sip of her coffee. "I see you discovered my friend's coffee truck," she said with a nod towards the matching coffee that Tess held.

Tess glanced down at the label on the paper cup, Red Truck Coffee, and took a quick sip. The coffee was rich and delicious. "This is your friend's place?"

Hannah nodded. "My friend Cammi started that little coffee truck the summer after we finished high school. She initially did it just for some extra cash, but she makes damn good coffee, so it took off and now it's all she's been doing in the summer for years. Misty Mountain Café is probably the only other place to get really good coffee in town, but that's more of a sit down place. Red Truck is where everyone goes when they're headed out on the water."

"Well, her coffee is amazing. Diamond Creek could compete with big cities when it comes to food, coffee, and shopping," Tess said. "Not that I'm from a big city. We're from North Carolina, near the coast."

Hannah tilted her head with a smile. "Really? I was born in North Carolina, but we moved here when I was six, so Diamond Creek and Alaska are home to me. Before we moved here, we lived in Chapel Hill but I have memories of going to the beach there. So different from the beaches here."

"That's for sure," Tess said. "We're from New Bern, which isn't on the ocean, but about a half hour away. Here though, it's amazing that the ocean is right up against the mountains. The views are like nothing I've ever seen."

Hannah nodded and looked out towards Mount Augustine, standing tall in the early morning. "The views are hard to beat. I went to grad school in Massachusetts and didn't realize how much I missed looking out and seeing the mountains everyday until I moved back home."

Tess followed Hannah's gaze to the volcano sitting quietly in the bay. The morning sun was high in the sky despite the early hour. In the few days they'd been in Alaska, she discovered that that trying to go to bed before the sun had set was an odd feeling. It was midsummer and the sun didn't set until after midnight and was up before Tess rose.

Nathan and his brothers untied the boat and within minutes, the boat motor rumbled and Jared was steering the boat out of the harbor into the bay. Though the breeze picked up, the warmth from the sun took the edge of the wind off. Tess took another sip of her coffee followed by a deep breath, the fresh air invigorating. Simon sat on a cooler beside the bench.

"So sis, what do you think of Alaska so far?" he asked.

"So far, so good. The fishing has been great and it's beautiful. I'm glad dad finally made this trip happen."

"I'll second that. Jordan's having the time of his life. He's determined to catch a king salmon today."

Hannah chimed in. "Well, he's with the right crew if he's hoping for that. I can't call favorites or I'd be in the middle of a war of brothers, but Luke and his brothers know how to find fish and catch them."

"They're also great with Jordan. Not sure how dad found out about their business, but we couldn't be happier," Simon said.

Hannah opened her mouth to respond when Jordan called out, "Look!"

Jordan was pointing out ahead in the water. Tess didn't see anything, but the ocean surface was disturbed where he was pointing.

"Dad there was a whale! Did you see it?" Jordan asked.

Simon stood and walked towards Jordan. Simon shared her father's dark, straight hair and chocolate eyes, which he'd passed on to Jordan. Simon was two years her senior, had been her tormentor in childhood and now her overprotective brother in adulthood. Since he'd watched her relationship with Chad dissolve, he'd become doting to the point of annoying sometimes. He knelt beside Jordan.

Just as she was about to turn away, the water surface rippled and broke about fifty feet ahead of them, a whale's tail flicking up out of the water, followed by the whale's body curling against the water and dipping back under. Tess stood to get a better view. Jordan jumped up and down, clapping. "See! I told y'all there was a whale. What kind of whale is that?" he asked.

"That's a humpback," Jared said. "They put on a show sometimes. Glad you got to see that."

Tess sensed Nathan beside her before she saw him. She turned away from the water to find he had tugged the cooler nearby a little closer and was sitting down.

"We aim to please when we take people out, but not everyone gets to see a whale like that," he said, catching her eyes. He nodded towards Hannah. "Right, Hannah?"

"True. Plenty of tourists pay small fortunes to go on whale sighting tours, but there's never a guarantee. How long are you here?" she asked, directing her question to Tess.

"Three weeks. My dad has wanted to come to Alaska to go fishing for years and we finally got around to it. I'm not sure how he decided on Diamond Creek, but we love it so far," she said.

Hannah and Nathan alternated with filling her in on all things Alaska and Diamond Creek. Being the only woman usually when they went fishing, it was nice to have feminine company. Hannah had a practical sense to her that Tess appreciated. It was clear that she was considered just as expert on fishing as any of the brothers. As the boat rolled across the water in a rocking motion, she watched Nathan banter with Hannah.

"You've ruined my guaranteed coffee from Luke. It's hit or miss now—have to plan for myself. It's rough," Nathan said.

"Yeah and that's probably good for you. Between Jared and Luke, you've been coddled. Stopping to get your own coffee might train you up to do it for the woman that you'll eventually meet and fall for," Hannah replied.

Nathan looked aggrieved. "Hey, I'm not that bad."

"I know you're not, but you tend to create this impression of stumbling through life when you're steady and stable, even though you won't admit it," Hannah said, a teasing look on her face.

"Okay…Luke fell hard, which is why, in case you forgot, I made sure he realized how amazing you are," Nathan retorted. "You two have been nothing but sugar and sunshine since you got married. And you went and had John last year, so now mom and dad aren't pressuring me and Jared to marry up and produce grandkids."

Listening to Hannah's comments only added to Tess's curiosity about Nathan. Sitting with them gave her a chance to casually take him in. His presence was potent. He radiated a sense of strength, along with being handsome and sexy as hell. And those eyes…she just wanted to dive in to the heat that swirled whenever he looked at her. Although she'd let herself say yes to dinner, it didn't change the fact that she couldn't figure out what he saw in her.

Despite her tendency to dwell, the day didn't allow it. It wasn't long before they arrived at what Jared deemed a good spot to try to catch a king salmon. Many hours later, Jordan's sought after king salmon had been caught. Tess had caught two more halibut with Hannah's help before the boat headed back for Otter Cove. While Hannah was at her side, offering pointers, Tess missed Nathan's assistance. His arms brushing her side, his steady focus, his black curls falling over those blue eyes, his confidence—radiating a strength that disarmed her, melted her defenses. Hannah stood beside Luke towards the front of the boat, one of his arms resting around her waist, his thumb hooked in a belt loop. Tess experienced another prick of envy. She didn't think she'd ever have something like what she saw between Luke and Hannah.

Tess rode the remainder of the boat ride quietly on one of the benches. Jared, as Nathan had noted on their last trip, drove the boat all day. Nathan was seated with her father, brother and Jordan, casually talking. He occasionally glanced her way, winking once or twice with a quick smile. The sun was just starting to dip in the sky. Light flickered across the water, striking sparks on the surface. Looking towards the shore, Diamond Creek sat against the cliffs, surrounded by deep green spruce forest. Tess took a deep breath of the clean ocean air and tilted her head back, her curls catching in the breeze. For the first time in a while, she relished a moment of peace.

CHAPTER 3

Nathan stood in the shower, letting hot water rush over him. As much as he loved fishing, it was always work and today had been no exception. His muscles loosened in the steam, the heat washing away his exhaustion. A few minutes later, he strode into the kitchen in worn sweatpants and a flannel shirt. He found Jared staring inside the refrigerator.

"Don't tell me there's nothing good to eat," he said.

"Can you remember the last time one of us went to the grocery store?"

Nathan thought for a moment and shook his head. "Can't say that I do. Luke was usually better about that than us, huh?"

Jared closed the refrigerator with a wry smile. "Guess so. Let's order pizza. I'm starving and too tired to drive to town for anything."

"Want me to call?" Nathan asked.

At Jared's nod, Nathan made the quick call to place their order. He and Jared lived together in a house they'd bought with Luke when they all moved up to Diamond Creek together. Luke had moved out last winter when he married Hannah. Nathan found himself trying a little harder to be responsible with Luke gone. As the baby in the family, he knew he'd gotten a lot of slack from his parents as well as from Jared and Luke. Much as Nathan enjoyed teasing Jared for being the serious one, he had always looked up to Jared. It was Jared's organization and planning that helped them get their commercial fishing business off the ground in Seattle and kept it going here in Alaska. Nathan knew he and Luke contributed just as much, but Jared was the motivator and took care of the logistical details without complaint.

Jared had switched on the television and was scrolling through channels. Nathan glanced around the house. He wondered what would happen if he or Jared found someone the way Luke had. The house was a gorgeous timber-frame home overlooking Kachemak Bay with a clear view of the mountains and a glacier. The kitchen and living room area had a wall of windows with French doors in the center overlooking the bay. A house without a view in Diamond Creek was uncommon with mountains in all directions. But when it came to the views, there was competition for which parts of town had the best view. Nathan happened to think they were on the better side of town, and he knew just about anyone he mentioned this to would spend the next few minutes explaining why the part of town where they lived actually had the best view.

He stepped onto the deck. The sun was setting with the time close to ten. Streaks of pink and lavender mingled with shafts of soft gold light. The mountains were dark across the water. Mount Augustine was shrouded at its peak with clouds shot through with the colors from the sky. He loved this time of day.

Until recently, Nathan used to head out to one of the local bars at about this time, Sally's being his favorite, to knock back a few beers and find some fun. Lately, he found himself less and less interested in the casual encounters he used to seek out. He knew Jared and Luke, and probably plenty of others, thought he had flings left and right. In reality, he loved to flirt and loved the fun of casual relationships, but only with a few women had he exchanged more than kisses. Though he'd happily assumed the role of flirt, he didn't take anyone's feelings lightly. If he thought someone was interested in much more than a brief fling, he made sure not to be misleading.

Something about Luke moving out had shaken him out of the idea that he would be young forever. He was past thirty now. His parents had a good marriage and were still solid all these years later. While he knew that wasn't old or even considered middle age these days, he had enough sense to know if he wanted a chance at what his parents and Luke had, he might need to take life a little more seriously. Although he'd be damned if he let himself get as serious as Jared.

He took a long look at the setting sun and turned to walk inside. Though a good baseball game was on, Jared had his laptop out and was poring over a spreadsheet. Nathan shook his head.

"Do you ever take a break?"

Jared looked up quickly. "I'll put this away when the pizza gets here. Just want to enter a few things."

Nathan held his gaze. "Yeah, I'm sure that couldn't wait until tomorrow morning. You work too hard. Maybe you want to blow me off because I'm your baby brother, but cut yourself some slack."

He flopped down on the couch near Jared and grabbed the remote only to have the doorbell ring.

"There's the pizza. You…" he paused with a deliberate look at Jared, "…put away your computer and take a break."

Jared rolled his eyes, but complied. With a few clicks, he

shut the computer and carried it downstairs while Nathan paid the delivery guy. When Jared returned, they carted the pizza into the living room and ate while watching the game.

"Another good trip with the Stanton family today," Jared commented. "Nice group. Michael sure loves to fish. Between him and the rest of them, they have enough experience that it's easier for us."

There was a long pause and Nathan turned toward Jared, tearing off a bite of pizza. Jared watched him with a gleam in his eyes. "What's that look for?" Nathan asked, the words coming out in a mumble as he chewed.

"You seem to find Tess a little more interesting than our usual customers," Jared said with a sly smile.

Nathan paused, mid bite and glared at Jared. He swallowed before speaking. "Seriously dude? I'm friendly to her just like I am to all of our customers."

He didn't know why, but he was uncomfortable that Jared had noticed anything. Although he should have known better. Jared was quiet and observant and only occasionally let on to what he noticed. He wasn't ready to tell Jared that he'd asked Tess out to dinner, or to admit that he found her intriguing and wanted to get to know her better. Not to mention that he found himself thinking about her golden brown eyes and lush curves quite a bit.

"Look, she's nice and cute as hell. But other than that, it's just me being me. You know I like to flirt," he explained, falling back on the hope that his reputation for being a flirt would throw Jared off the scent.

Jared quirked one of his dark brows. "You explaining yourself tells me a lot more than anything else would."

Nathan rolled his eyes and sighed. "Fine, think what you want. Just being nice. Is it okay to be nice to our customers or is that now a problem for you?"

Jared returned his eye roll. "Uh...no, being nice to our customers is not a problem. But if you're gonna flirt, be careful. Tess seems nice and probably not your usual type. Don't think she came to Alaska for a fling. Not to mention that having the hots for our customer's daughter isn't so good for business," he said, his eyes getting serious.

Nathan took Jared's words in with another bite of pizza and a sip of beer. "Agree with you there. I wouldn't try to have a fling with her. And give me some credit, I'm not a jerk. I've just had a few years of fun."

"I know you're not a jerk, which is why I said something. You sell yourself short, by the way. More to you than just flirting. I get to say things like that because I'm your oldest brother," Jared replied.

Nathan wouldn't admit it, but he appreciated what Jared said. With a nod, he turned the tables. "Since you're busy telling me to give myself more credit, do I get to point out that your plan to keep all relationships off the table is dumb? Not to mention that it breaks mom's heart." When he saw that Jared hadn't blown up yet, he took it further. "Plus, you need to lighten up and a little fun just might do the trick," he said with a wink.

Jared gave him a light punch on the arm. The moment passed and they moved on to eating through most of both pizzas and arguing over whether the Red Sox or Yankees would win the season series.

THE NEXT DAY, Nathan drove to town in the late morning. The air was cool with the sun shrouded behind clouds. Without the sun, summer days in Alaska didn't feel much like summer. Nathan had thrown on a fleece jacket with his jeans to knock the chill off. He was going to town to meet a family friend, Travis Wilkes, to help him clean the bottom of his boat. Travis had fished with them a few times over the years and was a solid guy. He often helped them out when needed, so Nathan was glad to return the favor.

Their house was situated on the top of one side of a hill that ran behind the town section of Diamond Creek. The bay was slate gray under the clouds, the mountaintops just visible above some of the clouds. Mount Augustine was shrouded. A hint of coming rain hung in the air. It wasn't the best day to scrape barnacles off the bottom of a boat, but then planning around the weather in Alaska didn't offer too many options. Most residents just worked through whatever came along.

Tess passed through Nathan's mind. He wondered what she and her family were doing today. He moved on to wondering about Jared's comment that there was more to him than flirting. He wouldn't admit it to Jared, but much as he wanted to flirt with Tess, the spark between them burned much brighter and with an indefinable quality that alternately drew him towards her and, if he could admit it for even a second, scared him a little.

With a hard shake of his head, he downshifted his truck and slowed as he approached the bottom of the hill. He tried to consciously think about something other than Tess. The effort was a spectacular failure, as he promptly moved on to picturing her ginger eyes, tousled honey curls and that lush little body. He swung the truck onto the highway into town and laughed to himself. He wished she'd call soon. He'd managed to get her cell number from her the other day, but sensed that he should let her take the initiative to call about dinner. He'd done the asking and she'd said she would find out when would be a good time and call. Her family had two more trips scheduled with them but not until next week. He gave himself two more days before he would consider calling her.

The old square red truck that housed Red Truck Coffee came into view. Nathan swung into the small parking lot.

As usual, cars were spilling out of the lot and parked along the road. Cammi, the woman who owned Red Truck Coffee and a friend of theirs, ran a brisk business all summer. He stepped out of his truck and walked to wait in the line filled with the usual mix of tourists and locals. Cammi was fast and kept the line moving. Her friend, Dara, was there with her this morning.

"Nathan! So good to see you," she said with a smile when he reached the front of the line. Cammi radiated warmth and an earnest sweetness. She wore her light brown hair in a pixie cut, her soft blue eyes tilted up at the corners whenever she smiled, which was most of the time.

"Hey Cammi, always good to see you. Can't tell you how awesome it is that your truck is right here where I need it on my way to the harbor."

"Of course it's right where you need it," she replied. "That's why I picked this spot. Have to admit though—when I started this business that first summer after high school, I had no idea when I asked for the permit to park here that it would take off as well as it did."

"You're smarter than you let on is what I think," Nathan said with a wink.

"I'll take that as a compliment," she said, her smile widening. "Saw your buddy Travis on his way out this morning too. I used to see Luke more often, but ever since he married Hannah…" her words trailed off.

"Oh no need to point that out. Trust me, I know how often Luke used to come by because he always got my coffee for me. But…the coffee's better when I get it for myself."

Cammi giggled as she handed him his coffee. "I can't pretend I do anything differently, but I'm glad you like it."

Holding his cup aloft, he waved as he left. A few sips of coffee and the morning looked brighter. Travis saw him once he stepped onto the dock and waved. Nathan paused for a moment at the top of the dock and looked across the harbor. Iris, their commercial boat, and their guiding boat sat quietly in their slips. Pride filled him whenever he saw Iris. He and his brothers had borrowed money from their father to purchase that boat to start their commercial fishing business. Within two seasons in Seattle, fishing from there up into Alaska, they'd been able to repay their father and start making a solid living. He couldn't have done it without his brothers, but he was damn proud of being a part of their small business. He loved the fishing and being outdoors. He'd had many odd jobs over the years, but he enjoyed being able to call his own shots, not because he wanted to be in charge, but because he enjoyed the independence.

He took a long sip of coffee and a deep breath of ocean air before walking towards Travis. When he reached the boat, he found Travis getting the boat ready to drive over the ramp and pull out of the water.

"So do you want to be the boat driver or the truck driver today?" Travis asked by way of greeting.

"My choice, huh? I'll take the boat. Not used to how your truck handles with a boat trailer on it."

Travis nodded. "Good enough. Already have the trailer hitched on. How about I head on up and meet you at the ramp in a few minutes?"

Nathan nodded. "Keys in the boat?"

At Travis's nod, he grabbed one of the boat lines and tugged the boat close enough to step in. Travis started the engine just as Nathan stepped onto the boat.

"So how about you untie her and toss me the lines?" Nathan asked, setting his coffee in a cup holder by the steering wheel.

"Yup. I'll meet you at the ramp in a few," came Travis's quick response.

Travis hopped out of the boat and moved quickly

around, untying the four lines that held the boat in its slip. Nathan neatly coiled the lines as Travis tossed them over. Nathan took the wheel and put the boat in gear to slowly move forward. He kept the boat speed slow, obeying the 'No wake' signs posted throughout the harbor. Even at the slow speed, he beat Travis to the ramp area. He idled the boat and sipped his coffee until he saw Travis's truck reach the top of the ramp. In minutes, they had the boat on the trailer and in place. He hopped in the truck with Travis.

"You can drop me off at my truck now, or you can bring me back later. Up to you," Nathan said.

Travis shrugged. "How about I bring you back when we're done?"

"Didn't I just say it was up to you?" Nathan asked wryly.

Travis rolled his eyes in return. "Just being polite, man." He put the truck in gear and drove slowly towards the road that led away from the harbor.

"So how've you been lately?" Travis asked. "Haven't had more than a few minutes to chat these past few weeks."

"Summer busy is what we've been. When we're not guiding, we've got something going on. How about you?"

"Same here," Travis responded. "The usual busy in summer. Headed up to dipnet in Kenai next week. They open the river for dipnetting next Sunday at midnight. You guys do that every year, right?"

Nathan nodded vigorously as he swallowed a gulp of coffee. "Hell yeah! Wouldn't miss it."

Dipnetting for wild salmon was a summer ritual in Alaska. It involved catching salmon by dipping a net in the water and scooping them out. There were a number of areas in Alaska where residents were permitted to dipnet. On the Kenai Peninsula, this included the Kenai and Kasilof rivers, both north of Diamond Creek. At the rivers, some people stood in the water that surged from the ocean into the mouths of the rivers while others rode in the rivers by boat, nets hanging over the sides. Nathan and his brothers had tried the options when they became Alaskan residents and tended to head to the Kenai River and stand in the water's edge.

"When do you plan to head to Kenai?" he asked Travis. "We usually keep an eye on the fish count from Fish & Game and head up when it starts to spike."

"Same here. I like to go the first week it's open just to see how I do. If I catch my limit, then I'm done. If not, I've got three more weeks to try again."

"Well, let me know when you decide to go. We have a few trips scheduled next week, but I might join you if I can."

Travis nodded. "Of course."

Once at boat storage yard, they spent the next few hours scraping barnacles off the bottom of Travis's boat. Nathan didn't know why, but it was the type of work that he found satisfying despite its tedium. He loved a good clean boat. While they worked, Tess crossed his mind again. He kept thinking about showing her all the different aspects of Diamond Creek and...that lush mouth of hers and those curves that made him itch to touch her.

When Travis was driving back to the harbor to drop him off, Nathan saw a small cluster of tourists stopped near the road, some tourists milling outside of their cars. In the field adjacent to the road, a mother moose and two calves were nibbling on alders. His stomach coiled in tension because tourists and moose could be a dangerous mix. Moose were frequently in town and could give the impression they were quite tame. Problem was, they were nearsighted and by the time someone was close enough for them to see, the person in question was dangerously close. Moose were deceptively quick. Their legs were so long, they tended to look as if they moved slowly. In reality, the length of their stride covered a lot of ground. At a slow jog, a moose could be on top of a person in seconds. A mother moose protective of her calves was particularly dangerous.

As he scanned the small group of people, he thought one of the cars was familiar and realized it looked like the rental car Tess and her family were using. He hoped they had enough sense to stay in the car.

"Hey Travis, you mind pulling over? Worried we might have a problem if we don't let these tourist know they need to keep their distance."

"Already trying to find a spot. We're on the same wavelength."

Travis parked just beyond the cluster of cars. They both stepped out and began to walk towards the small group. Nathan hoped they could just let people know they should keep their distance and that would be enough. As they approached, Nathan saw a small form dart out. His stomach fell when he realized it was Tess's nephew, Jordan. He quickly judged the distance between Jordan and the mother moose and her calves. If Jordan kept moving in her direction, he was likely to prompt her to charge. Nathan glanced back towards the car where Jordan had been and saw Simon stepping out to call to Jordan with Tess following and moving in Jordan's direction.

Nathan waved in their direction, but neither noticed, both had their eyes on Jordan who kept moving towards the moose. Nathan started to jog over, hoping to intercept Jordan. In what seemed to be no time, he saw the mother moose turn away from the alder, noticing Jordan.

"Jordan," he called. "Stop!"

Between his call and Simon's, Jordan finally stopped walking although he didn't turn back. In the meantime, the mother moose went from ignoring the small cluster of people to snorting and turning in their direction. All but Jordan were close enough to hop in their cars and most had the sense to do so. Tess, on the other hand, was focused on getting Jordan to safety. Nathan went from a jog to a run, going against his instincts to head in the direction of the moose. In a flash, the moose was charging directly at Jordan. Nathan got to Jordan seconds before Tess, grabbing Jordan by the edge of his shirt and firmly tugging him back into his grasp. Tess collided with them just as the moose stopped within a few strides of them. Nathan grabbed Tess by the arm and swung her behind him. Dust kicked up where the moose pawed the ground. Nathan kept moving quickly in the opposite direction of the moose, pulling Jordan and Tess along with him.

"If we keep moving away, she'll stop. Moose aren't predatory, but as you just found out, a mama moose will charge if you get too close to her calves," he said, trying to catch his breath.

He had Jordan by one hand now and Tess by the arm. She didn't question him. Her breath came in short gasps. Nathan glanced back as they continued moving away and saw that the moose had stopped in place. She snorted again, but remained still. Nathan's breath slowed, but he kept a rapid pace as they approached the cars. When they finally got to the car, he saw Simon, along with Michael, and a woman he assumed to be Tess's mother. All three had climbed out of the car.

Travis was waiting with them and caught Nathan's eye. "Since it was clear you had that in hand, I stayed here to make sure everyone else stayed put. Mama there seems to have decided it's okay now," Travis said with a nod in the direction of the moose.

Nathan looked back to see the moose had headed back toward the alder and her two calves, both of whom had watched and waited by the trees. As the mother moose reached them, she nuzzled them each and kept ambling, moving further into the field.

"Jordan, what were you thinking?! We told you it wasn't good to get too close," Tess said, her voice at high pitch.

Her eyes were dark with fear and adrenaline. Her chest rose and fell as her breath came in shallow gasps. Without realizing it, his arm went around her shoulders, unconsciously wanting to offer comfort. Tess didn't appear to notice, focused as she was on Jordan. Just as he became aware of what he did, she stepped away and knelt in front of Jordan whose eyes were welling with tears, overwhelmed with the cluster of adults exclaiming their worry.

Tess gave Jordan a quick hug and stood up. Nathan wanted to comfort her again, which startled him more than his attraction to her did. He felt out of sorts, still running on his own shot of adrenaline. Moose encounters were common, but they could occasionally cause true harm. He was beyond relieved that the moose had backed off and none of them were hurt.

Travis was talking calmly with Michael, assuring him that Jordan's impulsive action was not that unusual given how tame moose could appear. Simon had stepped over to Tess and Jordan, calmly tugging Jordan to his side for a quick hug and defusing the tension radiating from Tess. The other people lingering to watch the moose remained in their cars, some finally driving away. Nathan stepped over to Michael who surprised Nathan by clapping him on the shoulder and pulling him in for a quick hug. Releasing him, Michael held his gaze.

"Can't thank you enough Nathan. Don't know what Jordan was thinking. Thank God for you and Tess," Michael said with a shake of his head. "Just glad their okay. You okay?"

Nathan nodded. "I'm fine. Just did what I could."

The woman standing beside Michael reached over for his hand and held it in both of hers. "We haven't met. I'm Celine, mother, grandmother and wife to the crew here, not in order of importance," she said with a sidelong smile to Michael. "As Michael said, we can't thank you enough. Jordan loves wildlife and he's more used to deer where we live. They generally stay put if they don't run off in the other direction. I think he just thought that's what moose would do."

Nathan could see where Tess got her eyes and her curls. Celine was an older version of Tess, carrying herself with grace and warmth. Her curls were shot through with streaks of silver, and her eyes twinkled with smile lines.

"Nice to meet you," Nathan replied. "Sorry it was under these circumstances. I've gotten to know your family a little when we've been out fishing this week."

"I've heard all about your and your brothers. You've been the best fishing guides Michael could have found. I love to fish, but I have to stay on land since I get seasick. I'm always hoping that when the rest of them head out on the water that they're in good hands. After all I've heard, I know they are. Not to mention that now I know you'll put yourself in danger to make sure my grandson is okay, you're my favorite fishing guide," Celine said with a soft smile. She gave Nathan's hand another squeeze before releasing it.

Tess had stepped over to join them. Celine turned to her and tucked her hand in Tess's elbow. "Honey, Jordan's fine. You're fine. That's all that matters."

Tess looked at her mother. "I know, Mom." She turned to Nathan. "Thank you. You got us out of there quick." She held his gaze, her eyes uncertain.

"Of course," Nathan responded. "Just tried to get you two moving in the opposite direction as fast as I could. And don't give Jordan too much grief. He's one of many, including local Alaskans, that underestimate how fast a moose can move and think they seem more tame than they are."

Tess nodded but didn't say anything else—her eyes still

dark, her mouth in a tight line. In the midst of her family and Travis, Nathan wished there was a way to have a moment alone with her, but he couldn't find a chance.

Back in Travis's truck as they headed to the harbor, Travis made a few comments about tourists and moose and then. "So you couldn't seem to keep your eyes off Tess."

Nathan glanced to Travis and caught a sly smile. "Don't know what you mean," he said, opting for evasion.

"Just noticed that you paid her a bit of attention. I know you'd have run out and grabbed anyone that ended up in that situation, but afterwards, you seemed a tad distracted by her. That's what I mean."

Nathan shifted in his seat and was relieved that they were just about at the harbor. He wasn't up to questions about noticing Tess, seeing as he seemed to be more obvious than usual. He reverted to type and rolled his eyes. "You know I like women and I like to flirt. She's cute."

Travis chuckled. "Wouldn't call that flirting, more like you couldn't keep your eyes off of her. If you want to insist you were flirting, go ahead."

Travis turned into the harbor parking lot and came to a stop behind Nathan's truck, a bright red Toyota pickup. Nathan ignored Travis's last comment.

"As usual, thanks for the help. Cleaning barnacles is boring stuff. You made it go twice as fast if not more," Travis said. He seemed content to let the subject of Tess go.

"No problem," Nathan replied as he stepped out of Travis's truck. Closing the door, he leaned into the window. "Don't forget to call me when you head up to dipnet next week. "

"You got it." With a nod, Travis drove away.

Nathan stood in the parking lot for a moment and looked around. It was late afternoon, and there was a hum of activity from the docks. No matter the time of day, the docks and harbor were busy in the summer. Restless, he walked down towards their boats. He climbed aboard Iris and did a quick check. They didn't worry too much, but the harbor was so busy in the summer with a large transient population that came through Diamond Creek, there were occasional thefts from boats. After checking Iris and making sure the cabin was locked, he hopped on the guide boat and did the same.

Climbing back onto the dock, he paused to look out into Kachemak Bay. The bay was busy, filled with boats moving in and out of the harbor and fishing in the distance. Gulls circled overhead and eagles perched on dock pilings. Nathan took a deep breath and tried to exhale Tess out of his mind—to no avail. Much as he didn't want to admit it, Travis was right, he hadn't been flirting with Tess. He'd been worried about her and wanted to protect and comfort her.

CHAPTER 4

ess walked down the hallway of the hotel where they were staying, Midnight Sun Lodges. The hotel sat high on the bluff by the ocean, overlooking Kachemak Bay with a clear view of the mountains and glaciers across the bay. She reached the lobby to find her mother seated in a chair looking out over the water. Tess sat down beside her.

"Amazing, isn't it?" Tess asked with a nod towards the view when her mother turned toward her.

"It certainly is amazing. I wish we'd come here years ago. Your father's been fantasizing about fishing in Alaska since you were a little girl and he read a story about it in one of his fishing magazines." Celine said with a smile. She paused for a moment and reached over to place her hand on Tess's shoulder. "You're still worrying about what happened with Jordan and that moose. I can see it. Let it go darling. He's just a boy and he's fine. You're fine."

Tess sighed. "I know, Mom. I wasn't worrying about that."

Celine tiled her head and gave her a smile, her hand

sliding off of Tess's shoulder. "I know you and you were worrying."

Tess mimicked her mother's head tilt and widened her eyes. "Okay Mom, I'll fess up. It was a close call," she said with a shake of her head. What she didn't say aloud was that she couldn't stop thinking about how good it had felt to have Nathan rush in and protect her and Jordan. She was already deep into a crush on him, and it seemed every interaction they had only pushed her deeper. *That* worried her. She prided herself on being practical and sensible. Her feelings for Nathan were anything but.

Celine gave her another long glance but made no further comment. She looked back out toward the bay before turning to Tess again. "Let's go have the ladies dinner I promised you. The boys are on their own. My guess is they'll have pizza," she said with a small laugh.

Tess watched her mother as she stood. Celine had the same curls she did, although they were less unruly. She had also passed on her curves to Tess, although Tess had always thought her mother carried herself more elegantly than she did. On her mother, the curves seemed sensual, rather than the 'too much' Tess often felt. Celine wore a jewel green lightweight sweater over jeans with a purple silk scarf draped across her shoulders. Silver hoops winked at her ears with a chunky stone necklace resting on her breastbone. Her mother somehow managed to pull off a casual polished look under almost any circumstances. Tess chalked it up to her southern upbringing. In the South, appearances mattered a lot. Her mother seemed to have mastered this without losing her sense of self in the process.

Tess had struggled to master how she carried herself. In childhood, she'd been a strong personality, a tomboy stomping through life, always trying to impress her brother and father. When adolescence and high school came upon her, social pressures of which she'd previously been oblivious were overwhelming. Her confidence leached away in increments while she shielded the feeling behind sarcasm. She'd entered college and managed to make it through as a stellar student. Good manners had been drilled into her, along with pride in her ability to do well in school. Her surface was put together while inside, doubt held sway. Those kernels of self-doubt bloomed after she became involved with Chad. Her doubts convinced her that his cutting comments about her appearance were accurate. She wanted to reach into that mettle and find the woman she used to think she might become, all those years ago when she'd stormed through childhood, barreling through whatever frightened her.

She'd been lost in her thoughts for a moment too long and glanced to her mother, who was patiently waiting with a smile. Tess stood quickly and brushed an errant curl out of her eyes. She held her arm out. "Let's go. Where did you pick for us to go tonight?"

Celine slipped her hand in Tess's elbow and gave her arm a squeeze. "The Boathouse Café. While y'all have been out fishing, I've visited the local galleries and shops and gotten all the suggestions. Everyone has suggested The Boathouse Café. Supposed to have a great all round menu and excellent seafood. My seasickness may keep me off the water, but it doesn't stop me from loving good seafood. I figure we're here for three weeks, so you and I get the first shot and then we'll come with the boys."

Celine drove while Tess watched the scenery along the short ride. She imagined that living here felt like living in a postcard. The views were constant, along with routine sightings of eagles, moose, ravens, and more. Where they lived in North Carolina was lovely, although far more developed. There were quiet areas to be found, but fewer and much farther between. Coastal North Carolina was fairly flat with the occasional low hill. The stark mountains in Alaska were majestic in their presence. The soft warmth of North Carolina created a mellow, moist green scent that mingled with the warm salty coastal air. Here in Alaska, the ocean air was sharp and salty with its cool gusts. The air crackled with life and contrasts.

The Boathouse Café sat just at the edge of the bluff that overlooked the bay. The café was in an updated older building. Its siding was weathered clapboard accented with bright fuchsia trim. The parking lot was filled, despite the early hour. They entered a cluster of people waiting to be seated. The restaurant had a warm feeling, simultaneously homey and modern. The kitchen grill was open and adjacent to part of the bar, which was a polished mahogany. Copper cookware hung above and mahogany shelving lined the wall behind the grill. A wide selection of wines was visible. Seating was comprised of polished wooden tables and booths with crisp white linens. A variety of rich colored curtains added a dash of vibrancy.

Although there was a line, Celine whispered to Tess that she'd made reservations. Once they made it through the crowd waiting in front, they were whisked to the only open booth that Tess could see. A young woman with a blonde ponytail introduced herself as Kate and took their drink order. Her mother loved good wine and ordered a bottle for them to share. Tess perused the menu and noticed that the seafood choices were lengthy and all fresh. Salmon, halibut and Alaskan king crab were offered in various preparations. They settled on an appetizer of mini halibut tacos with her mother opting for a crab dish and Tess going with king salmon. She loved dinners with her mother. Since she'd gone off to college in Maryland and followed a job to Greenville, North Carolina afterwards, she and her mother tried to get together for dinner every few months, taking turns for who drove to visit whom. In the months after her miscarriage and breakup with Chad, her mother had been one of her biggest supports.

Once their wine arrived, Tess poured for both of them and her mother raised her glass for a toast.

"To you, my dear girl. It's time for you to shake the dust off after what happened with Chad. So here's to that little wild child I raised and seeing that spark in your eyes again," her mother said with a twinkle in her eyes.

Tess was taken aback, but she lifted her glass for a small clink. They hadn't spoken about Chad for a while now. She should have known her mother was just waiting for a chance to bring it up again. God love her, but her mother was as nosy and opinionated as they came. This quality was aggravated by the reality that her mother was subtle and sly, so she could fool most anyone. Even though Tess knew better, she'd hoped her mother assumed she had pulled herself together. On the surface, Tess had. She just wished the part of her that had the courage to break up with Chad would shock her confidence back into her. Part of her wanted to make the toast and move on, but Celine was sharp. She'd notice Tess was avoiding.

"What makes you bring that up tonight?" Tess asked.

Her mother gave her a long look, her eyes warm and kind. "I bring it up because you act like you've moved on, but I know you. Even though you didn't plan that pregnancy, you were obviously hurting when you miscarried. I had a miscarriage once too, like I told you. It's not easy, especially without support from Chad. And even though you don't say a word about it, you're beating yourself up for not seeing him for who he was to begin with."

Tess started to respond, but stopped when her mother continued.

"I raised you and your brother to give people a chance and trust in the better parts of others. That's just what you did with Chad. The downside to that is…once in a while, it bites you. That's how I look at what happened."

Tears pricked Tess's eyes. "Okay, maybe you're right. Just wishing I had more sense about Chad sooner. And yeah, the miscarriage was hard, much harder than I could have imagined for a baby I never planned. For crying out loud, I was on birth control," she said ruefully.

Her mother took a sip of wine while she looked around the restaurant. "I hope you don't mind that I mentioned it. I realize we're on vacation and it's supposed to be all fun, but it's been on my mind the last few days. I haven't seen you smile in months, not the way you have since we've been here. I'd like to see more of that. I'd also like to see you move on in more ways than one," she said with a wink.

Tess rolled her eyes. "Really Mom? You're gonna go there already." Celine just smiled wider and nodded. Tess shook her head and took a breath. "I'm working on it. The part about smiling more. No other promises."

"Maybe you should stop working on it and just let life happen. That's something else I know about you. You always tried so hard when you were a little girl. If you thought you needed to learn something, or do something better, you just kept at it. I love that about you, but…" Her mother tilted her head with a small smile. "You had a hard lesson to learn this time, but it doesn't mean you need to 'work' on anything. Time helps a lot. Along with not beating yourself up."

Tess took another deep breath. "You've been waiting to say all this to me, haven't you?"

Celine was never one to shy away. "I was just waiting for the right time. But I've said my piece. Let's enjoy dinner."

Tess allowed herself to relax and just enjoy being where she was. The restaurant had an almost panoramic view of Kachemak Bay and the mountains across. The sun had started to set, albeit slowly. Sunsets in Alaska lasted for hours due to the proximity to the earth's northern pole. Rays of light cast long beams across the water, mingling with subtle rose and lavender streaks. She wondered what it would be like to see the northern lights in the winter. She'd heard about them and seen photos, but found it hard to imagine that the dark night sky could be filled with color.

The appetizer of halibut tacos was sumptuous. The king salmon was unlike any salmon Tess had eaten. She thought she knew what good salmon was but realized other salmon she'd had didn't even compare. It had been prepared in a basic way, baked over a cedar plank, flavored with a touch of lemon and garlic. Her mother became lyrical in her exclamations over the Alaskan king crab, which was served simply with butter. As Tess was laughing at her mother's abandonment over the crab, she looked up to see Nathan walking towards their booth. Jared and Luke were just behind him. Much as Nathan looked like his brothers, all Tess noticed was him. Her breath hitched, a flush rising at the mere sight of him.

Celine followed Tess's gaze. "Oh it's Nathan. Such a nice man! He was so kind today. Those must be his brothers. I mean, my god, the three of them are like peas in a pod. So handsome," she said with a wink towards Tess.

Nathan approached their table. "Hello there. You two found one of the best places in town for dinner."

"So nice to see you again, Nathan. These must be your brothers," her mother said with a nod towards Jared and Luke who came to stand to one side of Nathan. "I can't imagine who else they'd be."

"You guessed right. This is Jared and Luke," he said, gesturing towards each. He turned towards her mother. "And this is Celine. Tess's and Simon's mother, Michael's wife and Jordan's grandmother all in one."

Jared and Luke politely greeted Celine and made casual conversation with them. Tess's eyes kept straying towards

Nathan. He was freshly shaved and his thick black curls were damp and less wild than when he was out on the water. He wore a blue flannel shirt over jeans. The blue brought out the blue in his eyes, which were bright enough on their own.

She wished she could find a way to have some time alone with him. She pushed back against the strong pull, annoyed with herself for tumbling deeper into this crush. She didn't doubt that Nathan was accustomed to women fawning over him. It wasn't Nathan's fault that his downright handsome, sexy manner led her to shy away. While he was a far cry from Chad, they shared a magnetic charisma that drew women.

A wave of bitterness washed through Tess. Ignoring it, she called on the manners drilled into her, engaging in polite conversation. She caught a passing sharp glance from her mother, but ignored it. Within a few minutes, the hostess came to let the brothers know a booth was ready. Nathan gave her an assessing look as he turned away. After dinner, Tess guessed her mother discerned something was amiss with her, but she had the sense to let it lie for now. Tess was relieved that Nathan and his brothers had been seated on the far side of the restaurant, far enough away that she could more easily tune out the draw she felt and the disquiet it provoked.

* * *

HOURS LATER, Tess sat by the window in her room, watching the sun finally dip behind the mountains. The sky was barely light, a deep pink radiating above the mountains. She was restless, had been since they'd returned from dinner. She regretted that she'd told Nathan she'd have dinner and berated herself for worrying about it. His pull was a little too strong for her sanity. She didn't need to fall for some handsome guy again. Her inner agitation prompted her into motion. Tugging her windbreaker out of the closet, she stepped into her running shoes and slipped out of her room, heading to walk on the beach.

The early night air was sharp and brisk. A soft breeze came off the bay, the earthy fragrance of saltwater and ocean life almost instantly soothing her. The waves rolled into shore in a quiet rhythm. She took several slow breaths and stopped to look out over the water. The deep pink in the sky had faded to just a whisper of color. The half-moon sat high in the sky, its light reflecting on the water.

Tess walked slowly along the edge of the water where the sand was firm. She could hear distant voices from other areas on the beach and the harbor docks. Their hotel was situated just down the road from Otter Cove Harbor. Though out of sight, the reflections from the lights lining the docks spilled out from the cove, the water shimmering in the almost dark. The soft sound of water lapping the shore lulled her.

As Tess walked, she heard muted footsteps approaching. She glanced up to see Nathan walking towards her. Her stomach clenched, heat swirled to life and her pulse thrummed. "Damn," she said, not meaning to speak aloud.

Nathan didn't appear to have seen her up to that point. His head whipped up when she spoke.

"Tess?"

She sighed and stopped in her tracks. "Yup. It's me."

"I didn't expect to see you out here," Nathan said, sounding legitimately surprised. "Where are you staying?" he asked, striding towards her, coming to a stop a few feet in front of her.

It took a moment for her eyes to adjust and discern his features. Tess nodded her head in the direction of their hotel. "We're just back there at Midnight Sun Lodges. Dad wanted to be close to the harbor and from what I can tell, that's about as close as you can get. What brings you out here at this hour?"

Nathan shrugged. "Can't beat a walk on the beach. I love it here just about anytime of the day or night. What about you?"

Tess wasn't about to tell him that she was restless and discombobulated, mostly because of him. "Just wanted to take a walk. It's beautiful out tonight."

She hoped Nathan would move on quickly, although she wasn't sure how to gracefully make her exit. Being this close to him keyed her up, her pulse so rapid she worried he could hear it.

Nathan was quiet long enough that Tess glanced over and saw that he was looking out over the bay where the moon hung above. He appeared pensive. Despite the pull to fill the silence, she remained quiet.

Tess stared toward the water and was startled to hear the surface of the water break nearby. A sleek rounded shape lifted out of the water and held still.

She jumped slightly. Nathan turned quickly toward her.

"What's that?" she asked.

"Looks like a seal. They come pretty close to shore. Surprised you haven't seen one yet. They're nosy and love to watch people. If you walk on the beach during the day, don't be surprised if a few follow you along in the water, checking on you every now and then. Once in a while, they pull up and sun themselves on the docks."

Tess quietly watched the seal, which held still in the water. It couldn't have been more than fifteen feet away in the dark. She sensed Nathan move closer to her. The tension that radiated through her ratcheted up a notch.

Tess dared to look in Nathan's direction. Her focus narrowed to this very moment. A gust of wind blew her curls wilder than they already were. In the scant light, his eyes locked with hers, dark and intent. Unable to look away, heat rushed through her, her chest rose and fell with her rapid breath. His mere gaze wiped all thought from her mind. Nathan stepped closer until he was inches from her. Another gust of salty air blew a curl across her eyes. He reached up and brushed it away, his hand sliding into her hair and down along the side of her neck, his thumb gently passing over the beat of her pulse.

Before she could form a coherent thought, she was wrapped in Nathan's strong embrace and his lips came against hers. His kiss was a slow burn, initially cautious and then rocketing into a heat that she hadn't known she craved. One of her hands slipped into his black curls and the other around his neck, pulling him closer. She would have crawled into him if she could, completely engulfed in the moment. Thought abandoned her and she reveled in sensation.

One of Nathan's hands slipped under the back of her shirt, the warm roughness of his palm sent sparks skittering through her. His tongue delved into her mouth, meeting hers in a heated tangle. Her nerves were alight, vibrating to the tune of his touch. Heat smoldered in her center, pulsing through her. Without the strength of his arms holding her up, she'd have fallen.

She needed to be closer. She tugged at his flannel shirt, tearing the buttons open and slipping her hands inside. She sighed into his mouth at the feel of his skin. She ran her hands over his chest, feeling his heartbeat against her hand, pounding in a rapid rhythm.

Slick moisture built inside of her. Nathan's lips traveled down the side of her neck, leaving chills in their wake. Tess was flushed inside to the point of madness. She tugged him against her pelvis, sighing when she felt his hard cock press into her. He unhooked her bra and slipped his hands around to caress her breasts. Her breasts were heavy with desire, aching for his touch, craving the relief it offered. She gasped into his mouth. He dragged his thumbs across her nipples, slowly curling his hands around to cup both of her breasts, holding them with the lightest touch. She arched her back, her shirt slipping open and breasts spilling out.

Nathan sucked his breath in. "Tess!"

His whispered exclamation filtered through the fog of desire that had swamped her. Before she could form a thought, his lips closed over one nipple. She fell back into the fog, sensation overtaking her. He slowly licked and nibbled on both of her breasts. His hands kept busy with soft strokes, caressing her nipples with the barest grazes of his thumbs and soft pinches. Tess tumbled into a pool of feeling—her pulse careening out of control, her breath shallow, her desire building to a fevered pitch. Somewhere in a distant corner of her mind, she was stunned with how much she wanted him and wanted *this*.

She dragged her hand against his cock, felt it pulse against her hand through his jeans. She wanted him inside of her and wanted it *now*.

She started to unbutton his jeans, only to feel one of his hands come against hers and hold it still. She paused, her breath coming in gasps.

"Tess," he said, a questioning tone to his voice.

She held still, the haze clearing in her mind. She was relieved her eyes were closed because she couldn't believe she had been about to yank Nathan's jeans down and much more.

"What?" she asked finally.

"You have to know that I want you. I want you *now*. But…I didn't mean for this to happen this fast. Not because I don't want to. Trust me, I do. It's just that…" he paused and took a breath. "I don't want you to do something you might regret later."

Tess was relieved for the dark so Nathan couldn't see her blush. Now that the haze she'd fallen into had cleared, she was mortified. Her hand was still against the front of jeans. She could feel the heat from his cock, straining against his jeans. The hand he'd placed over hers remained there. She slowly pulled her hand away, feeling his gaze on her. Her eyes traveled down, taking in her unbuttoned blouse, his hand cupping one of her breasts. Her nipples tight and peaked with desire, both damp from his lips.

With a quick shake of her head, she stepped back abruptly, creating a pocket of space between them. His hands fell away. She looked up and saw the chest she'd just been caressing. As she had guessed, he had a body many women would give anything to get their hands on. His chest was fluid and muscled, a light dusting of black curls. His abdomen was sculpted. Her eyes followed the trail of dark hair to where his jeans hung low on his hips. His jeans pulled tight across his erect cock. Only the top button was open. Despite reality slapping her in the face, she still wanted to tear his jeans open. She couldn't believe she'd let this happen, much less how much she wanted him. If she let herself be honest for a moment, the desire she felt for him was unlike any she'd felt before. Her experiences with sex were best described as mediocre. Nothing horrible, but nothing great either. These few moments with Nathan were a wildfire she couldn't contain and didn't know what to make of.

She finally tilted her head back far enough to see his face. He had tucked his hands in his pockets. His chest rose and fell quickly. She waited a beat before speaking. "Well… that kind of just…happened."

Nathan gave a soft laugh. "You could say that again."

He looked over at her in the darkness. He appeared to be waiting for her to say something. Tess was lost. But she was nothing if not polite and since he seemed expectant, she tried to come up with something.

"I don't know what to say," she said and paused with a

small laugh when she realized how honest her statement was. "I didn't mean for that to happen."

Nathan nodded. "Me neither," he responded, giving her a long look that turned the heat up a notch inside of her. "But I won't pretend I didn't enjoy every second of it," he continued with a slow smile, his eyes flicking down towards her breasts and back to her face.

Tess thought she might melt into a puddle at his feet. Her nipples had tightened

in response to his glance. She instinctively tugged her shirt closed and looked away, breaking free from his gaze. She was surprised when his hands carefully started buttoning her shirt for her. Her breath, which had finally started to slow, became shallow again, her heart racing just to have his hands buttoning her shirt. Stepping back when he finished, he quickly buttoned his own shirt, hiding away that glorious chest.

She tucked her hands in the pockets of her windbreaker, uncertain of what to say next. Although the silence could have been uncomfortable, it wasn't. The sound of the ocean water lapping against the sand calmed her. She looked out over the water. The seal had disappeared.

Nathan's voice broke through the quiet. "Guess it's good we're in agreement we didn't plan that. Can I persuade you to have dinner with me now?"

Looking over, she saw a flash of uncertainty in his gaze. He continued, "I get the feeling that you said you'd have dinner with me but that maybe you'd let the next few weeks go by without actually letting it happen. After this, well… let's just say I want a chance to get to know you." His said this with an earnest quality.

She wanted to tell him that he wasn't right, but that would have been a lie. She had wished maybe she could just ignore his request and put it off. She took a long breath again as anxiety built in her.

"I wasn't planning to ignore that you wanted to go to dinner. But I won't pretend I wasn't sure about it, still aren't sure about it. I'm only here three weeks. I don't know… about *this*." She gestured between them.

He nodded. "Me neither. Don't see what it hurts just to maybe get to know each other. All I know is that I'll be bummed out if we can't even have dinner." He sounded almost boyish.

A giggle burst out, the sound foreign to her, it had been so long since any man had made her giggle. She glanced away for a moment, looking out over the dark water. Turning back she nodded. "Okay, you wanted dinner, you'll get dinner. Lord knows, I wouldn't want to bum you out," she said with another giggle.

"You say when," came his quick response.

She considered what she could tell her family and then decided not to worry about it. "How about tomorrow night? You can pick me up at the hotel. We fish with you and your brothers again the day after."

Nathan nodded in quick ascent. "You got it. Seeing as I can tell your mom's already scoping out what's good, any requests for where we go?"

She shook her head. "You pick. Say six o'clock?"

Another nod from him. "Do you want me to walk you back to the hotel?" he asked.

She shook her head. "No thanks. I want to walk some more."

"Got it. Watch out for seals," he said with a smile.

They stood for a moment. Tess had the urge to lean over to kiss him but wasn't ready to face the fire that he kindled. He reached a hand up and tucked a stray hair behind her ear. "I'll see you tomorrow," was all he said before his hand dropped. Her ear tingled where he'd briefly touched it.

"Good night," she called softly as he turned away.

He glanced over his shoulder. "Good night."

Tess watched Nathan walk away in the dark, his form slowly fading. When she lost sight of him once he rounded the corner of the beach into the harbor, she turned to face the ocean. The moon had risen higher in the sky. It was almost perfectly at half fullness, a half circle of light casting a glow on the water, the waves rippling in its shimmer. Her heart finally slowed, her breath following suit. She laughed to herself, considering that she'd come out here to get her mind off of Nathan. That was about impossible now. In what couldn't have been more than a few minutes, he'd turned her world upside down. She'd never felt what she'd felt with him and it terrified her.

She started walking back towards the hotel at a slow pace. The cool temperature was a balm to the flush she felt inside and out. She heard a sound in the water and looked out to see a seal surface again. Just as before, the seal held its head above the water and appeared to be watching her. In a moment, the seal curled and dove back under the water, only to surface again a few feet ahead of her. Tess made her way along the edge of the water towards the hotel. As Nathan had described, the seal followed her along the way. It would pause at points, holding still in the water, its rounded head above the surface, bobbing in the small waves that rolled into shore. It repeatedly dove back under the water and surfaced ahead of her. When she reached the walkway for the hotel and turned to walk up, she looked to the ocean once more. There was just enough light cast from the hotel lights that the seal was visible, watching from the water just beyond the end of the walkway.

CHAPTER 5

*N*athan came awake gradually, warm from the sun shining directly onto his bed. He hadn't been thinking too clearly after running into Tess on the beach and had forgotten to close the shades last night. Replaying those few minutes with her over and over, he'd been forced to take a cool shower to shake off the yearning for her. He lay still, disoriented from being deep in sleep. He heard his door push open and the sound of dog paws padding across the carpet. With a smile, he rolled to the side, expecting to see Jessie, Hannah and Luke's dog. Luke must have stopped by with her. In a moment, Jessie came around the side of his bed and started wagging her tail like mad. She'd stayed with them a few weeks when Luke first found her, and he and Jared took care of her whenever Luke and Hannah were out of town. She sidled up to the bed, rubbing against his hand. She was a lovely girl, black with soft gold markings and wavy long fur.

"Hey there girl," he greeted her. "You've decided it's time for me to get up huh?"

Jessie responded by wagging her tail faster and nuzzling

his hand. He stroked her back and rested in the sun for a moment. With a deep breath, he pushed himself up and swung his feet to the floor.

"Alright girl, I'm up."

Striding to his dresser, he tugged a T-shirt out. He didn't bother changing out of the sweatpants he'd fallen asleep in last night. Jessie followed him a half step behind as he walked out to the kitchen and living room area. He found Jared seated at the kitchen table with Luke and Hannah.

"Good morning," he said with a small wave. He swiped at his curls for a moment, pointlessly attempting to bring order to them.

Hannah grinned. "Hey there Nathan. Looks like you're personal alarm clock woke you. If you're not around in the morning when we come by with Jessie, she goes to find you right away."

Nathan glanced over to Jessie who'd flopped down in the middle of the kitchen, her tail still wagging with small thumps against the floor.

"I think I'm her favorite uncle," he said with a sly smile towards Jared.

Jared shook his head. "Nope, that's me."

"Jessie loves everybody," Hannah said with a laugh. She gestured towards the coffee pot. "Fresh pot of coffee—waiting for you."

Nathan quickly poured coffee in a mug waiting on the counter, added a dash of cream and sat down at the table. He held his coffee aloft with a nod towards Hannah. "Guessing you're the one who got a mug out for me," he said with a smile, taking a sip of coffee. "And of course, the coffee is delicious."

"Of course, I got the mug out for you. Jared and Luke may sometimes take care of you, but I don't think they go that far," Hannah replied with a wink.

"Uh, definitely not," Jared said. "We might make coffee for him, but only because we're making it for ourselves."

Luke chuckled. Nathan took another few sips of coffee, savoring the rich taste. Hannah made coffee the way he liked—dark. Luke's arm rested across the back of Hannah's chair, hand curled around her shoulder, his thumb absently caressing her. Nathan thought back to last night—a part of him wishing his sense hadn't got the best of him. Tess's ginger eyes and honey curls and lush curves filled his mind. It had taken almost all the discipline he had to stop himself from taking her in the sand.

"How's it going?" Luke asked, his voice interrupting Nathan's thoughts, which was convenient because his cock twitched at the mere thought of Tess this morning.

"Just a little out of it. Coffee hasn't kicked in yet," he said, not about to share his train of thought with them. "Where's John?" he asked. John was Hannah and Luke's one-year old son.

"He's with Susie this morning. We've got a few errands to take care of and she offered to babysit. Errands are much quicker without a toddler," Hannah replied wryly before changing the subject. "When are you guys taking that family out fishing again? They were great. I enjoyed hanging out with Tess."

Nathan felt Hannah's gaze on him and looked over, answering before he thought about it. "They have another trip scheduled with us tomorrow."

"Since when did you ever remember who was scheduled with us?" Jared asked.

Jared's observation was on target because Nathan rarely paid attention to such details, particularly since Jared handled most of the scheduling.

"I remember sometimes. Plus, when we saw Tess and her mother at The Boathouse last night, they mentioned it," he responded, hoping they'd move on. He didn't want them catching on that he noticed just about everything to do with Tess.

Hannah's eyes took on a curious gleam, but she remained quiet. Luke glanced at her and then Nathan, but he kept quiet.

Jared, on the other hand, wasn't holding back. "Really? We run into people we take fishing when we're out all the damn time. Diamond Creek's the size of a thimble. Still don't think you ever pay much attention to who's heading out with us. Here's what I think, you can't keep your eyes off of Tess, so for once you're paying attention."

Nathan took a slow sip of coffee and shrugged. "Think what you want," he offered in return to Jared. He was in no mood to take this one up with Jared, exposed as he felt since last night. To say he was startled by how the slow burn between them exploded into white-hot passion last night was an understatement.

Hannah seemed to take pity on him. "Oh whatever, Jared. Even if Nathan's got the hots for Tess, it's not like he's going to chat about it over coffee. Leave him be for now."

Nathan gave her a grateful smile, which he immediately realized he'd done too soon when Hannah continued. "Although for what it's worth, I think she's awesome. A woman like her would be great for you. Might push you to do something other than flirt," she said with a sly smile.

"Could I just have my coffee in peace?" he asked wryly.

Luke barked a laugh. "Maybe, maybe not. I'll stay out of it for now, but I reserve the right to embarrass the hell out of you later."

Nathan rolled his eyes and pushed his chair back. "That's about all I can handle before a shower," he said as he stood. He opted to change the topic. "So what are you two up to today?" he asked Hannah and Luke.

Jessie had gotten up and sidled against him when he

stood. He reached down to stroke her head, slipping his fingers through her glossy hair.

"Not much. We came by for coffee before we head to town for errands," Luke replied.

"We have to get some fertilizer for the garden," Hannah added with a nudge of Luke's shoulder. "You promised we'd take care of the flower beds this week."

"So I did. Need anything?" Luke asked.

Jared and Nathan nodded in unison, which prompted a grin from Luke. "How about you do our grocery shopping for us?" Jared asked.

Nathan added, "You did a better job with groceries than we do."

Luke looked amused. "So I had to move out for you two to appreciate me? We can grab a few things for you today, but you're gonna have to figure this one out because I can't shop for you every week."

Luke and Hannah stood. Nathan experienced a moment of relief; they seemed to have moved on from needling him about Tess. Within a few minutes, Hannah was cleaning up in the kitchen and he was able to gracefully make his exit to shower. Entering his bedroom, he softly closed the door behind him. He looked out the window, which faced the bay. The sun was bright and the wind blowing, a steady roll of the waves on the water and a cluster of sailboats in the bay.

Once Nathan stepped in the shower, his thoughts turned to Tess again. For the first time since he'd asked her out to dinner, he pondered the fact that she didn't live here. When he'd originally asked her, he'd thought it would just be fun. After kissing her last night and almost tearing her clothes off, he wasn't so sure what he wanted.

* * *

IT WAS late afternoon when Nathan stopped in to grab a cup of coffee at Misty Mountain Café. He had spent most of the day helping Jared with yard work and then headed to town to stop by the post office to pick up their mail. He'd kept himself busy enough that he'd managed not to dwell on Tess, but thoughts of her danced in the corners of his mind. He stepped into the coffee shop and tipped his sunglasses on top of his head, taking a quick look around. The coffee shop was situated in an old Quonset hut, a relic from the days of World War II. The United States had set up strategic bases in Alaska during the war due to its location on the Pacific Ocean. As a result, Quonset huts were scattered around the state; some left where they were originally placed by the military and others relocated. The huts were half circles of corrugated steel, often fairly long, and resembled half-tubes on the ground. Inside, they felt open and airy. They held up well in the rough weather of Alaska. As with many, this one had been modernized inside with finished walls covering the steel and decorative timber beams crisscrossing the upper portion. The café was accented with a wide variation of bright colors from different colored window trim and curtains to bright table-cloths. Local artwork rotated through the café on its walls.

This month was a new series of photographs from a local photographer who was a friend of his, Shane Joseph. As he walked over to take a look, Susie Hammond, Hannah's best friend and a good friend of he and his brothers, waved to him from a corner table. He returned the wave and called out, "Be right over, let me grab a coffee first."

He got in line behind what appeared to be a few tourists, seeing as Nathan had never seen them around town. The local population of Diamond Creek wasn't too large, but the town exploded with tourists every summer. Anyone unfamiliar was most likely a tourist. Nathan thought back to when he and his brothers first moved to town a few years ago. The locals were welcoming, but it had taken a good year before Nathan felt like they'd genuinely been accepted. He learned over time that Alaskans were accustomed to people coming to the area with the intention of staying and then leaving within the first year, either daunted by the long winter and its short days, or having little understanding beyond the fantasy of living in Alaska.

Unlike other parts of the country, or the Lower 48, as Alaskans referred to the rest of the country, living in Alaska meant a degree of isolation that few grasped until they experienced it. In most of the United States, many areas considered themselves rural and they were; yet one could access populated areas within a few hours and by car. Most of Alaska was off the road system and urban areas took hours to reach by plane. Residents had to be prepared to tolerate this level of separation, along with the much higher costs of living. The payoff was the sense of community and caring that thrived in ways he hadn't seen elsewhere, along with a stunning beauty and a connection to nature that was honed and sharpened by the way life was shaped by the seasons.

After he got his coffee, he headed to Susie. Once she saw him approaching, she closed her laptop and tucked some papers in a folder. She greeted him a huge smile. "Nathan! Haven't seen you in weeks. How have you been?"

Nathan returned the smile and sat opposite her at the tiny table. Susie had wild brown curls and warm brown eyes. She was petite with an outsized personality, witty, outspoken and funny. She was also the best accountant in town and did the books for their fishing business. He took a gulp of his coffee and looked over at her.

"Just fine. Busy fishing, but I'm sure you figured that. How about you?"

Her curls bounced as she nodded. "Good, good. Busy keeping up with everyone's accounts. I came over here for a change of scenery and to eavesdrop and catch up on any gossip," she responded with a sly smile.

Nathan chuckled. "So, what's the latest news?"

"Well, if you must know..." she paused, her eyes taking on a mischievous glint. "There is some gossip about you, or perhaps it's better said that there's chatter about the fact that you seem to have changed your ways recently."

He rolled his eyes. "Why would anyone care what I'm doing?" he asked, feigning ignorance.

"Not long after you guys moved here, you became known as the fun one. Always out at the bars, flirting enough that you basically tortured half the single women in this town. You've lived here long enough that you might have a clue, but you have to realize that for those of us that grew up here, someone new in town is major news. Especially when they stay. With Jared so serious and keeping to himself, Luke now married to Hannah, all the girls had their hopes pinned on you. Not me, of course, because you're not my type. But now word is that you're not out that much anymore. Sooooo...the guessing game has been whether or not you got serious with someone. I know you can't be because Hannah would have told me, but you should know plenty of people are wondering."

Nathan sighed inside and looked over at Susie. The downside to a tiny town in Alaska was that everyone noticed everything. "Maybe I haven't been out as much lately but don't read too much into that. Just haven't been in the mood these days," he said with a shrug, not about to get into the fact that he wasn't so sure being the local flirt was what he wanted for the foreseeable future.

Susie was sharp, but she didn't push. "Well, I just thought you'd want to know. No worry that you're the only subject of gossip. There's plenty more. Like the fact that the couple that moved to town and opened The Boathouse Café are getting a divorce now and planning to sell the restaurant. I can assure you that news is getting way more traction."

"Oh, that's too bad. Don't really know them. Hope whoever buys the restaurant has enough sense to keep it the way it is. I love that place," he said.

"You and me and pretty much everyone in town," Susie said with a nod. "Anyway, that's the main news. On another subject, I just closed out the books from the last two months for you guys. The One That Didn't Get Away is in good shape this year."

Nathan experienced a flash of pride. No matter how many years they did this, he loved the fact that their business was doing so well. "That's awesome! Knew we were busy, but since I don't do the books...Thank God you do, by the way," he said with a nod to her. "We don't really know how the numbers shake out until after everything tallied up and expenses are covered. I'll let Jared know when I head home. He's always impatient to get the final numbers."

Susie shook her head. "You can say that again," she said wryly. "You guys are easy to work with for the most part, but Jared wants everything right away. He forgets that I can't balance everything out until all the receipts are in, and I have a chance to enter expenses. I've learned to be ready for him though. He's so uptight about it that I try to beat him to calling me every time."

Nathan threw back his head with a laugh. Susie gave Jared a run for his money. He'd watched her needle Jared time and again. "Awesome! Now I can enjoy the fact that I'll be able to give him an update before he even called you."

Still laughing, Nathan pushed his chair back and stood. "I gotta get going Susie. As usual, great to see you."

As Nathan drove home, he pondered the fact that he'd unwittingly become a small topic of town gossip. While he had previously shrugged off what people thought of him, he wasn't too comfortable that his patterns were so obvious. A glance at the clock on his dashboard and he realized he'd be meeting Tess for dinner in just over two hours. His stomach coiled and his heart picked up. The anticipation of seeing her sharpened his desire so quickly that he flushed. He felt like a teenage boy with his first crush. He wanted her so much that he would have preferred to skip dinner entirely and take her straight to bed. Somehow, he didn't think that would help him convince her he wasn't just a playboy.

He sensed a hesitance with her, as if she didn't believe he was genuinely interested in her. As naturally beautiful and sexy as she was, he was curious about how oblivious she appeared to her appeal. The thought occurred to him that he would usually blow by any woman that didn't seem easy-going. Tess had an edge to her and tended to be reserved. And yet, the side he'd seen of her in those blurred moments of passion on the beach was wild, unrestrained and so passionate, he'd thought she was about to burst into flames in his arms, right along with him. The contrast of how she felt in his arms with the guardedness she exuded at other times puzzled him. The fact that he was persisting in his pursuit of Tess in spite of this and that her hesitance only sparked his interest and determination was a new experience.

CHAPTER 6

ess fiddled with her hair, trying to get an errant curl to stay in place. After her futile attempts failed, she let her hands fall to the edge of the bathroom counter. Accepting what she'd known for years, that her hair had a mind of its own, she sighed and quickly applied a soft pink lipstick before turning away. She had about a half hour before Nathan was due to pick her up and was pondering whether to ask her mother to make excuses for the rest of her family as to why she wasn't having dinner with them this evening. She'd delayed until the last minute. While she adored her family, they were prone to have strong opinions about what she should do, especially when it came to men, all of which had been exacerbated since she'd broken up with Chad. She decided to tell her mother and ask her to cover with the rest of the family. She couldn't fool her mother. Otherwise, she knew she'd get found out and then lose all chances to manage the narrative. Picking up her phone, she dialed.

Her mother picked up on the second ring.

"Hello dear! We're going to head out in about an hour. Will you be ready?"

Tess took a breath, bracing for the interrogation that was sure to come. "Hey Mom, that's what I was calling about. Do you have a minute to come to my room?"

The line went silent in her ear. Just as Tess hit the button to end the call, she heard a rapid knock at her door and laughed. Her room was four doors down from her parents, so her mother must have run down the hall. Opening the door, she could see the speculation whirring in her mother's mind as Celine gave Tess a quick perusal.

"Yes?" Celine asked.

"Come in Mom, let's not chat in the hallway," Tess responded with a small laugh.

Once Tess had the door closed, she sat on the side of the bed. "Here's the thing, Mom. I'm asking you to keep this to yourself so you better promise before I say another word."

Celine's eyes took on a curious gleam. "Of course! Whenever you've asked me to keep something to myself, I have. You should know that by now," she said, a touch of affront in her tone.

"I know, Mom, but I have to make sure. That's all," Tess replied. She took another deep breath, seeing as she seemed to be taking those a lot these days. She looked over at her mother and felt her shoulders relax. Despite her mother's tendency to be overinvolved and to worry, Tess knew she was blessed to be so loved. Celine looked worried and curious. Tess put her out of her misery. "Nathan asked me out to dinner and I said yes," she blurted out.

Celine squealed. "Oh, he's such a nice man and so handsome! He's perfect for you. Tess, this is wonderful!"

Tess rolled her eyes. "I know he's nice, Mom, and I won't pretend he's not handsome, but could you please not marry us off just yet? This is just dinner and he lives here—in Alaska, nowhere near North Carolina. I like him anyway and I need to have a little fun. You said so yourself. He's asked a few times, and I finally said yes."

Celine visibly tamped down her excitement, but her smile just grew wider. "Just like I said the other night, it's time for you to move on. A date with someone like him could lead to all sorts of things. I just don't want you to rule anything out. Have fun, enjoy him," she implored, her gaze growing serious.

"Mom, it's just one date. I'm telling you this because it's tonight and I want you to cover for me with dad, Simon and Jordan."

Celine nodded, a gleam in her eyes. She loved feeling like she was in on something. "Of course! Do you know where you're going so I can make sure we don't accidentally end up at the same place?"

Tess shook her head. "I didn't think that far ahead. How about you tell me where you're going and I can rule that out if Nathan suggests it?"

"We were planning to go to The Boathouse Café again. Your father wants to try it. Since you loved it, I figured you wouldn't mind going again."

"What are you gonna tell them about why I'm not with y'all?"

"Oh that's easy. I'll just tell them you decided to get one of the spa packages here. Those take hours and hours. The guys will never think twice about it."

"You are too good at this, Mom," Tess said wryly.

"You forget that I have three older brothers. They may seem like nice uncles to you, but they were hell on me when I started dating, all the way into my marriage with your dad. Once they decided he was okay, they finally stopped nosing into everything. I became the master at coming up with good excuses for what I might be doing," Celine explained with a sly smile. She gave Tess a long look. "You look lovely, but then you usually do." She walked over to Tess and loosely tousled Tess' curls and turned her to look in the mirror sitting over the dresser. "You need to stop trying to make your curls behave and just embrace that they are wild. Took me years to do that with my own curls, but ever since it's much easier." She tousled Tess' curls more and straightened a dangly earring she'd tangled in the process.

Tess looked at her reflection and saw that her mother was right. The less she tried to rein in her curls, the better they looked. Her mother's mussing had left her honey gold curls in a soft rumple, the light catching on the brighter shades.

She looked up at her mother. "Thanks, Mom. I should have mentioned it sooner, but it was only yesterday that I agreed to have dinner with Nathan." She decided not to let her mother in on the few moments of frenzied passion with Nathan last night. Those moments loomed so large that even a second of thinking about them flushed her, just as it did now.

Celine was still busy with her hair. She made a few more adjustments to Tess' curls, tugging and tousling until she appeared content. She stepped away. "I wouldn't be anything other than a good sport about this. I want you to have fun and enjoy yourself. Anytime you want to clue me in, feel free. I'll keep this quiet no matter what, but if you feel like filling me in tomorrow, that would be just fine," she said with a wink, her soft Southern drawl peaking at the end.

Tess threw her head back with a laugh. "Oh Mom, I'll fill you in. I know you'll find a way to get answers even if I'm not so sure I want to tell you," she said. She glanced at the clock on the nightstand. "Okay, Nathan's supposed to pick me up in about fifteen minutes. You need to get back to your room and keep dad, Simon and Jordan occupied."

Celine nodded, all business now. "You got it girl, I'm on my way." She strode to the door and turned back just before she opened it. "You're beautiful inside and out. Nathan's lucky to have even one dinner with you. Don't forget that," she said. With an emphatic nod, she swung the door open and stepped out.

Tess looked in the mirror again, taking in the way her mother had just carelessly undone her efforts to subdue her curls, leaving them wild and free. She stood and smoothed down the pants she was wearing. After obsessing over what to wear, she'd settled on the only pair of pants that she'd packed that weren't jeans. They were soft and silky, a deep green shade and flared to swing around her ankles. She'd paired them with a cream-colored gauzy cotton blouse. She wore a choker around her throat, a lightweight silver chain with a large round blue lapis stone that sat in the juncture between her collarbones. She'd paired that with a hammered silver cuff on one arm and a set of matched earrings of the blue lapis. Predicting it would be cool, she planned to bring a windproof fleece jacket. Just as she glanced at the clock again, her phone rang.

"Hello," she said, bringing the phone to her ear.

"Tess? It's Nathan."

"Hey there," she replied, her heart speeding up at the sound of his voice.

"Just calling to let you know I'm pulling into the parking lot if you want to meet me out front," Nathan said.

Tess was on her way to the door when she abruptly stepped into the bathroom. She grabbed the small bottle of perfume oil sitting on the bathroom counter—an amber scented oil she loved to wear but rarely did. She dabbed the oil on the insides of her wrists and elbows and on her neck and refused to think about why it mattered just now.

* * *

TESS SAT in the passenger seat and looked out over a field

where Nathan had pulled over. They were on the way to what Nathan described as the best local brewery in Alaska: Diamond Creek Brewery. Nathan assured her that the brewery also had amazing food. He insisted on taking her on a quick tour of Diamond Creek highlights before they had dinner. They were presently looking at an open field filled with fuchsia colored flowers. The field sat atop one of the hills in town. The hillside dropped down behind the field, opening up an expansive view of Kachemak Bay and the mountains beyond. Mount Augustine sat towards the left of the view, tall and regal as it rose out of the water, a cluster of clouds circling its peak. The field was flanked by spruce trees, the deep green a contrast to the bright flowers, which swayed in a breeze that came off the bay. Tess caught her breath at the sight of the flowers with the bay spilling out behind them where the hillside dipped down. The sky was slightly overcast, its slate gray brightening the contrast of the flowers.

"What are those flowers?" she asked.

"Fireweed. Prettiest weed I ever saw," Nathan said. He glanced towards her and smiled. "Beautiful huh?"

She nodded. "If something could be more than beautiful, this is. The fireweed is amazing. I can't believe it's just a weed. And the view," she said with a sigh.

"Fireweed is everywhere in Alaska. It blooms towards the last part of summer and usually lasts about a month. The first time we came fishing up here, we stayed here in Diamond Creek just when the fireweed was in bloom. It's part of why I fell in love with Alaska," he said. He started the truck. "Thought you might like to see it."

Tess finally turned away from the view. "Thank you for bringing me up here. I've seen a few patches of the flowers in town, but it's nothing like seeing a field full of it."

Nathan's dimples joined his smile as he shifted gears and turned on a road that led down the hill to town. Tess took advantage of his attention to the road and took a good long look. His black curls were a tad less unruly than when he was out fishing but not by much. His blue eyes were just that—so blue that it was like diving in for a swim to look at them too long. His mouth was sensual, his lips full and mobile. He had a resting grin expression. She figured he probably had a half smile even in his sleep. His features were strong; sculpted cheekbones, a strong nose that looked as if he'd broken it at some point with a jog in the bridge and dark slashes for eyebrows. She turned away, realizing that looking at Nathan too much made her wonder yet again why a man as gorgeous as him would be interested in her.

In the few minutes since they'd driven down from the top of the hill, clouds had burgeoned in the already overcast sky. A soft drizzle started to fall. Tess was glad she'd brought her windbreaker. Nathan's truck, a bright red Toyota, had a jumble of jackets and boots in the small cab behind the front seats. Nathan came around a corner in the road.

"What the hell?!" Nathan exclaimed.

Tess saw a blur of brown and heard the squeal of tires. Fear rose in her throat when she realized two vehicles were ahead of them on the road: a small truck on its roof in the middle of the road with a compact car on its side in the ditch. Nathan swore a few more times as he steered the truck to a stop, inches from the overturned truck. When they came to a stop, Tess finally let out the breath she hadn't realized she was holding, her heart hammering in her chest. They sat in the silence for a moment, the rumble of the truck's motor the only sound. Tess looked to the side of the road to see the blur of brown was a moose. It disappeared into the trees that flanked the road.

"You okay?" Nathan asked, his voice slicing through the silence.

Tess nodded and turned to look at him. She realized she had one hand clenched around his forearm. She'd curled her other hand tight on the edge of her seat. She slowly released her hands and rubbed them together. "I'm fine. You?"

"Fine," he said.

Tess automatically unbuckled her seatbelt and went to see if they could help. Clambering out of the truck, she ran over to the truck in the road. She heard Nathan calling 911. She knelt down to see that there were two people inside. A young woman appeared unconscious, but Tess couldn't see much else, other than that the woman was jammed to one side of her seat in the upside down vehicle. The other passenger was a man who was conscious, his eyes wide and dark. Blood ran down his cheek in a trickle. Broken glass was scattered all over him. His shoulder pressed against the doorframe. He was bracing himself with his free arm against the ceiling.

"I know you may be hurting, but can you wait until the ambulance gets here?" Tess asked. "I'm afraid to try to move you too much—we need to be careful," she explained.

The man nodded. "I can wait, but I'm worried about Paige. Can you tell if she's okay?" He tried to turn to see, grimacing as he did.

"Don't do that," Tess said. "I'll go around. What your name?" she asked.

"It's Finn. Paige is my sister," he said, his eyes catching hers, dark with fear.

"I'm Tess," she said, thinking that she didn't want to be nameless to him. She stood and glanced to Nathan who'd gone to check on the other vehicle. She could hear him talking to the 911 operator, providing a running commentary.

"Nathan," she called, walking around to the other side of the truck.

He looked up and tilted the phone away from his mouth.

"These guys are a little banged up but okay. How about over there?"

She didn't want to speculate, but she was worried about the woman. She shrugged instead. "How long until help gets here?"

Nathan relayed her question and called back. "About three minutes away now according to dispatch."

Tess knelt down to see if she could get a better sense of Paige's injuries. After long look, she still couldn't tell if Paige was breathing. Tess's stomach felt hollow and her chest tight. She wanted to tear the truck door open and pull Paige out to make sure she was okay. One look at the doorframe, and she knew that was impossible. It was crushed against the truck's roof, the metal wrinkled into a tight jam. The window was broken, yet just as with Finn, she worried that if she tried to pull Paige out, she'd hurt her even more.

She heard Finn's voice. "Paige? How are you? I can't turn my head to see you," he said. "Can you see if she's okay?" he asked, directing his question to Tess.

Tess waited a beat before responding. Part of her wanted to reassure him, but she didn't want to pretend she knew something she didn't. She chose honesty. "I can't tell. She's not conscious, but I think you may have guessed that. She must have hit her head."

Finn was silent for a moment. When he spoke, his voice was tinged with fear and desperation, tugging at Tess's heart. "She'll be okay. She has to be."

Tess waited beside the truck, kneeling by Paige. She reached a hand out and carefully maneuvered it through the broken window, placing it on Paige's shoulder, this woman she'd never even met. After a moment, she felt the subtle rise and fall of Paige's breath. It was shallow but she was breathing. Tess said a silent hallelujah. She looked around. The truck's roof was crumpled. The compact car lay on its side, smashed against the ditch embankment. She could hear Nathan talking with the passengers, asking them both to wait until help came. A raven called nearby, a magpie responding with a burst of chatter, both flying out above the wreckage.

As Tess looked up at the two birds, she heard the ambulance siren barreling up the hill toward them. She kept her hand on Paige's shoulder, holding on to the soft rhythm of her breath. The ambulance came to a quick stop just below the accident. In seconds, the crew was in full swing. Tess quickly deduced she would be in the way if she stayed by Paige, so she gave Paige's shoulder a gentle squeeze and stepped away from the truck. The next few minutes passed in a rapid blur.

The police arrived on the heels of the ambulance. In questioning Nathan and the two young men from the compact car, who had been pulled out within minutes and aside from a few cuts and bruises looked fine, Tess learned that two moose had run across the road. With both vehicles trying to dodge the moose, they collided. Tess wondered if the moose she and Nathan had seen was one of them. The thought that they had just missed being in an accident elicited a wave of feeling—she was just getting to know Nathan and the thought of him being hurt terrified her. She quickly shook her head, uneasy with how much he mattered to her.

It wasn't much longer before the emergency crew had gotten Finn and Paige out of the truck. Finn was shaken and sported a few cuts and bruises. He hovered by the ambulance stretcher, asking questions and constantly checking Paige's face. While one of the crew as attempting to reassure Finn, Paige's eyes flicked open. She appeared disoriented but clearly relieved.

Despite Paige's protests, Finn and the crew insisted she go to the hospital to be cleared. She appeared to think that since she was conscious, she was fine. Another few minutes and the ambulance headed back down the hill carrying Paige with Finn accompanying her. Tess looked towards Nathan who was standing with the two young guys from the car. The two police officers were conferring by their car, one on the phone with a tow company.

Tess walked to Nathan's side. "Well, all's well that ends well. Seems like everyone will be okay," she said.

Nathan started to speak, but was distracted by a loud rustle in the trees. All heads turned towards the trees in unison. In a few seconds, a moose came ambling out of the trees, followed by two more. Tess glanced around, gauging where Nathan's truck was in relation to the moose—not close enough for comfort. The moose seemed completely unconcerned by the presence of four people right by them and an additional two just down the road. One of the moose stepped close to the compact car on its side, reaching its nose out to sniff at a tire.

Tess felt Nathan step closer to her, his hand sliding around hers, the vital strength comforting her. Just as one of the moose stepped into the road and nosed the over-turned truck, a loud crackling sound came over the cop's radio. The first moose that had stepped out of the trees swung its head in the direction of the cop car, its attention focused on the sound from the radio. Another second and the moose started moving in the direction of the cops who appeared not to have noticed as one was leaning into the cruiser, talking on the radio, and the other had his back to them.

Nathan called out in the direction of the cops. "Hey!"

At this point, the moose stopped in the road and turned back towards Nathan and the rest of them. In slow motion, Tess watched the moose start to jog back to them, seeming to cover an enormous amount of ground in slow motion. The cluster that they had formed broke apart. The two guys clambered on top of their wrecked car, Nathan dashed towards the overturned truck, much closer than his, dragging Tess with him. Next thing Tess knew, she was trying to gain her footing on the undercarriage of the upside down truck. There were two islands of people on wrecked vehicles with three moose staring at them. The cops had wisely climbed back in their car. She burst out laughing.

One of the cops leaned out the window. "Hey there! No worries, we're not leaving, just hanging tight 'til these moose get over their curiosity."

Tess only laughed harder. She considered that perhaps she should be afraid, but didn't think the moose could do much to them where they were.

Nathan caught her eye, looking bemused. "Well damn if this isn't silly. Staying put is the smartest thing to do, but we look ridiculous." He looked toward the cops. "Glad to see you guys are safe and tight there. Any ideas on how to break up this moose party?"

The two guys across from them were laughing too. One of them leaned down from his perch to grab a stick. He stood and tossed it towards the moose that had led the way out of the woods. The stick landed with a thud. The moose's only response was to lean down and nose at the stick.

Tess was laughing so hard at this point, tears rolled down her cheeks. She sat down on one of the tires. Nathan looked over at her. "You seem to be enjoying this."

Her shoulders shook with laughter. "This is just so ridiculous! I thought I'd see wildlife when we came to Alaska, but I never could have imagined this." Giggles kept bursting out.

She jumped when she heard the police siren come on. They flashed their lights in conjunction with a few more blasts of the siren. The three moose were finally jolted enough to start moving. In another few minutes, the three moose disappeared into the trees across from where they had appeared. They waited a few more minutes before climbing down from the respective vehicles. Just as they did, two tow trucks appeared. The cops finally got back out of their car and stood by while the tow truck drivers started to get the vehicles loaded. Nathan and Tess said their good-byes to the police and the two guys who hopped in the back of the cop car for a free ride to town.

Once they were in Nathan's truck, Tess was overcome with the giggles again. Nathan looked at her askance and just shook his head. "Well you definitely have a story after this," he said with a chuckle.

Tess took several deep breaths and watched while the crushed truck was slowly levered into place on a tow truck bed. She thought about the moose, standing on the bottom of the truck, the fear in Finn's eyes and the relief she experienced when she felt Paige's breathing. She looked at Nathan, a wave of feeling rushing through her. Between the accident, the worry of whether everyone would be okay and then the moose, she was awash in adrenaline.

"I'm just glad everyone's okay," she said, sobering for a moment. "I didn't say anything, but I was scared for Paige for a few minutes there. It was hard to tell how she was since she was unconscious. I wasn't sure she was breathing at first. I'm so glad she came out of it okay, at least as far as we can tell."

Nathan held her gaze. "You looked worried when you were waiting beside the truck. Damn glad she's okay. I know her and Finn a little. She's his younger sister." He gave her an assessing look. "Are you okay? You didn't hesitate to jump right in to help. And then, of course, those damn moose," he said with a shake of his head.

"I'm okay. Just overwhelmed I guess. And the moose, well that was just funny. I know they can be dangerous, but once we were on the truck and the guys were on the car, we were fine."

Nathan nodded, his eyes crinkling with a smile. He

glanced up and started the truck. "Looks like we can finally get through."

Tess looked away from him to see the rear of the last tow truck rolling forward. Nathan shifted the truck into gear and slowly followed the two tow trucks toward town.

"Still up for dinner at the brewery?" he asked. "I'd understand if you weren't. It's been a pretty eventful drive to dinner."

Tess didn't hesitate. "Oh yeah. I'm up for dinner. If everything hadn't turned out okay, perhaps not," she responded. "Plus, you've talked this place up so much that now I'm ready to see if the food and beer is as amazing as you say."

She felt Nathan's grin before she looked over. He kept his eyes on the road. "Guessing I'll hear about it if it doesn't meet your standards."

athan held the door for Tess when they entered Diamond Creek Brewery. After the hostess advised it would be a few minutes, he waited beside Tess in the small and crowded entryway.

"I wouldn't have thought a brewery in Diamond Creek would have a hostess," Tess remarked.

"Only in the summer. Gets so busy that if they don't have someone managing the front, it's a mess. Seeing as you're here in the midst of tourist season, probably hard to imagine that the town only has about a quarter of the summer population year-round. Much quieter in the winter," he explained, his eyes traveling around the restaurant to see if he recognized anyone.

The brewery was in an old refurbished plane hangar. What had once been a cavernous space, large enough to accommodate two small planes was now an expansive restaurant and brewery. The back end of the building housed the brewery part of the business, the stainless steel brewing equipment partially visible behind a brick wall that separated the area. A decorative copper storage vessel sat beside the entrance into the brewery area. The high open space afforded in the hangar was broken up with elaborate model planes hanging from the ceiling, most of them models of the small two to six-seater planes used throughout Alaska. The hangar had been modified with additional windows cut into the walls, offering a view of an adjacent marshy field where moose were often seen against a backdrop of the bay and mountains in the distance. The restaurant area had booths lining the walls and a large grouping of tables scattered in the middle. The kitchen was against the far wall, a bar separating it from the rest of the room. The restaurant was at capacity, tables and booths filled with a crowded bar. What could have been a noisy space was softened with a plethora of fabric wall hangings and colorful rugs under every table and booth.

Nathan saw a few friends at the bar, including Travis who offered a quick wave. Returning the wave, he realized he'd better be ready for some teasing from Travis and his brothers. Seeing as Travis had already discerned Nathan might be interested Tess, Nathan's presence with her tonight would only add to that speculation.

Nathan sighed internally and purposefully looked away from Travis, only to have his eyes land on Tess, who appeared lost in thought. He took advantage of the moment to take a long look at her. Her hair was a rumpled cluster of honey-gold curls, the light catching in them, creating bright shimmers when she moved. Nathan found himself picturing how mussed her hair would look if he ever had a chance to make love to her. That thought led directly to the memory of the feel of her lips against his. Given the reticent vibe she gave off, he hadn't expected her to throw herself into a kiss that way. Yet she hadn't held anything back. Neither had he —only to force himself to stop when it was the last thing he'd wanted to do. He still wasn't quite sure how he'd managed that, calling on every ounce of restraint he had.

Though he wasn't sure of much, he had a good hunch that if they'd gone much further, it would have been near to impossible to stop. He thought Tess would've regretted that later and likely doubled her resistance to getting to know him. He wasn't sure what lay behind it, but she had a strong wall of reserve with a hint of bitterness to it. Nathan wanted to know the seeds of that reserve and bitterness. He also felt spurred by the challenge to erase it.

Tess lifted her eyes to his—almost cat-like, corners tipped up, that tawny ginger color hypnotizing him. Nathan held her gaze for a moment, heat arced between them.

An eyebrow quirked. "Yes?" she asked.

With a mental shake, Nathan pushed his heated thoughts about Tess away. "Just looking around."

Tess looked doubtful, but she didn't push. "I'm so glad everyone ended up okay after that accident," she said.

"You and me both. Could have been much worse given how banged up both vehicles were. That's one thing I've learned here—watch out for moose."

"I didn't really get it when I read that moose were so common around here. I figured they were mostly in the woods. We have deer everywhere in North Carolina, so I guess I should have realized moose were like that here. Just that deer are a lot smaller and pretty shy."

"Moose are damn near everywhere. It's cool to see 'em, but steering clear is the way to go. Between today and the little run-in you and Jordan had the other day, you've had your quota. Promise me you'll go the other direction if you see another one," Nathan said.

Tess nodded vigorously, her curls bouncing on her shoulders. "Oh, I promise. I've had my fill of close encounters of the moose kind."

Nathan thought back to the recent afternoon when he'd intercepted her and Jordan when that moose had charged and again to the accident they'd encountered this evening. A protective feeling toward her surged in him, ruffling his composure. He started to respond only to have the hostess call his name, the interruption a welcome relief.

The next few minutes passed with getting seated at a booth, a waitress taking their drink orders and reciting dinner specials—all the while Nathan wondering what to do with his feelings. He'd known he wanted a chance at something more after watching Luke fall for Hannah. He'd consciously pulled back from his casual partying for a reason. Yet he hadn't expected to be drawn to a woman like Tess, nor to feel that he couldn't control the sense of protectiveness that swelled whenever she was near—not to mention a craving for her that went beyond the physical. These thoughts ran through his mind while he reminded himself that she was only here for two more weeks, she didn't live here, and she'd made it pretty damn clear she wasn't looking for a relationship. Against this backdrop, he'd desperately wanted her to go to dinner with him. He wanted to dissolve her defenses and expunge the traces of bitterness he sensed in her. And damn if he wasn't sure what to do about how much he wanted that.

Nathan stared blankly at the menu and didn't notice that Travis had walked up to their booth.

"Hello there," Travis said.

Nathan reeled his thoughts in fast and looked up to see Travis with a glint in his eyes. Tess might not notice, but Nathan knew damn well Travis was enjoying this moment.

"Hey man. What's up?" Nathan asked, aiming for casual.

Travis took a swig of beer and held his glass up. "Enjoying a delicious Diamond Creek Alpine Brown—my favorite." He turned toward Tess. "Nice to see you again. No more moose encounters, I hope. Nathan's brought you to the best brewery in Alaska. Enjoy it."

Tess grinned at Nathan, exchanging a look of amusement with him before turning her smile to Travis. "He swears it's the best. I've noticed most of the food in Diamond Creek is good though, so I'm guessing this place will be too. As for moose, well…"

Nathan interjected. "On the way here, we came upon a fresh car accident—two moose and two cars swerving. Ran right into each other, the cars, that is. Not a scratch for the moose."

Travis's gaze sharpened, a look of concern flashing.

"Everyone's okay, but we had a scare, complete with us having to wait on top of the overturned truck while a few moose milled about," Nathan said, his gaze lingering on Tess for a moment.

Travis lifted his eyebrows. "You're getting your fill of moose. Had enough yet?" he asked wryly with a nod to Tess.

"Seeing them from a distance from now on would be just fine with me," Tess replied with a soft laugh. Occasionally, Tess's soft southern drawl was more evident. Nathan could have listened to her say some words all day long and 'fine' was one of them. Her tongue lingered on the i, drawing it out and warming it up.

Travis turned his gaze to Nathan, an eyebrow lifting. "I'd ask what you're up to, but it appears to be dinner with Tess."

"Hard to miss that," Nathan replied. Right about now, he was hoping Travis would take the hint and move on.

Just as that thought crossed Nathan's mind, another fishing buddy stopped by their table, Samuel Perkins. Samuel was the best cook to be found for fishing trips and a frequent presence at local bars. He'd likely have noticed Nathan's absence lately, but he wasn't one to comment. As Samuel was greeting them, Maggie and Jason Matthews appeared, another pair of local friends. They were high school sweethearts who reunited and married after college. Maggie had short black hair and dark eyes. Jason's shaggy blonde hair and blue eyes were a contrast, yet they both tended to look as if they'd just walked off a hiking trail, typically attired in fleece outdoor gear, ruddy cheeked, and almost always entwined with each other. Their construction company was the one that had built the home Nathan and his brothers purchased. Nathan realized he needed to change gears fast and accept that this would not be a private dinner with Tess.

Travis seemed to read his mind. He leaned over. "There goes your private dinner," he said just above a whisper.

Nathan looked askance at Travis to catch him grinning. Knowing he couldn't say much without Tess wondering what Travis was talking about, he ignored him and made introductions for Tess. Over the next few minutes, he watched Tess relax in a way she hadn't with him. She was naturally inquisitive and had gracious manners that drew others out in conversation. She had Samuel explaining the challenges of cooking at sea, and Jason and Maggie expounding upon the best way to create a sustainable energy home. Having met Tess's mother, who was the epitome of the famed gracious Southern manners, this didn't surprise Nathan. Yet, it illuminated the guarded quality he experienced when they were alone. That reserve only heightened the contrast with her unrestrained passion when they'd kissed. He wanted to break through that reserve—again and again and again.

While Tess was busy chatting with Maggie, Travis tugged a chair to his side. "So, still just flirting with Tess?" he asked.

"Dude, let up, would you? It's just dinner. I didn't deny that I thought she was cute as hell. So, I asked her to dinner. That's it," Nathan replied. He shifted his shoulders, restless at Travis's curiosity.

"Hmm. If it wasn't so obvious that it bothered you for anyone to notice you were interested in her, it wouldn't be so tempting to give you a hard time," Travis said, his eyes holding a teasing glint.

Nathan sighed and looked over at Tess. Her honey curls moved with her gestures. She had expressive hands. Her eyes were warm and lively as she talked. Just watching her lips move raised his temperature. Her mouth was a perfect bow, her lips plump and soft. He wished they were alone, so he could kiss those decadent lips and feel her go wild in his arms, that polite reserve dissolving.

"Okay, trying to be helpful here. If you don't want the whole damn town to notice that you're totally into Tess, you might want to stop staring at her like that," Travis said, his voice low.

Travis's words cut into Nathan's train of thought. Much as he didn't want to admit anything to Travis, he knew Travis was right. His attraction to Tess went well beyond superficial. While he couldn't have explained it, he knew that what lay between them was special. His body thrummed with electricity any time she was near, and he just wanted...to know her...on every level. He chuckled softly.

"Good point," Nathan said. With a mental shake, he looked to Travis and past him around the restaurant. "Did you decide what day you're headed up to dipnet?" he asked, abruptly changing the subject.

"Aiming for Wednesday. Anything scheduled for you guys?"

Nathan thought for a moment, realizing the only trip he knew for certain was with Tess's family. "Not that I know of. Let me check with Jared tomorrow. I'll call to confirm but should be able to go."

Samuel joined their talk of dipnetting. Nathan was relieved to get off the topic of Tess and back onto the familiar terrain of fishing. In the meantime, their food arrived; talk turning to how good it was and the various recommendations for Tess of every local restaurant her family should try while they were in Diamond Creek. Just as he thought he was in safe territory and back in control, Maggie cut into their conversation. He'd gotten to know Maggie and Jason mostly through Hannah, Luke's wife. They'd grown up in Diamond Creek. Though he enjoyed Maggie, she tended to think everyone's business was hers.

"So Nathan, rumor has it you haven't been out and about much lately. Word on the street is you must be flying solo with someone. Is Tess the lucky girl?" Maggie asked.

Nathan flinched internally and silently cursed Maggie. She was known for her utter lack of tact in social situations. Glancing around the table, he saw Jason elbow Maggie, Samuel lift his eyebrows, and Travis visibly choke back a laugh. As for Tess, her reserve was back in full force, her gaze guarded and questioning.

"Damn, can't do much of anything around here without people coming up with all kinds of ideas," Nathan said, deciding deflection was his best option, especially with Maggie. She'd just keep on with the questions if he didn't redirect her. "We've taken Tess and her family out fishing twice now. Thought she outta see what Diamond Creek had to offer beyond good fishing, so we're just having dinner. As for my evening habits...seriously? So I haven't been out as much lately—didn't know anyone cared all that much."

"Do I have to worry about the rumor mill if I breathe the wrong way?" Travis asked. "I've seen plenty of Nathan lately, and not much has changed far as I can tell."

Nathan sent a silent thanks to Travis. Much as he knew he'd have to put up with all kinds of teasing for this, the rumor mill in Diamond Creek was a sore point for Travis. He'd once had a relationship go south after a few incorrect assumptions blossomed into a breakup. As such, he went out of his way to deter it.

Between Jason's elbow practically dislocating her rib and Travis's comment, Maggie looked apologetic. "Sorry Nathan. You know me, just sticking my foot in my mouth over rumors. If anyone knows better, it's me. If I'd listened to the local gossip, I'd have never believed Jason still loved me and we wouldn't even be together now," Maggie said dramatically. She proceeded to throw her arms around Jason who returned the hug, all the while shaking his head.

"Babe, love you too," Jason said, in reply to Maggie's declaration.

Nathan took the chance to look in Tess's direction again. The guarded look had eased a little. He didn't want her speculating about Maggie comment and running with it. Not for the first time, he wished his penchant for being a flirt wasn't typically interpreted as him being a player. He didn't like to explain himself to others so he'd allowed that perception to stick. Now he just hoped Tess wouldn't believe his false persona and could see through it, see who he really was.

Between Travis and Jason, they got the conversation back off of Maggie's questions. Within minutes, Travis was saying his goodbyes with the rest following in his wake. Somehow, the time he'd hoped to get to know Tess had turned into a mini social hour. Dinner had come and gone. He felt like he'd lost something, he'd wanted a chance to actually talk to her, start to know who she was underneath that reserve. Her head was turned as she looked out the window. She must have sensed him looking at her because she turned toward him with a smile, her gaze open, that guarded look gone for a moment. Just a look from her and his stomach clenched and desire coursed through him.

* * *

Approaching nine in the evening, the sun was on its way to sliding behind the mountains when Nathan turned the truck into the parking lot at the harbor. He'd persuaded Tess that she should see the late sunset from the harbor.

She'd been somewhat quiet on the ride from the brewery, commenting only that the food and beer had been as good as he'd promised. The quiet allowed him to ponder the missed chance to get to know her, to woo her, over dinner. The missed opportunity sharpened his interest. Several moments later, Nathan followed Tess onto the deck of Iris, their commercial fishing vessel. The view was better on the boat, high enough to see past the smaller boats that filled the dock slips. This time of evening, the docks were quiet, the hustle and bustle of summer days ebbed with the setting sun. A few boats had cabin lights on in the fading light.

Tess had stepped to the bow, her hands curled over the railing. "Wow...beautiful. I'd want to live out here in the summer," she said, turning to glance over her shoulder at him.

Nathan tucked his hands in his pockets and strode to her side. "Some do," he said, tilting his head in the direction of one of the boats with lights on. "We used to stay on the boat in the summer when we came up from Seattle before we moved here. Loved it myself, but it gets damn cold come fall. Not practical beyond summer." He leaned against the railing, angled toward Tess.

She nodded and pointed toward Mount Augustine, one of several volcanoes that could be seen from Diamond Creek. "Mount Augustine seems to have its own clouds every day," she said.

Nathan followed her gaze to a cluster of clouds arrayed around its peak. At the moment, they were swirled with colors—a deep red shot through with streaks of gold. The volcano was dark in the fading light. "Augustine usually does have its own clouds. Not sure why, probably because it's the only thing out in the middle of the bay." Her nearness ratcheted up his desire, it pulsed through him in waves. His eyes traveled back to her, drawn to those kissable lips.

Tess nodded. "Were you here the last time it erupted? I

read that it was only a few years ago." She seemed entirely unaware that volcanoes were the last thing on his mind. He had to force himself to focus on her words.

"Yup. Not too eventful, although they had to reroute some airplane traffic due to visibility problems from the ash. Not to mention that the ash can clog up an engine in a second. About all I noticed was the ash on the snow and the plumes coming out of the top."

Tess nodded again, her eyes on Mount Augustine in the distance. Her curls fluttered around her face in the soft breeze. Turning to him, she caught his gaze. Their eyes locked onto each other. Nathan felt a deep physical tug, the pulse of desire humming through him. His hands itched to reach over, cup her cheeks and pull her close enough to kiss. His mind flashed back to the feel of her lips under his the other night. A current flared to life between them. She was close enough that he caught a whiff of her perfume, a sensual earthy scent that surprised him, if only because it was at odds with the reserve she maintained. His hand unconsciously rose to tuck an errant curl behind one ear. The moment he touched her, he didn't want to stop. He cupped her cheek, pausing for a moment. She looked back at him, her eyes darkening, though they held a hint of vulnerability. Knowing that words would only shatter this moment, he tried to convey with his eyes that she needn't worry, *ever*, with him. He held those tawny eyes with his and slowly leaned in for a kiss. Much as he didn't want to give her a chance to stop him, it was important that she knew he would give her that chance.

For a split second, Nathan thought Tess might pull away —that hint of vulnerability flashing. Just as he wondered what she might do, she leaned into him. Capturing her lips, he began a heated exploration, tracing the shape of her lips with his tongue, her mouth falling open on a sigh. His heart hammered and heat built between them, his tongue slipped inside her mouth, engaging hers in a slow dance. He turned his back to the boat railing, pulling her tight against him, reveling in the feeling of her lush curves. His erection strained against his jeans. With a groan, he slid his hands to her hips and pressed into them. Tess sighed into his mouth, one of her hands curling around his neck and tangling in his hair, the other tearing at the buttons of his flannel shirt.

Nathan was functioning solely on sensation at this point. The moment Tess's hand slid against his skin, pleasure arced so strongly that he gasped. Just as she had the other night, she threw herself into this kiss, into this moment. All traces of reserve were gone. She was a living flame in his arms, flexing against him. Not realizing it, Nathan must have unbuttoned her blouse because next thing he knew, he was looking down at the tops of her luscious breasts, barely held in by a lacy bra of green silk—another surprise. The practicality that she tried to exude was given up by her sensual perfume and oh-so-feminine bra. He broke away from their kiss and closed his lips over a peaked nipple through the lace. Tess gasped and arched. He lingered over that nipple, teasing the other through the lace with soft pinches.

"Oh *my*…Nathan…please…" Tess choked out. Her abandon pushing his desire up, the heat between them so strong, he could hardly think straight. He forced himself to remember where they were.

Nathan paused to look at her. Her lips were swollen and rosy red, her eyes closed, her honey curls in disarray and her chest rising and falling in fitful breaths. He gave both of her nipples a small tug, his cock straining even harder against his jeans when she let out a deep sigh. Leaning down, he gave his attention to her other nipple, sucking it through the lace, pulling back to blow softly on both nipples. Tess's hand slid down his abdomen, quickly unbuttoning his jeans and sliding her hand inside his boxer briefs to curl around his cock. He sucked his breath in and tried to think through the fervor he felt. His control was fragile, blown to bits by the incendiary passion between them.

Attempting to pull back, what little control he had left dissolved when Tess used her free hand to unclasp her bra in the front, the insignificant scraps of lace falling apart and her voluptuous breasts tumbled into view. Nathan slipped his hands around her breasts, the feel of her luscious skin and the tightening of her nipples against his palms wiping all thought clear of his mind. Tess's hand slowly stroked his cock and pressed against him, bringing her bare breasts flush to his chest. Once again, he reminded himself to think, to remember someone might see them. He started to pull back, only to have Tess tug him close.

"Don't stop," she pleaded.

Nathan captured her lips quickly, gentling his kiss almost immediately. With a fraction of space between their lips, he whispered, "Trust me, I don't want to stop. But we need to get out of view." He swiveled his head, taking a quick glance around, catching sight of a few people in the distance on a boat two docks over.

Returning his gaze, Nathan looked down into Tess's face. Her ginger eyes looked back at him, slightly unfocused and wide. Her breasts were in their glory for him to see, her nipples a deep pink, damp and taut from his lips. Not breaking their embrace, he started to walk them back from the railing, eyes on hers every step. A hint of a smile tipped the corners of her mouth up. He nipped at one of her nipples as he kept walking them away from the railing towards the boat cabin. Tess giggled and gave his cock, still clasped in her hand, a quick stroke as he maneuvered them. When they reached the door to the cabin, he fumbled for his keys with one hand.

Another giggle burst from Tess. "Think you're a multi-tasker huh? We'll see about that."

Just as Nathan managed to get his keys out of his pocket with one hand, Tess dropped to her knees in front of him, tugging his jeans and boxers open. She was completely shielded from view fortunately because the next thing she did erased what little control Nathan had. She freed his cock and dragged her tongue along one side and then the other.

"Tess," he choked out. "We need..." His next words sputtered as her mouth closed around his cock, warmth and wetness pulsating around his shaft.

Nathan threw his head back with a groan. *Sweet Jesus... Tess...oh my god.*

She explored his cock with strokes of her tongue and drew him deep in her mouth. He felt bereft when she pulled back and cool air replaced her mouth.

"Thought you were gonna open that door," she said, her voice husky with passion.

Nathan looked down at her, breathless and desperate for her in a way he'd never been for any woman. Tess returned his gaze, her honey curls tumbling around her shoulders, her lower lip caught in a small bite, her eyes teasing. Not breaking her gaze, he deliberately reached around her and unlocked the door. In a blur, they were inside the boat cabin, and Nathan had turned Tess around with her back to the door. He flicked the lights on. Driven by sensation, he pushed her against the door, plastering his body to hers, grinding his hips into her pelvis. Tess gasped into his mouth as Nathan tugged at her pants. She shimmied her way out of them, all the while pushing his jeans down. Reaching under her hips, he caught a glimpse of honey gold curls at the juncture between her thighs. He lifted her against the door, positioned himself and was about to slide into her when he forced himself to pause.

"Tess?"

Her eyes were closed, her head against the door. With

obvious reluctance, she opened her eyes. "Didn't we agree you didn't want to stop?" she asked, a trace of annoyance flashing in her eyes.

Nathan chuckled, his cock pounding from frustration. "I don't...two things though...just want to make sure you really want this and..." he paused and took a much needed gulp of air. "Need some protection..."

Tess held his gaze, her breasts rising and falling with her breath, making it incredibly hard for him to remember he needed to know she wanted this, that he wanted her to want this.

"If it isn't obvious, I *want* this and I want it *now*...and I'm gonna lose it if you don't have a condom somewhere," she said emphatically.

His eyes completely on hers, Nathan freed one hand and fumbled for his wallet in his jeans.

"See? Multi-tasking...not so bad at it," he said, tugging out the sole condom he carried in his wallet. He didn't have time to contemplate what it might mean that he was so consumed with desire for Tess that any caution had evaporated. She tore the condom out of his hands and slipped it on, guiding him into her warmth. Closing his eyes, he captured her lips just as he drove to the hilt. She gasped into his mouth and wrapped her legs around his hips. She felt *soooo* good around his cock, a warm, fitted embrace.

Tess's head fell back against the door, her breath coming in pants. He slipped his hand to the space where their bodies joined, caressing the tiny bud that rested just above where his cock continued to sink into her.

She arched against the door. "Nathan...oh god...don't stop...don't stop...*please*..." She came in a burst, calling his name again in a throaty voice, convulsing tightly around him. Unable to slow down, much as he didn't want this to end, he pounded into her warmth, his own climax coming in a roar as he pulsed into her.

As the pulses of his orgasm slowed, Nathan leaned his forehead against hers. The feel of her heartbeat against his chest grounded him. Gradually, their labored breathing slowed. He leaned back to look at Tess. Her eyes were closed. He brushed a curl out of her face. Not wanting to pull out, but realizing she would get uncomfortable soon if they remained where they were, Nathan wrapped both arms around her and leaned away from the door.

"Hold on," he said softly, carefully stepping away from the door, holding her securely. In a few steps, he sat down on a bench against one wall, Tess's knees coming to rest on either side of his hips. Fluid in his arms, she fell against him, her head resting on one of his shoulders.

They remained that way for several long moments. Tess finally lifted her head and sat back a little. Nathan took a good long look. Her breasts were so lovely and luscious, weighted and round with deep pink nipples. She tilted her head to the side and crinkled her nose.

"What?" he asked.

She shrugged and smiled, a blush blooming across her cheeks. A small giggle escaped her. "Let's just say I didn't expect this," Tess said, her expression sobering.

Nathan waited a beat. "I didn't either. But...I won't pretend I wasn't interested. Have been since the day I met you."

Tess's blush deepened. She broke their gaze, her eyes skating around the boat cabin. Nathan sensed it was best to let her take the lead in this conversation. Not to mention that he was navigating uncharted waters emotionally. He'd never experienced passion like what lay between him and Tess—it was a living, breathing, vital incandescence. The intensity gave him pause, yet it also enlivened him. He was emotionally and sensually drained while he also felt a current of vitality thrumming between them.

Tess finally returned her gaze to him, her lower lip

caught between her teeth. Nathan wanted to lean over and kiss her luscious mouth again. Instead, he waited. Her chest rose and fell with a deep breath. She opened her mouth to speak, closing it again immediately. A tear slid down her cheek.

"Tess? You okay?" Nathan asked, his hands sliding up her arms in a soothing caress.

Tess brought her hands to her face for a moment, taking several long shaky breaths. With a rapid shake of her head, she wiped the tear away and lifted her chin.

"I'm fine...I just...I don't know..." she said, her words trailing off.

Nathan wanted to ask all kinds of questions, but Tess seemed to be walling him away, pulling herself within. He allowed himself one question. "Can you tell me what's going on here?"

She laughed softly, a bitter edge to the sound. "Not just now. I'm sorry."

He nodded slowly. "Okay. Just so you know, this pretty much blew my mind here," he said, gesturing between them. "Not something I make a habit of doing on a first date. I know you didn't expect this, neither did I. How about we not overthink it for now?"

Tess looked away again, before bringing her eyes to meet his. "You got it. Not overthinking is a great plan," she replied with a firm nod and a small smile. Much as Nathan wanted to push, he knew now was not the time.

The next few moments gave Nathan a chance to pull himself together between the buttoning of shirts and tidying of hair. When they stepped out of the boat cabin onto the deck, all that was left of the sun was a curved sliver above the mountains, deep red and surrounded with fading rays reaching into the sky. The moon was rising to one side, bright in the almost-dark sky. When he pulled up the Tess's hotel, he looked over at her, her lips were still swollen, her curls a rumple around her face. Before she had a chance to think, he leaned over and kissed her just as she turned in his direction. "See you tomorrow," he said, pulling back to look into her ginger eyes.

Tess nodded. "Good night," she said, stepping out of the truck. She started to turn away and swiveled back. "Dinner was great." For a split second, Nathan saw a deep vulnerability flash through her eyes, gone just as quickly as it came.

"Glad you enjoyed it," was his only reply. He watched as Tess walked to the entrance of the hotel, putting the truck in gear and pulling away when she opened the door.

CHAPTER 8

At three in the morning, Tess gave in and got out of bed. After Nathan had dropped her off last night, she'd fallen into a deep sleep for several hours until she woke to go to the bathroom. Since then, she'd been restive, coming in and out of sleep, thoughts of Nathan and those moments of heedless passion running in circles in her mind.

After a long shower, she flipped open her laptop to review numbers on one of her fundraising projects. With the news on low volume in the background, she scanned through her email and downloaded the latest reports to update her spreadsheet—all in the hope she could chase thoughts of Nathan out of her mind. However, her body seemed to be running the show. One minute, she was focused on the data in front of her, the next she was remembering the feel of Nathan's lips closing around a nipple and his cock sliding inside of her.

Time and again, her thoughts wandered back to that moment when she'd been overwhelmed with the reality that she hadn't been intimate, not even a kiss, with a man since she'd broken up with Chad. On top of that, she couldn't seem to recall the last time she'd had an orgasm with anyone other than herself making it happen. Sex with Chad had been less than thrilling. He was pretty focused on himself. As for the men that had come before him...meh. But with Nathan—a mere kiss was like stepping into a living flame. Landing from the electrifying ride with Nathan, she'd been awash in sensation, waves crashing through her. She'd just had the best sex of her life and loved every minute of it. Sitting there in his arms, the afterglow of passion shimmered between them—pulsing, vibrant.

Next thing she knew, her face was in her hands and she was trying to stop the tears. She'd been so walled off from any feelings, she could hardly face that what had just happened with Nathan involved much more than lust. Although she had a long list of doubts about herself with any man and about Nathan, she didn't doubt that he'd been concerned. His concern only heightened the well of feelings rushing through her. She desperately wanted to know that he had been just as shaken by their encounter, but she didn't know...and hadn't the courage to ask. She had *not* planned on this. She wouldn't be in Alaska much longer and hadn't expected her heart to get involved. It was supposed to have been just a dinner date. Now her well-constructed defenses appeared to be a sham with Nathan.

* * *

TESS PERUSED the early bird menu in the hotel restaurant. At five o'clock sharp, she was the first customer this morning. Within the hour, her family would be meeting in the lobby to head out on today's fishing trip. The thought of spending the day with Nathan in his element elicited confusion. Just thinking of him, those moments between them, kicked her heart into gear. Closing her eyes, she pictured his blue eyes, dark with passion—and all she wanted was him to herself.

And yet…the depth of how much she wanted him dismayed her because she had *no* idea what could come of it.

"Good morning, darlin'," Celine said, walking to the table where Tess sat and immediately sitting down across from her.

Tess looked over and suppressed a sigh. Her mother's eyes were bright and she could barely contain her smile. Tess knew her mother was just about beside herself to hear how her evening with Nathan went. Much as she wanted to avoid it, that was impossible.

"Hey Mom. How was dinner last night?"

"Lovely. I had one of the salmon dishes, which was just sumptuous. Your father and Simon loved it." Celine leaned forward with a conspiratorial grin. "I didn't give anything away. They have *no* idea you were on a dinner date with Nathan. So how was it?" she asked, abandoning any effort to delay her questions.

A flash of heat coursed through Tess as she pondered how the evening went. Should she tell her mother that what started with a kiss had morphed into the hottest moments of her life, that she'd never really understood the concept of passion the way she did now, and that she wanted Nathan in a way she'd never wanted any man in her life? Tess kept her eyes on the menu, attempting to appear distracted. Which she was, just not because of the menu.

"Well?" Celine prompted.

Tess looked over at her mother and almost started laughing aloud. If she told her mother the bare truth, Celine would probably do cartwheels on the spot. Her mother wasn't one to be shy. Long before most of her peers, Tess had been subject to a practical discussion of what to expect from her body and from sex as she faced the cusp of adolescence. Her parents had always been openly affectionate and loving, her mother comfortable in her skin, evoking an earthy sensuality. And yet, Tess didn't want to share such details with her mother. They were too private, and she was too discombobulated.

"Dinner was great. Nathan took me to Diamond Creek Brewery. Food was delicious and the beer was quite good," Tess said, hoping her mother might be satisfied.

"I've heard of the brewery. Do you think your father would like it?" Celine asked.

Tess nodded just as the waitress arrived, setting a cup of coffee in front of Tess and taking the rest of her order. Taking a welcome sip, Tess waited while her mother ordered a coffee and breakfast. Once the waitress walked away, Celine leaned back and gave Tess a long look.

"Dinner was great, that's all I get?" Celine asked.

Tess tilted her head to the side and returned her mother's long look. "Seriously Mom? Just what do you think I might have to add?"

Celine turned when the waitress returned and accepted her own cup of coffee. Taking a swallow, she returned her sharp eyes to Tess. "Oh, let's see. Your first date in what… over a year since you broke it off with Chad after two years with him. Technically, that makes this your first date with someone new in over three years. I could find out how good the brewery is by eating there myself," she said, a hint of sarcasm in her soft drawl.

Tess sighed audibly. "Mom, dinner was great. Nathan seems like a nice guy. I'm sure you have all kinds of ideas about what this date might mean, but the reality is…we'll be back in North Carolina soon, and Nathan will still be here in Diamond Creek. Not much chance that this will turn into more than a few dates." What Tess didn't add was that the very reality she was using as an excuse to hold her mother's questions at bay made her long for the circumstances to be different. *That* scared the hell out of her. For the first time in a while, the self-doubt she'd worn like a cloak of protection and avoidance felt like a hindrance, something holding her back.

Celine still didn't look convinced, but just as she started to ask another question, Simon and Jordan entered the restaurant, Jordan skipping his way over to their table. The hour passed quickly, her father joining them minutes after Simon and Jordan. On the way to the harbor, they stopped at Red Truck Coffee. Tess held a warm cup of coffee in her hands while she waited for everyone to get served. The morning air was brisk, a swift breeze coming off the bay. She jumped at the sound of Nathan's voice.

"Morning Tess," Nathan said.

Tess turned to find Nathan standing a few feet away. A jolt of heat sparked in her center. A blush crept up her neck, her cheeks becoming warm.

"Good morning," she replied, aiming to sound nonchalant.

A slow smile came across Nathan's face as he stood before her. His eyes were sharp blue in the crisp morning, darker than the sky. Tess couldn't help but recall the heated look in his eyes last night, which only deepened her flush.

"How are you?" Nathan asked.

Her manners did their job as she managed an answer. "Pretty good. Looking forward to getting out on the water. How are you?"

Nathan gave her an assessing look. "Pretty damn good. Looking forward to a day on the water with...*you*," he responded with a teasing glint in his eyes.

Just as Tess was contemplating how to keep their conversation in safe territory, her father joined them.

"Mornin' Nathan. Good to see ya," Michael said, giving Nathan a casual pat on the shoulder. "Lookin' forward to catching another king salmon today."

Tess allowed her father to take over the conversation as

the rest of her family joined them. Celine paid a little too much attention to Nathan, going so far as to ask him about his opinion on Diamond Creek Brewery, which earned her a questioning glance from him. Before long, they were aboard the boat. Tess was pleased that Hannah was joining them again for the day. The rest of the day passed in a blur. Tess was grateful for the distraction offered by her family and Nathan's brothers. Much as she wanted to tamp it down, the attraction between her and Nathan was even more potent after last night. She caught herself staring at him time and again, appreciating the flex of his muscles when he moved. He was rangy and compelling, a bundle of unapologetic masculinity at home in the outdoors, his sensual features made more so with the knowledge of how his lips felt against hers and the touch of his strong and sure hands on her body.

It was late afternoon when they walked into the harbor parking lot. A cluster of people stood near the entrance to the parking lot, all appeared familiar with Nathan and his brothers. Jared made introductions for them. Talk turned to fish, as was to be expected. Tess was tired, her lack of sleep finally catching up to her. She stifled a yawn. One of the men in the group, Alan, gestured to Nathan.

"Dude, what's up? Haven't seen you out in months," Alan said.

Tess glanced at Nathan, her interest piqued. Last night, Nathan's friend, Maggie, had also commented in this vein, implying that rumor had it Nathan must be exclusive with someone and wondered if it was Tess. Nathan and his friend, Travis, had breezed the comment away. Tess had tucked it in the back of her mind.

Nathan shrugged. "Not much, just haven't been out as much lately." He smoothly redirected the conversation onto fishing.

Tess sensed a hint of discomfort from him, yet he was adept at keeping conversations where he wanted them. A quick look around and Tess caught Hannah's expression, her eyes sharp and speculative. Tess watched Hannah exchange a quick look with Luke who gave a small shake of his head. Hannah bit her lip, appearing to hold back a laugh.

Tess was acutely aware of every move Nathan made, even when all he did was kick a pebble. Although she had consciously avoided opportunities alone with Nathan—to keep a lid on her rampant desire and to keep her mother from speculating more than she already was—she felt adrift watching him walk away with his brothers as she climbed into the rental car with the rest of her family.

* * *

Tess sat propped in a pile of pillows on her hotel, idly flipping through the channels. Slightly tipsy from a tad too much wine at dinner with her family, she giggled when she came across Deadliest Catch, realizing that Nathan would make a good addition to the show with his rugged sensuality and handsome looks. Her smartphone vibrated on the night table. Reaching for the phone, Tess almost tumbled off the bed. Righting herself, she glanced at the screen seeing the banner announcing a text from Nathan.

When can I see you again?

Tess stared at the message, ecstatic that he wanted to see her again and annoyed that she cared this much. She counted how many days they had left in Alaska. Though it may have been the wine, she decided to ignore her unofficial policy of avoiding all things risky with men because in a mere two weeks, she would be flying back to North Carolina. She had enough sense to know this could be nothing more than a fling, so she'd enjoy it.

Now? Tess typed in reply.

Ten minutes. Meet me out front.

Eight minutes later, to be exact, Tess stood in the lobby

of the hotel by the door. She hadn't bothered to change so when she caught sight of herself in the mirror in the lobby, she giggled and hoped Nathan didn't plan to take her anywhere important. She was attired in flared cotton pants and a tank top with a lightweight fleece jacket. Her hair was mussed, the curls a disorderly frame for her face.

Headlights reflected in the mirror. Seeing the outline of Nathan's truck, she stepped outside. Nathan opened the door from the inside of the truck. As soon as she'd closed the door, he leaned across the armrest and kissed her, cupping her cheek with his palm. Tess fell into his kiss, heat building in her core instantly. Nathan stroked deeply with his tongue, his thumb running along the edge of her jaw and down the side of her neck. When he pulled back, she felt bereft, not ready for the moment to end. Her breath was shallow, her heart hammering against her ribs. Nathan's thumb brushed softly against the pulse in her neck. Opening her eyes, Tess looked into the rich blue of his, which were just inches away.

"Damn," Nathan said, his voice just a whisper. "Been wanting to do that all day. You have no idea what you do to me."

His eyes glittered in the soft glow from the parking lot lights. With the wine having softened her defenses, Tess didn't stop to consider her reply.

"You and me both."

Nathan didn't move away, his thumb idly stroking the side of her neck. Tess subtly arched into him like a cat, her body on fire and desire thrumming through her.

"Where are we going?" she asked.

Nathan shrugged and pulled away, shifting the truck into gear and starting to drive. "Didn't think that far ahead. Wasn't sure you'd even answer my text," he replied, glancing her direction with an eyebrow lifted.

Tess bit her lip, wondering what to tell him—that last

night he'd given her the best sex of her life, that she didn't know what to do about how she felt about him, that all she wanted to do was listen to her body, ignore her mind and dive into whatever lay between them. She swatted her thoughts away, reminding herself that thinking would just interfere.

"I wanted to see you again," she said with a shrug. "I'm only here two more weeks, you know." As those words left her lips, she wondered why she felt the need to point that out for Nathan.

"I know. That's why I want to see you every chance I get." Nathan turned the truck into the harbor parking lot.

Tess took his words in and for a few moments, decided to just let herself believe that he wanted her as much as she wanted him. Before she knew it, they were walking through the wispy dusk onto the docks and onto Iris, the commercial fishing boat. Nathan's hand held hers in a warm, strong clasp. Just as he unlocked the boat cabin door, she experienced a wave of uncertainty. She wasn't the kind of woman that a man like Nathan would fall for. She was too curvy, too reserved and carried too much baggage. When she didn't follow him immediately through the door, Nathan turned back to face her. Holding her gaze with deliberation, his eyes simmering, he softly tugged on her hand. Never breaking her gaze, he closed the door and pulled her tight against him into the shelter of his embrace.

Tess inhaled deeply, absorbing the sharp scent of him, a mix of fresh air with a hint of salt and spruce. The warmth of his body seeped into hers. Nathan nuzzled her neck, speaking quietly. "Stop thinking so much, just let this happen."

Chills chased by heat coursed through her. Nathan tangled his hand in her curls and kissed her. Her mind went blank, obedient not to his words, but to his body and the incandescent flame of feeling between them—passion laced with a depth of longing that Tess could hardly bear. She pressed against him and opened her mouth on a deep sigh. Their tongues stroking and hands tearing clothes off, they somehow made it into a small room inside the cabin. It was tucked into the bow of the boat, a v-shaped mattress fitted perfectly into the bow. Nathan walked back until her knees hit the edge of the mattress and she tumbled back. Nathan knelt in front of her. All that was left of her clothes were her panties, a scrap of navy lace. His eyes traveled across her body and up to her face. When he looked at her, she flushed through. His eyes were dark with passion, a hint of a smile at his mouth. She caught her breath when he leaned forward and licked one nipple and then the other.

"I don't think you have any idea what you do to me," he said huskily. His hands cupped her breasts, thumbs teasing the peaked nipples as he brought his gaze back to hers.

Wordlessly, Tess shook her head. Nathan dipped his head again and lavished one breast with attention, dragging his tongue in a searing circle before his lips closed over the nipple with a soft suction. She looked down at his dark head bent over her breasts, one of her hands tangled in his curls. He turned his attention to her other breast as she arched against him, awash in sensation. Slick heat built in her core.

"Nathan," she gasped, her voice breaking.

He slowly pushed her back and tugged her panties off. Spreading her legs, he slipped one finger and then another into her dripping channel. She sighed with relief only to protest when his fingers slid out and he commenced to toy with the damp flesh, dragging his thumb back and forth across her clit. Heat continued to build, a mist of passion sweat covering her. Tess gasped again and again, pleading again and again as Nathan teased and toyed with her. Only occasionally would he dip a finger inside. His mouth joined his fingers, nibbling and licking at her, suckling on the tiny bud and licking deep inside. Tension built until Tess was begging. She pushed herself up and tugged him to her, tearing his jeans and boxers off, wrapping her hands around his velvety cock, her mouth following.

Nathan only tolerated a moment before pushing her back. "Too much," he choked out. "I need to be inside you."

He fumbled in the pocket of his jeans on the floor. Tess swatted his hands away and pulled him to her. "Doesn't matter, I'm on the pill." She kissed him hard, leaning back with him.

Nathan's body covered hers. As her back hit the mattress, he clasped both hands and curled them into his, stretching her arms back above her head, just as he slid home inside of her. Tess gasped into his mouth, the relief of having him stretch and fill her acute. Nathan slowly began to drive into her, pulling back again and again until just the tip of his cock teased the entrance of her drenched channel. She pressed her hips into his, helpless and desperate against the flood of feeling. The tension built inside her until she climaxed in noisy rush, Nathan following her with a final deep thrust before collapsing against her.

He shifted his weight to one side and rolled them over so she lay across him. They were still joined, his cock pulsing inside her. She rested her head on his shoulder and absently ran her hand across his chest through the dark curls scattered across. She thought perhaps if she could just have these moments with Nathan, she might forget to worry.

CHAPTER 9

"*H*ey, hand me that wrench," Nathan said, shaking his hair out of his eyes.

He felt the cool metal of the wrench land in his outstretched palm. He was tucked under the side deck at Luke and Hannah's house, helping Luke install new decking.

"Thanks." He quickly worked to wrench the bolts loose where the decking joined one of the pilings. "Remind me how come I'm the one under the deck here," he said, his knees cramping from being bent over under the deck for the last half hour.

"No good reason other than you're a good sport," Luke replied with a chuckle. "Soon as I get these last few boards in place, you can come on out."

They worked quickly and in a few more minutes, Nathan stood on the deck with Luke, inspecting their work. "Looks good. You shouldn't have to replace this again. It's that synthetic stuff, right?"

Luke wiped his face on his sleeve. "Yup. Don't want to have to worry about doing it again."

Nathan nodded and took a look around the yard. Hannah loved flowers with the yard scattered with flower beds, stone walkways meandering among them. At the moment, many of her flowers were in bloom, the yard a mix of color amidst the dark green of the spruce trees. The sky was clear today and the wind up, the bay choppy with waves.

"Let's get some lunch," Luke said, turning to open the door.

Following him inside, Nathan kicked off his shoes and walked into the kitchen. Hannah and Luke lived in her childhood home, which was passed on to her when her parents died in a plane crash. The home was a timber frame style home, as many were in Alaska. Most of the first floor was wide open space—the kitchen and living room flowing into each other. Exposed beams angled across the ceiling. A soapstone woodstove anchored the living room, which was toward the front of the home and offered a view of the bay and mountains.

Nathan headed straight for the kitchen table where Luke was already sliding a chair out. Hannah was puttering in the kitchen and had made them lunch—sandwiches along with salmon spread and crackers. He sat down with a sigh and immediately shoveled a few crackers with dip in his mouth.

"Hungry, Nathan?" Hannah asked with a teasing grin.

He nodded and took a sip of the water she set beside him. "Your hubby made me do all the shitty work under the deck. Now I'm starving."

Hannah giggled, looking toward Luke. "So you had him on his knees huh?

Luke nodded, swallowing a bite of his sandwich before speaking. "Hey, he offered. Wasn't gonna say no," he said with a shrug.

Hannah asked a few questions about the decking, and they chatted generally about the remaining summer projects to handle before fall set in. Winter came quickly once summer ended, so every year it felt like a race to cram in outdoor projects. Nathan concentrated on eating, not paying much attention to what they were saying. When Hannah got up to get Luke something else to drink, her hand slid across Luke's shoulders in an absentminded caress. That simple gesture brought Tess to mind, although just about anything seemed to bring her to mind these days. Last night had felt *soooo* damn good—Nathan was left adrift with what to do about it.

Being with Hannah and Luke reminded him of how easy he'd thought it should have been for Luke when Hannah came along. He'd found Luke's confusion over what to do a silly distraction. For his own set of reasons, Nathan contemplated that relationships weren't so simple. He wanted Tess like he'd never wanted any women in his life and yet...it was complicated. One major factor being that she lived clear across the country. While he'd been busy trying to persuade her to have dinner with him, he'd thought she was cute, it would be fun and light and not much more than that. Sure, he'd pulled back from the frequency of his flirting and hoped to eventually settle down like Luke, but that hadn't been on his mind when he'd first noticed Tess. If he were honest with himself, he likely wouldn't have been so persistent with her if she hadn't been so guarded. The challenge served to bolster her allure, rather than dissuade him.

"Yoo hoo," Hannah said, her tone teasing as she waved a hand in front of Nathan's face.

He dragged his mind off of Tess. "What?" he asked, mildly irritated.

"Just wondering why you're so out of it," Hannah replied.

Luke didn't say a word, just lifted an eyebrow and took another bite of his sandwich.

"I'm not out of it, just enjoying my lunch," Nathan said.

Hannah tilted her head. "Um, you ignored Luke when he asked you *twice* if you were going dipnetting with Travis tomorrow. That's out of it. My guess is you've got Tess on the brain," she said, her eyes twinkling.

Nathan took another bite of his sandwich before replying. Chewing slowly, he looked askance at Luke who was grinning. A giggle burst from Hannah.

Nathan shrugged. "So what if Tess is on my mind? She's cute."

"You didn't bother mentioning that you took her out the other night. Travis told us he ran into you with her at the brewery. Seeing as you haven't been out much lately, and you can't keep your eyes off of her when they've been fishing with us…" Luke trailed off with a small chuckle.

Nathan decided it wasn't worth trying to sidestep with them. "Yeah, I took her to dinner. I like her—a lot more than I planned on. Don't know what the hell to do about it though. She doesn't even live here."

Hannah's eyes sobered, and she glanced to Luke. "Told you he really liked her," she said before turning back to Nathan. "Not sure what to say about the fact that she doesn't live anywhere near here. Maybe you should just play it by ear."

Luke looked to Hannah. "So he really likes her, she doesn't live anywhere close to here and you want him to play it by ear?" he asked with a shake of his head. "Hon, this is Nathan. He plays everything by ear. I'm guessing he wants some concrete advice, or he'd still be playing it cool with us."

Hannah swatted Luke's shoulder. "Hey! What do I tell him? He's right, she lives across the damn country." She turned to Nathan, leaning her elbows on the table. "I like Tess. I'm glad you like her, but I don't know what to tell you," she said earnestly.

Nathan shrugged and picked up another cracker,

scooping a generous amount of salmon dip into his mouth. "Damn if I know what to do. Seriously, I just thought she was cute, so I asked her to dinner. She got all prickly about it and it made me want to persuade her. I finally did and then…" he paused, getting flustered.

Luke interjected. "She's more than just cute for you. She's got you all tied up. Way I see it, you have two choices: make the most of the next week or so that she's here, or back off. Whatever you do, be decent to her. She's the good kind."

"I'm decent to everyone," Nathan replied, aggrieved with Luke. "And what the hell do you mean—the good kind?"

"Not saying you aren't decent. And the good kind, well that's the kind of woman worth fighting for. Like Hannah," he said, reaching to clasp Hannah's hand. "Dude, you're the one that helped me realize what an idiot I was about to be. Remember all that stuff you said about how awesome Hannah was?" Luke asked.

Hannah smiled wide and leaned her head on Luke's shoulder. "Awww, I love it when you remind me that I'm worth it. Especially when John kept me up almost all night."

Luke rubbed her hair. Hannah lifted her head, and Luke leaned in for a lingering kiss. Witnessing the easy intimacy between them made Nathan wish he could leapfrog to that point with Tess. With a mental shake, he reminded himself that he'd had a single dinner with her, a few days of fishing and two nights of unbelievable passion.

Luke looked back to Nathan. "So yeah, Tess is the good kind. Don't get all defensive about it. Might as well admit you want to enjoy what little time you have with her, so stop worrying about it so much."

Nathan nodded, his chest tightening at the thought of seeing Tess again. Deciding it was best to get off the topic, he belatedly addressed Hannah's earlier comment. "Back to dipnetting—I plan to head up to Kenai with Travis tomorrow. Wanna come?"

"Sure. Why don't you see if Tess can come too?" Luke asked with a wink.

Hannah giggled. Nathan glared at her. "Oh god, Nathan. Just teasing. I can't help it. It's fun to see someone matter to you. But seriously," she said, giggles subsiding. "Taking her dipnetting is an awesome idea. She can't do anything but watch, but it's sight to behold, especially for people that love to fish. I'll go too. That way, she won't be stuck with three men all day. I'll even call to invite her," Hannah offered with a grin.

"You will?" Nathan asked.

"You got it! I got her number the other day because I wanted to invite her for coffee." Hannah stood and fetched her phone, calling before Nathan had a chance to respond.

Luke rolled his eyes. "Better watch out, man. If you want Hannah to back off, say so fast."

Nathan shrugged. For the moment, he didn't mind her meddling. Not to mention that it was impossible for him to say no to any chance to see Tess, the pull was too strong. "No need...for now," he replied, his heartbeat kicking up.

Hannah walked back into the kitchen, slipping her phone in her pocket. "She's meeting us at Misty Mountain tomorrow morning. Who's driving?"

* * *

A FISHING NET snapped out of the water, right into Nathan's chin. The salmon that had been in it sailed just beyond his shoulder and landed in the water with a splash —a flick of silver and the salmon was gone. Nathan reflexively grabbed the net when it tumbled into the water. Fortunately, the net was light aluminum, so getting whacked in the face by it was more a nuisance than anything else. Nathan turned to find Luke laughing a few feet away. They were standing waist-deep in the mouth of the Kenai River where the water from Cook Inlet was rushing upriver, sockeye salmon following the tide to spawn further up the river. The Kenai River was one of several choices for dipnetting, and Nathan's personal favorite. The mouth of the river faced Cook Inlet and the mountains across. Along with the view, the sockeye that came through here were sizable—it wasn't unusual to catch salmon that were twenty pounds or more. Usually one good day of dipnetting, and he and his brothers caught enough to almost fill a chest freezer.

"Yours?" he asked, holding up the offending net and looking to Luke.

Still laughing, Luke nodded and waded in his direction. "Damn fish caught me off guard. Hit the net so hard, I lost my grip."

Nathan handed the net back to Luke. "Just don't keep throwing your net at me and catch some salmon," he said, shaking his head.

"Almost have our limit. Thinking we won't be here much longer," Luke replied.

"I know, fish are running today," Nathan said. He glanced over his shoulder to the shore. Tess and Hannah were seated on two coolers on the beach. Hannah had started out dipnetting with them, but they were catching them so fast, she stayed on shore to gut and clean the salmon.

"She's not going anywhere, man," Travis said, a hint of sarcasm in his tone. He'd been standing silently beside Nathan and Luke, holding his net in the water.

Nathan whipped his head around and glared at Travis. "Like I didn't know that," Nathan replied sardonically.

"Wouldn't know it by how often you keep looking over there. You're usually so slick, always playing it cool. Can't keep it together around Tess though," Travis said, not missing a beat.

Luke piled on. "It's almost embarrassing, man. You can't keep your eyes off of her. How 'bout you just go sit with them and we'll get the rest of the salmon for you?"

Travis and Luke took turns teasing Nathan for another few minutes. Nathan tolerated their ribbing with a few return jabs, but he found it harder to deflect them when they were pointing out an uncomfortable truth. While Nathan had never purposefully tried to play it cool and slick, he'd never encountered a woman who threw him off of his casual, fun-loving flirt attitude. He kept looking at Tess because he couldn't seem *not* to.

"Enough guys," Nathan said, finally annoyed enough. "Can you cut me a little slack here? Maybe I notice Tess a little more than usual, but could we just leave it alone for now?"

Travis looked toward Luke with a grin. "Wow, now we've pissed him off."

Luke chuckled and looked to Nathan. "Maybe a little, but he wants us to play nice around Tess, so he's not gonna say too much about it."

Nathan shook his head. "Guys, could we *please* move on?"

Just as Luke started to reply, Nathan felt the sudden tug of a salmon swimming right into his net. He yanked his net into the current, forcing the fish into the back of the net. As he turned to walk to shore, he spoke over his shoulder. "Will it get you guys to back off if I just admit I have a thing for her?"

Travis chuckled. "Okay. But only 'cause you admitted it."

As he trudged through the cold, rushing water, he heard Luke's reply. "Damn, didn't think he'd fess up that fast."

Reaching the shore, Nathan dragged the net, fish safely inside, onto the sand. He felt Tess before he saw her. She had a subtle, but lively presence. She clearly loved the outdoors and loved fishing. She'd asked tons of questions when they'd first gotten here. He could tell it was hard for her that she had to be a spectator today, but dipnetting was for residents only. The beach was crowded with dipnetters. The season was short, a month usually, and could be impacted by the fish runs. If numbers were low, sometimes the season was shortened or cancelled. The result that when it was time to dipnet, residents came from all over the state. There were hundreds of people crowding the area today. Tess had ambled around, chatting, admiring salmon and making the best of her spectator status.

Nathan was glad Hannah had come along. Once they got going, Hannah had spent most of the morning with Tess in between gutting and cleaning fish. Seconds after he glanced up to greet Tess, Hannah joined them. She deftly took the fish from him, gutting it and cleaning it within minutes. Gulls and eagles circled above, diving down for scraps scattered around the beach.

Hannah walked over to their cluster of coolers to tuck the fish inside one of the coolers and shift ice on top. Tess stood to his side, looking out over the water, a hand shading her eyes. Nathan took the moment to look at her. Sun-kissed and wind-blown, her curls blew in a tousle around her face and neck, the bright sun glinting in the gold. Her cheeks were rosy. She was attired in colorful striped rubber boots, loose red capris and a beige cotton shirt. Her arms were dusted with sand. Who'd have thought he'd think rubber boots were sexy? On Tess, they just added to the charm. She was carefree, sultry and sexy—without even trying. Nathan wanted to pull her in his arms and kiss her.

Tess turned away from the water, catching his gaze. The reserve that she so often displayed held for just a moment and then dissolved. Her lips tipped in a small smile. She held his eyes for a moment before a giggle burst out of her.

He tilted his head to the side. "What was that for?"

She shrugged, the small smile widening. "Don't know. It's just fun to be here."

Nathan stood in place. They were surrounded by people, a bustle of activity. The waves crashed into the shore, voices carried across the water, a salty mist blew off the water, a gull dove down and landed at his feet, pecking at the edge of his fishing net. A gust of wind blew sand across them. Tess pushed her curls behind her ears and they immediately blew wild. She laughed again. Nathan took two steps to reach her side and leaned over to kiss her. Her lips were cool and salty. He forgot where they were, every sense funneled toward her. Holding her lips in a light kiss, he slid a hand down her back, nudging her closer.

CHAPTER 10

ess's mind was wiped blank. She leaned into Nathan, her breasts brushing against his chest. The voices surrounding them faded, she heard only the rhythmic sound of the ocean waves rolling into shore and felt the mist drifting off the water. The bubbly joy she'd felt just before Nathan kissed her morphed into that frenzied heat he elicited in her. His palm slid down her spine. Nathan deepened the kiss, his tongue slipping into her mouth, tangling with hers in lazy strokes. She loved kissing him—he was leisurely and thorough, nipping, nibbling and stroking.

Nathan abruptly pulled away. "Damn," he swore softly.

Tess looked up into his blue eyes, momentarily dazed. The sounds around them came back into the fore. Glancing around, the reality of where they were returned—they stood in the middle of fishing nets, people and gulls. She took a step back.

A sharp whistle came from the water. Tess saw Luke wave at them. "Nathan?"

He held still, holding her eyes for a long moment, heat arcing between them. "What?" he asked.

Tess nodded toward the water, just as Luke whistled again. "I think Luke's trying to get your attention," she explained. She had to bite her lip to keep from laughing. Nathan appeared just as dazed as she felt.

He turned to the water. "Yeah?"

By this point, Luke was wading toward the shore, net in tow. "Got another salmon," he called out.

Nathan met Luke at the water's edge, returning with a salmon. Hannah startled Tess when she spoke just at her shoulder. "I got it," Hannah said, reaching over to take the salmon.

A moment of awkward silence passed when Hannah walked back to the coolers. A tumble of thoughts danced through Tess's mind. Part of her wanted, *desperately wanted*, to have Nathan to herself just now, to keep kissing him, to spiral into that place he took her where nothing but sensation reigned. It was like a drug she'd never had. Another part of her kept interjecting that she needed to keep her distance, needed to remember that this was just a fling, that she'd be back in North Carolina soon, that this couldn't amount to anything more.

Nathan stood quietly, just watching her. His black curls were messy, his eyes such a bright blue, the masculine angles of his features stark in the shadows from the sun. Tess had surreptitiously watched him most of the day, savoring the moments when the whites of his teeth flashed in a smile against his sun-burnished skin.

He cleared his throat. "Think I should head back out to catch a few more salmon," he said.

Tess nodded.

Nathan held her gaze. "I'd rather just keep on kissing you...But wrong place, wrong time," he said with a sheepish smile.

Tess bit her lip. "I know. Go fish," she said, giving him a push on the chest. Nathan curled his hand around hers and lifted it, turning it over to place a soft kiss in the center of her palm. Tess thought she might melt, right there on the beach, surrounded by salmon being cleaned and gutted, gulls swooping, and people, all focused on something to do with fish. Her heart hammering, she stepped back when Nathan let go of her hand. He gave her a last look and waded back into the water.

"Hope you aren't trying to hide the fact that you are *seriously* into Nathan," Hannah said as soon as Tess sat down on the cooler across from Hannah.

Tess felt her face redden and wished for the one-millionth time that she wasn't a blusher. Looking to Hannah, she caught her warm eyes and smiled ruefully.

"Guess it's kinda obvious, huh?"

Hannah pursed her lips and feigned thoughtfulness for a moment before nodding emphatically. "Yeah, it's way obvious. On the upside, Nathan's just as bad as you," Hannah said.

Tess couldn't help herself. "Really? How can you tell?" Her curiosity about Nathan was growing by the second, and she'd had no chance to get to know anything about him from anyone else.

"Oh, let's see. I can tell because the guy can't keep his eyes off of you, he's like a teenager, all starry eyed. He takes every chance he can get to be near you, and he just forgot you were in the middle of this..." Hannah paused and gestured around. "And kissed you right here. I was worried for a second that you two were about to go a step too far for public consumption."

Tess's blush deepened. It was hard to admit, but it felt damn good to hear that Nathan couldn't keep his eyes off of her. She had tons of other questions but wasn't sure whether it was okay to pry.

Hannah's eyes held an assessing look. With a shrug, she continued. "I'm guessing you have some questions about Nathan."

Tess glanced toward Nathan who stood between Luke and Travis again, his back to the shore. Looking back toward Hannah, she blushed again. She had plenty of questions, but she didn't even know where to start.

Hannah nodded even though Tess didn't say anything. "Here's the thing, Nathan's a sweetheart, but he doesn't let that show too much. He's the baby of his brothers, if you didn't know that already." At Tess's nod, Hannah continued. "He just turned thirty-one this year."

"He's only thirty-one—he's three years younger than me! Oh dear god," Tess exclaimed, interrupting Hannah. "I've never dated anyone younger than me. Now I'm gonna feel old." She shook her head. Three years didn't seem much, but handsome as Nathan was, it made her question how he viewed her even more.

Hannah rolled her eyes. "Oh who cares? It's three years. Not like that makes all that much difference. If he was three years older, you wouldn't think twice. Don't be silly."

Tess looked over at Hannah and realized she might be reacting a bit much. She just had assumed Nathan was her age or older. "Okay, maybe I am. I just hadn't thought about it and don't want to feel like the old one."

Hannah quirked an eyebrow at her. "Since when is thirty-four old? I'm guessing that how old you are if Nathan's three years younger."

Tess shrugged sheepishly. "I guess it's not. I just hadn't thought about how old Nathan was…that's all. Honestly, I hadn't thought I'd be doing much of anything with anyone on this trip. I sure as hell didn't plan on going out on any dates, much less more than one. This whole situation with Nathan has been…a surprise. I'm not so sure what to do about it." Tess closed her eyes for a moment, wondering just how she'd ended up here, sitting on a cooler, longing for a moment of privacy with Nathan, a man she'd definitely *not* expected to fall for. Sifting through her feelings led only to further confusion, complicated by the realities of the situation. In another week, she'd be back in North Carolina. Nathan would remain here, in Alaska, roughly five thousand miles away, give or take.

The teasing manner faded from Hannah's eyes, her soft blue eyes empathetic. "Yeah, I can see that. You just didn't know you'd meet Nathan. He might be the baby, but those Winters brothers are all pretty damn easy on the eyes. Seeing as I married one, I get the draw."

Hannah's words drew a chuckle from Tess. "Yeah, he is seriously easy on the eyes. I have to say I've wondered how come Nathan was even single. It's not like he couldn't have his pick of women," Tess commented.

"He could. I had the same kind of questions when I met Luke. But, trust me, Nathan's a good guy. He's a flirt, I won't deny that. But I've always thought he just needed to find the right person. I realize there's all kinds of things in the way—mainly that you don't even live here—but I think you're great with Nathan," Hannah said earnestly.

"Kind of hard to figure out the 'not living' here part of that equation. But I'm curious...a couple of people have mentioned that Nathan hasn't been out much lately. He blows it off, but what's that about?" Tess asked.

Hannah gave her a sharp look before responding. "Well, like I said, Nathan's a flirt. He used to be on the local bar scene more often. He's not a heavy duty partier, just used to run with the fun crowd. I can't say why, but he's laid pretty low for the last year or so. In a town like Diamond Creek—small and nosy—people notice things like that. He tended to keep things casual with women. Come to think of it though, he hasn't dated anyone, even casually, in a while. Luke says Nathan has *never* been the way he is with you. So, make what you will of that, but I hope you don't think Nathan makes a habit of getting involved with women the way he has with you. It's pretty obvious you mean a lot to him."

Tess felt warm all over, a flush blooming from the inside. Her heart did a little jig at Hannah's words. Much as she didn't want to admit it, she was in deep with Nathan. Just as she allowed this feeling to wash over her, the familiar defenses she'd built jostled for attention. What was she doing falling for a man that she had no practical chance with, given the geography of their circumstances? And shouldn't she be worried about the fact that she was probably just a novelty to him? Once the haze of lust faded, what would happen? Though she didn't like to think about it, Chad had been handsome and charming at first. What had seemed wonderful at first left a bitter taste now.

Tess gave her head a hard shake. Hannah waited quietly, seeming to realize that Tess needed a moment. Tess could imagine she and Hannah would be good friends if they lived near each other. Hannah was down to earth, easy going, practical and kind.

Tess looked at Nathan again. Even at a distance, he was handsome. She caught the flash of his teeth, which she loved, as he laughed at something Travis said. Turning back, she blushed when she realized she was fawning over Nathan like a teenage girl.

"I don't know what to do," Tess said, her voice sounding as confused as she felt.

Hannah nodded slowly. "Look, I don't know what to tell you. I don't know you all that well, but I like you. I think you should just try to stop worrying and enjoy what you can with Nathan. There's no way to know what could happen in the future. He's totally into you and you're into him. Enjoy the moment. I realize that might sound corny but it fits."

Much as Tess wanted a better answer than that, particularly the part of her heart that was scarred from her failed relationship with Chad, she knew it was the only answer for the moment. Or the only answer that didn't mean pushing Nathan away. As strong as the urge to do that was, the feeling that existed between her and Nathan was stronger.

"It is corny, but I see your point," Tess said, nibbling the inside of her cheek. "As for the future…I guess I'll just take it a day at a time."

"If you need to talk some more, I'm here," Hannah said. "Consider me your Alaskan go-to friend," she said with a smile. "But, for now, we've got more fish to deal with." Hannah stood and grabbed the fish whacker leaning against one of the coolers as she strode off to meet Luke at the edge of the water. Nathan and Travis were close behind Luke, dragging their nets through the water.

* * *

TESS STOOD at her hotel window looking out over the bay. Wind blew the rain sideways, creating a mist over the water. She had just returned from having an early dinner with her family. The sunny afternoon was long gone. The sky had clouded, wind, rain and much cooler air fast on its heels. With a sigh, she turned away from the window, sitting on the edge of the bed. They were flying out in two more days. Tess recalled that when her father had been planning this trip and her mother hounding her to come with them, she'd been worried that spending three weeks in a tiny town in Alaska would be too long. She'd never have expected to be wishing she had more time and certainly not because of a man.

Since the day she'd gone dipnetting with Nathan and his brothers, she'd abandoned any attempts to hide her fling with him from her family. She'd realized that she'd have far less chances to see Nathan if she tried to keep their relationship hidden. Her mother had been surprisingly well-behaved about the whole thing, only occasionally did her enthusiasm bubble over in public.

In the last week, Nathan had spent almost every night with her at the hotel. The nights were a blur of passion, tinged with a level of closeness that alarmed Tess if she let herself think about it. Early this morning, in the soft light of dawn, she'd woken curled on her side; Nathan spooned behind her, one hand curled on the underside of her breast, his palm warm against her bare skin. She remained still for a moment, luxuriating in the feel of being surrounded by his warmth. She breathed deeply, trying to inhale the moment. Nathan had woken, mumbling *Tess, mmm* into the back of her neck. She pressed her hand against the one that lay against her breast and held it tight, tears pushing against her closed eyelids.

Nathan's body tensed in a shivering stretch behind her before relaxing and curling more closely against her. Nathan nibbled on her neck, his lips tracing down her neck onto her shoulder. His warm hands skated across her body in light strokes, the roughened texture of his palms a soft abrasion that set her nerves afire. He slipped beneath the sheets, parting her thighs, his tongue delving into the center of her. Half-awake, Tess tumbled into the heat that flared between them. She climaxed in a burst against his mouth, gasping his name. He slid up her body, his lips leading the way, taking her mouth in a deep kiss, his tongue stroking into her mouth just as he slid his cock into her slick channel. He stroked in and out of her, again and again in a controlled pace. Tess became frantic against him, lifting her hips to meet his, urging him deeper and deeper. Nathan didn't break from the slow kiss until she came apart in his arms again, her orgasm so intense, it brought tears to her eyes. His forehead resting against hers, Nathan had followed her over the edge with one final thrust.

Just thinking about those moments brought a flush all over. Tess bit her lip and wondered just how she was going to handle the end of this time with Nathan. She'd taken Hannah's advice and thrown herself into enjoying the moments with Nathan. She kept trying to convince herself that this time with him would stay encapsulated here in Diamond Creek once she returned to North Carolina. As the days and nights passed, it was getting harder to believe. She feared she'd made herself too vulnerable.

A sharp knock on her hotel door broke into her train of thought. Opening the door, she found her mother waiting.

"Hello dear, let's go downstairs for a drink," Celine said immediately.

Before Tess had a chance to respond, her mother had slipped her hand through her elbow and was tugging her into the hallway.

"Okay, okay, Mom. Can I get my purse?" Tess asked with a small laugh, slipping her arm out of her mother's grasp.

Moments later, they were seated at a table by the windows that faced Kachemak Bay. The rain was blowing against the windows, obscuring any view. The weather suited her mood, a combination of dreary and chilled. Celine had ordered a bottle of red wine.

Once they were served, Celine sipped her wine, looking thoughtful.

"What, Mom?"

"What do you mean?" Celine parried.

Tess gave an exasperated sigh. "You dragged me down here for a reason, so let's not bother with small talk."

Celine smiled ruefully. "I lost the ability to trick you when you were a little girl. Not like your brother. I can still sweet talk him." Celine paused and looked over at Tess, her eyes concerned. "Honey, you know how happy I am that you've actually let yourself have a little fun."

Tess nodded, gesturing with her hand for her mother to

continue. She was impatient and anxious; she wanted this conversation over. She'd known it was coming because her mother could only keep her opinions to herself for so long.

"I'm thrilled to see you spending time with Nathan. I couldn't have picked a better guy for you. When he joined us for dinner the other day, it's obvious he adores you. And obvious that you're trying as hard as you can *not* to let it show that he might matter more than just a little. Much as I don't want to worry about you, I'm worried that you're going to try to convince yourself to forget all about Nathan when you go back to North Carolina. That's a mistake."

Tess took a gulp of wine. "So, you think it's great that I'm having a fling, but you think I shouldn't forget about him when we go home? Mom, I kinda have to," Tess replied. She couldn't bring herself to say aloud that she could hardly bear to consider keeping the door to her heart open. The only way she was getting through the intensity of her feelings for Nathan was by telling herself over and over and over that it was temporary. Because it was.

Celine shook her head. "Honey, you don't have to. If something's worth it, at least leave the door open for there to be a chance. I may be a romantic, but I'm not stupid. I'm not sayin' that being clear across the country is a good way to start a relationship. Just that I don't want to see you pretend Nathan doesn't mean anything to you. Who knows? Maybe he'll visit you in North Carolina. Maybe you'll come back to Diamond Creek again. Lord knows, your father would be thrilled to come back. Just…just don't close yourself up. That's all, that's what I'm worried about."

Tess's throat tightened with emotion. In her warm drawl, her mother was asking Tess to do the one thing she just didn't know if she could. What lay between her and Nathan was a curveball she hadn't expected. After the disaster that was her relationship with Chad and the way she'd felt about herself as a result, she had promised she wouldn't be stupid again. And here she was—falling for a guy where the geographic obstacles were large enough that the only way she could tolerate saying goodbye was by keeping her head and heart clear about what this fling was —temporary insanity.

"Mom, you're worried. I get it. Let me do what I gotta do here. Nathan *is* great, but I can't go home thinking something might come of it. I just can't," Tess said, flinching a little at her tone—hearing the tinge of desperation in it.

Celine pursed her lips, absently twining her necklace around her fingers, a thin chain of silver with a single amethyst set in silver. She wore matching earrings, the bright amethyst coordinated with a purple silk blouse, her silvery curls a contrast to the deep color. Celine nodded slowly. "Okay, I won't bother you about this for now, but no promises that I won't bring it up later."

Tess started to protest, but Celine held her hand up. "You might not like it, but I know you pretty darn well. Watching you shut down after what happened with Chad made me sad. I just don't want to see you wall yourself off even more over something good, like what you have with Nathan. I'm done...I'll keep out of it for now," Celine said with an emphatic nod. "Shall we talk about the weather?" she asked with a soft chuckle.

Tess sighed. She knew her mother meant well. It was just that her feelings were churned up enough already. She didn't have the emotional wherewithal to try to keep a door open in her heart when it was going to be a hell of a lot harder than she could ever have anticipated just to say goodbye to Nathan.

Tess looked over at her mother, taking in the kindness in her gaze. She knew it was hard for her mother to let this lie for now. "Mom, I get where you're coming from. I do. I might be able to talk about it later, just not now. Not while we're still here in Diamond Creek, and I'm trying to figure out how to deal with Nathan."

Celine nodded slowly and took a sip of wine. "Of course. I think Nathan's worth the trouble. He's damn handsome," she said, a twinkle in her eyes.

Tess gave a soft laugh. "That he is."

Celine deftly steered the conversation onto safer topics. Tess allowed herself to stop dwelling on Nathan and just enjoy the time with her mother.

AN HOUR OR SO LATER, Tess quietly closed her hotel door and leaned against it, sliding to the floor. She was tipsy from the wine. She slipped her phone out of her purse and glanced at the blank screen. She'd expected Nathan to call by now. He and his brothers had a guiding trip scheduled today. While their return times varied, she figured they would have headed back hours ago based on the rain and wind.

The phone vibrated in her hand, an unfamiliar number flashing across the screen. The area code was the only one for Alaska. She answered promptly.

"Tess?" Hannah asked.

"Yes?" Tess asked in return.

"It's Hannah. Just wondering if you've heard from Nathan."

A knot of anxiety formed in her belly. "No, no I haven't. Have you heard from Luke?"

There was a long pause. "Wish I could say that I had. I expected them back about an hour ago," Hannah said slowly, her worry evident in her voice. "I was hoping you'd have heard from Nathan by now."

A flash of panic reverberated through Tess's body, her chest became tight, her breath short. Forcing herself to stay calm, she remained still, seated on the floor, her back against the door. "Is there something we should do?" she asked, her anxiety blooming, her stomach hollow.

Tess heard Hannah speaking to someone else, her voice muffled. "I just asked my friend, Susie, to call down to the harbormaster and see if he's heard anything. Where are you?"

"I'm at the hotel where we're staying, Midnight Sun Lodges."

"Why don't Susie and I come down there? I'm sure it's nothing. They probably just got slowed down by the weather. I'd like to be by the harbor though so we can help unload when they get in," Hannah said.

"Sure, meet me here. I'll go get us a table in the lounge," Tess replied.

The tipsy feeling she'd had when she got to her room had disappeared with a rush of adrenaline and worry. She may not have known Hannah that long, but she knew Hannah wasn't one to overreact. If Hannah was calling, wondering where Luke and his brothers were, it was well past time that they should be back. Standing, Tess walked to the windows and looked out into the misty, gray sky. It was late evening now, but still light and would be for another few hours. The visibility was beyond poor. Tess could barely make out the shape of the walkway that led from the hotel to the beach. The rain was falling at a drenching pace, and the wind drove the rain sideways. She didn't like thinking how it must feel to be out on the water in weather like this—cold, wet and miserable.

Moments later, Tess returned to the lounge where she'd just been with her mother. The waiter gave her a questioning look when he came over. "Didn't I just see you?" he asked with a smile.

"Oh, just meeting a friend while we wait for someone to get in from fishing," she explained.

The waiter, a slender young man with stick-straight brown hair and matching brown eyes, gave her a sharp look. "Hope they make it in soon. Pretty bad weather to be out," he said.

The anxiety that Tess had been trying to keep at bay reared up, her chest tightening with worry for Nathan and his brothers. "It's not good out. They have a lot of experience though, so I'm sure they're just delayed," she said.

"I'm sure they'll make it in, just bad weather to be out," the waiter offered.

Much as Tess wanted another glass of wine to dull the sharp edge of her anxiety, she thought it best to be able to think clearly, so she ordered coffee. Hannah arrived with her friend, Susie, and another woman, who bore a clear resemblance to Hannah. Susie was a tiny burst of energy. She had wild brown curls that she kept carelessly pushing out of her face and bright brown eyes to match. She was an amusing contrast to Hannah, barely reaching Hannah's shoulder. Hannah quickly introduced Tess to Susie and Emma who turned out to be Hannah's sister. Emma shared Hannah's blue eyes and long, dark hair with less curl to it. She was somewhat reserved, although in comparison to Susie, almost anyone could seem reserved.

"Now would be the time that we should down a bottle of wine, but we need to keep our wits about us," Susie said wryly. "Nice to meet you, by the way," she continued with a nod to Tess. "I've been wondering who Nathan fell for. That man is gaga over you. Which is saying something because I've never seen Nathan like this about any woman."

Tess was startled, but she couldn't even assuage the curiosity Susie's comment elicited. She was too worried about Nathan. The waiter arrived, promptly serving them coffee. While he was pouring coffee, Tess recalled that Hannah had asked Susie to call the harbormaster.

"Any news from the harbormaster?" Tess asked.

Hannah shook her head, her eyes worried. She absently tucked her long dark hair behind her ears and took a sip of coffee.

"Harbormaster said they were scheduled to return two hours ago. The good news is that they didn't radio that they were having problems. The bad news is that they didn't radio anything, and they're two hours overdue," Susie said. She gave Hannah's hand a quick squeeze. "I know you're worried, but this is Alaska. Weather like this is pretty common. I'm sure they're just delayed because of poor visibility."

Hannah nodded. Emma slid an arm around Hannah's shoulders and gave her a squeeze. Tess didn't know what to say or what to do. Her hands curled tightly around the mug of coffee, the warmth grounding her. With all the questions that had been tumbling through her mind about Nathan, her doubts felt insignificant and silly now. Try as she might, she couldn't help but worry that something had gone horribly wrong in this weather. He meant far more to her than any man ever had. While she still didn't know what to do about the geographic distance between them, she knew she loved him. Worry tightened her chest, a flash of panic bubbling. While part of her tried to stay calm, she was terrified that she would lose the chance to let him know how she felt.

Tess was so wrapped up in her thoughts that she jumped when a phone rang. Susie grabbed her phone, sitting on the table between her and Hannah.

"Yes?" she asked quickly. "Okay, so they radioed?"

Hannah tugged at Susie's arm. Susie listened and nodded before turning to Hannah, her mouth away from the phone. "They radioed in. One of the engines went out when a wave washed over the back of the boat. Hang on, let me get more info."

Hannah nodded, one hand clenching her coffee mug and

the other holding tight to Susie's arm. Emma spoke quietly to Hannah, telling her to focus on the positive – that they were okay. Tess could only imagine how Hannah felt, given how Tess felt. Her heart was hammering, her throat tight. She just wanted to have Nathan here, on dry land again. They waited while Susie asked a few more questions and ended the call.

"They're okay, but the harbormaster's called the Coast Guard. There's too much water in the boat. The wave flooded one of the engines and they're busy bailing water. Shouldn't be too long," Susie said, flicking her eyes between Hannah, Emma and Tess.

Hannah sat silently, her hand still holding tightly to Susie's arm. Susie uncurled Hannah's hand from her arm and gave it a squeeze. "How about we focus on the good part? Listen to Emma. They are safe. The Coast Guard is on the way. Ted…" Susie glanced to Tess. "He's the harbormaster," she said and turned back to Hannah. "Ted got their location and everything, so it's not like the Coast Guard is flying blind to find them."

Hannah took a shaky breath. "I know, I know. I just hate knowing they're out there in this weather and the boat's taking on water. It's not good."

Tess took her own shaky breath, trying and failing to calm her heart. "Did Ted know roughly how long it should take the Coast Guard to get to them?" she asked.

Susie nodded. "He thought probably fifteen minutes by helicopter. They were heading out with two helicopters and one of their boats. He said he'll call as soon as he hears. The part we don't know is will they wait until the boat gets there and tow them in? Or will they need to airlift them out of there? If they do that, it means the boat can't be salvaged. He just didn't have enough info to know more than that right now."

It suddenly occurred to Tess that John wasn't with

Hannah. She'd been so wrapped up, she hadn't noticed. "Where's John?" she asked.

"Dropped him off with Susie's mom," Hannah explained. "I thought it'd be best if he wasn't here right now. I'm too worried and when they get in, we'll be busy helping. Not to mention that he doesn't need to see all me so worried. Plus, he loves Susie's mom."

Susie chuckled. "She spoils him rotten. She's his stand-in for a grandkid these days."

Tess took another breath, her mind promptly returning to wondering when they'd hear back and how Nathan and everyone else on the boat were doing.

They had been silent for several moments when Susie's phone rang again, the fork sitting beside the phone vibrating along with the phone. Susie snatched the phone, asking a few rapid questions.

She put her hand over the phone. "Coast Guard is on scene. Everyone is okay, but they're concerned about hypothermia because they're all wet so they're going to airlift them out. Sounds like they plan to tow the boat back."

Hannah's eyes filled with tears, the look of relief on her face evident. Tess felt her own tears press behind her eyelids. As relieved as she was, she didn't think she could relax until they were back on dry land. Looking out the window, she saw that they were losing the light. The gray was darker and thicker, the rain blowing in sheets, hitting the windows with sharp pelts. Thinking of Nathan out in this weather, on the ocean and probably soaked through, made her heart hurt.

"Tess honey, what's going on?"

Tess turned to see her mother walking over, her father at her side. They walked to the table, both looking curious. They had met Hannah when she'd helped on two of their guiding trips.

"We were just in the front getting some fresh towels and saw you in here," Celine said.

Much as Tess didn't want to explain, she saw no way out of it. She knew her parents would worry because they liked Nathan and his brothers. She wasn't prepared to be in the middle of battling her fear, her worry and the realization that she loved Nathan while she tried to keep it together in front of her parents.

Susie jumped in by introducing herself and explaining the situation. Tess gave Susie a silent thanks. She settled in for the long wait until Nathan and his brothers were back on dry land.

CHAPTER 11

The sound of helicopter blades blocked out everything else, slicing through the air in a rhythmic slap. Tess stood at the side of the landing strip— Hannah, Emma and Susie waiting alongside her. They had waited at the hotel lounge for a long hour before word came that the Coast Guard had airlifted everyone into the helicopter, and they were headed in to shore. Tess's nerves were worn. Her parents had waited with them for a while. To Tess's relief, they'd graciously bowed out when it was time to head over the airport where the helicopter would land, asking only that she call them with an update. Much as she appreciated their support, she didn't want to have a meltdown in their presence.

Rain fell steadily, the wind blew sideways with the helicopter adding a swirl to the wind as it slowly landed. Tess was soaked through, shivering against the cold. Looking around, she saw Hannah, Emma and Susie were in no better shape. Moments later, the helicopter settled firmly on the ground and the sound of pouring rain seemed quiet without the whir and whack of the helicopter blades.

Tess watched as one person after another stepped out into the rain. Hannah ran to Luke, Jared was tugged into the cluster with Susie and Emma. A few others stepped off next who Tess assumed to be the tourists the brothers had taken fishing for the day. Nathan finally stepped out, looking around, his eyes catching hers through the rain. She ran to his side, Nathan tugging her quickly into his embrace.

"Hey," he said, his voice muffled against her wet hair.

She burrowed against him and felt him shiver. Pulling back, she looked up. Tears slid down her cheeks. "You're cold, we need to get you somewhere warm."

His smile was tired, but true. "I know. Just glad to see you," he replied, keeping her tucked close to his side.

Despite or perhaps because of her overwhelming feelings, Tess became worried about what happened to their boat. "Is the boat okay?" she asked, looking up at Nathan through the rain.

He nodded. "It's gonna need some repairs because of the flooded engine, but it'll be alright. The Coast Guard is towing it to the dock for us."

The next few minutes were a bustle of activity. An ambulance had been waiting by the landing strip. Despite their protests, Nathan, Luke and Jared were ordered to go to the hospital to be cleared. After some haggling, the family who had gone fishing with them was escorted in the ambulance, and Emma drove the rest of them there.

The hospital waiting room, despite its typical sterility, was warm and comforting, a haven from the rain and wind. Nathan had been taken in for a quick exam, along with Luke and Jared, all three complaining it was unnecessary. The waiting was quiet and slow. The news droned on the sole television in the waiting area.

Another long hour and the brothers were cleared to go home. The teenage daughter of the family on the guiding trip was hypothermic and would remain for the night.

During the wait, Emma had driven Susie home to retrieve her car. Emma took Hannah and Luke home, while Susie took charge of Jared, Nathan and Tess. The ride to the hotel was quiet. No questions had been asked, it appeared everyone assumed Nathan would stay with Tess at the hotel. Tess wasn't sure what to think of that assumption, but she wasn't letting him out of her sight tonight.

Tess closed the door to her room, the thick carpet muffling its sound. She switched on the lamp by the bed, turning to look toward Nathan. "Shower," she said, pointing to the bathroom.

"Aw…I don't want a shower, just want to lay down with you," he whined.

She shook her head firmly. "You're soaked and so am I. Let's enjoy some hot water instead of freezing rain."

Nathan shrugged and offered a tired grin. "In that case…"

In the steaming shower, Tess soaped his back and turned him around to soap his chest. She ran her hands through the dark curls scattered across. Nathan leaned forward and captured her lips in a long kiss. A soft heat suffused Tess. Nathan stumbled a little. She pulled away, holding his eyes for a long moment. His eyes were bloodshot and droopy, his face haggard from exhaustion. "You are too tired for this. Out now," she directed.

"Geez, you're bossy." He tried to kiss her again, but his balance was off and he fell against the wall.

Her heart clenched. She didn't like seeing him this tired. Tess shook her head against the tears that threatened. She briskly turned off the shower and stepped out, immediately handing him a towel.

Hours later, in the thin light of dawn, Tess woke to the feel of Nathan's hand sliding down her hip, the other hand caressing her breasts, the feel of his roughened palm coasting across her nipples bringing a catch to her breath.

They made sleepy love, barely moving from their spooned position. Nathan slowly worked her into a heated frenzy with soft strokes and nibbles on her neck. He'd slipped his fingers into her moist center. Gasping his name when his fingers disappeared, she'd sighed in relief when he'd entered her from behind with a deep thrust. She tumbled into an orgasm the moment he delved a hand down the front of her body to caress her just above where he stroked deeply into her. Nathan followed her over the edge, holding her close as their breathing slowed. Tess fell back asleep and didn't wake until light sifted through the heavy hotel curtains. Nathan was still curled around her, his breathing soft and steady. Slowly untangling herself, she slipped out of bed and went to the bathroom. When she returned, she propped herself with pillows and sat beside Nathan, stroking his hair.

* * *

THE NEXT DAY, Tess stood by the windows in her hotel. The room was quiet and tense. Nathan wanted to drive her to the airport and she'd just told him no for the hundredth time. He sat on the edge of the bed, his hands raked in his black curls.

"All I'm asking is that you think about it. We don't have to let geography be a barrier. If you won't consider moving here, I'll move to North Carolina," Nathan said, his eyes determined.

She almost laughed aloud, not because it was funny, but because she couldn't believe that when he'd charmed her into dinner that this is where they ended up. She still hadn't adjusted to the power of her feelings during that long hour she'd waited for word on him and his brothers.

"You can't do that! I can't imagine you anywhere other than Diamond Creek. This place...it's you, it's your life. I'm not saying no, I'm just saying I don't know." Tess paused, tears choking her words.

Nathan's dark blue eyes held hers, almost daring her to ignore the practical side of herself. She gave her head a sharp shake.

"Nathan…" Her voice cracked, she took an unsteady breath. "We didn't plan on…*this*…" she gestured between them. "I didn't know that dinner would end up being so much more. I'm not trying to play this down. You mean *so* much to me. I just…I just need a little time. You have to understand; this was a vacation. I have a life, work, all kinds of things that I can't just toss away. Just like I'd never ask you to walk away from everything you have here. The thought of moving to Alaska never crossed my mind before I met you."

Nathan latched onto her last sentence. "So does that mean it has crossed your mind now?"

A tear rolled down her cheek as she nodded. "I just don't know what to do. Please just give this some time," she pleaded.

Nathan turned away, looking out the window, his profile stern, his emotions tightly held in check. He nodded firmly, as if to himself. "Okay, you have your time. But listen…" he turned and walked to stand in front of her. Placing his fingertips under her chin, he tipped her face towards his. Much as Tess wanted to look away from the raw emotion in his eyes, she looked straight into them, memorizing the feeling there. His words tore through her, her heart. "I love you."

"I love you too," she whispered.

Nathan wrapped her in his secure embrace and just held her for several long moments. There was a knock at the door. She knew it would be her mother. She called out that she'd be right there.

She looked up at Nathan, searching his eyes. "Just let me

say goodbye here." A tear slid down her cheek, the dampness cool on her skin.

Nathan nodded. "Promise me you'll think about what I asked."

Tess's throat tightened as she nodded. "I will...I promise."

There was another knock on the door, her mother's muffled voice reminding her they had to go. They were due to leave for the airport any moment. Nathan pulled her back into his embrace. His strong arms held her close. She breathed his scent in, memorizing it. He leaned back and held her gaze, those blue, blue eyes reading into her heart. "Don't you dare forget about me, Tess." He tapped his heart and then hers with one finger. "I know you didn't plan this, I know it's not convenient—but you are the woman for me. I love you." He leaned in for a slow kiss, his lips exploring hers in that slow, leisurely way of his—for that one moment, making her forget time.

Tess didn't look away when he broke their kiss. "I love you too. I won't forget you. I promise." Nathan released her gently. He stepped away, and she felt bereft out of his arms. Nathan braved his way through her mother's entrance into the room. With one quick kiss, *don't forget* whispered into her ear, Nathan left the room.

CHAPTER 12

Tess took a slow look around her condo. It was a small two-bedroom condo in a wooded area of Greenville. Tall loblolly pines surrounded the condo complex creating a shaded landscape. Her condo consisted of an open living room and kitchen area with hardwood flooring, granite counters in the kitchen, and a wall of windows with a sliding glass door that led to a small deck. A small alcove on one side led to two bedrooms and the sole bathroom. She'd decorated the apartment with her mother's help—bright purple curtains, a few framed photographs of the ocean and mountains and a painting by her grandmother of a field of lavender. An inviting sofa and chair set of soft green fabric and deep cushions with throw pillows and soft blankets completed the room.

Her friend, Deanna, had watered her plants while she was gone. The condo had the quiet, still feeling that places held when they'd been empty for a while. Tess went into action mode, unpacking her luggage, starting a load of laundry, and taking stock of what she had in the refrigerator. Since Nathan had left the hotel, she'd been in an emotional cocoon—her feelings distant and numb. Thoughts of her last few conversations with Nathan rotated through her mind. She'd slept through most of the long flight from Alaska.

Tess opened the sliding glass door, leaving the screen closed. The salty, moist, green scented air that was eastern North Carolina filled the room. She breathed deeply, inhaling the familiar essence. For a moment, she missed the crisp, bright air that was Diamond Creek. The salty scent there was sharper and cooler.

A few days later, just when she felt like she was getting caught up at work and somehow managing to tolerate the sharp spikes of feeling that tore through her when she thought of Nathan, her work phone rang.

"Tess Stanton," she said briskly, her mind half on the spreadsheet on her computer that outlined the current numbers on one of her fundraising projects.

"Hey Tess, it's Chad."

Tess had known that the second he'd spoken. She was silent for a moment, unprepared for his call. As she sat there, staring at her computer screen, she realized that hearing his voice didn't elicit much more than a brief flash of irritation and a lingering residue of shame.

"Yes?" she finally asked.

"How was your trip to Alaska?" Chad asked, his tone casual as if it was perfectly normal that he was calling her out of the blue.

"How did you know I was in Alaska?" Tess asked sharply.

"Geez, Tess. Your father's been planning it forever. It's not like we didn't talk about it," Chad replied, his tone conveying the sense that she was being silly to wonder about his question.

"It was fine. Why are you calling Chad?" she asked, deciding it was best to get right to the point.

"I thought maybe we could have dinner, catch up, that kind of thing."

Tess had absolutely no idea why Chad thought she'd even consider this. After she'd walked out, he had tried to persuade her to return off and on for a few months, but he hadn't called in over six months. She figured he'd finally gotten the clue that she wasn't going back and moved on. She'd never gotten too close to his circle of friends, so she hadn't heard much about him, which had been just fine with her.

"I don't think so, Chad. Like I said before, we're done. I learned more than I needed to know about what was going on behind my back when we were together, so I'm not really up for the whole friends thing with you."

Chad didn't miss a beat. "Tess, can't we just move past all that? We had something together for two years and went through a lot at the end there. I know the miscarriage was difficult for you, and I was there every step of the way. I don't see what's wrong with trying to be friendly and have dinner."

Tess thought back to the weeks after she'd learned she was pregnant and then miscarried. Chad had been barely supportive. He hadn't gone to the doctor with her, had spent most evenings watching television in the living room while she holed up in the bedroom. He'd made his usual comments about her weight and trying to put more effort into what she wore. Thinking about how Chad treated her brought Nathan to mind. He'd called last night as he had every night since she'd returned home. He was everything Chad wasn't – warm, supportive, curious about her daily life. She could barely stand to think about the way she felt when they were intimate. It was so foreign from the experiences she'd had with Chad; it almost felt like she was devaluing it to think about it in any context related to Chad.

"Chad, it's not going to happen. No dinner. Please don't

call me again," she said firmly and hung up the phone without waiting for his response.

Tess was irritated with Chad's call and aggravated that his intrusion flustered her. It didn't surprise her that he was oblivious enough to think that she might consider dinner with him, but it elicited lingering feelings of shame because she still couldn't believe how long it had taken her to see him for who he was. It puzzled her that he was trying to reconnect after all this time, but she shook off the sense of unease his call brought with it.

Time passed slowly and quickly in the weeks after her return from Alaska. She missed Nathan, and his calls were the highlight of every day. And yet, she was mired in indecision. She couldn't quite bring herself to seriously consider moving, while she couldn't imagine Nathan being anywhere other than Diamond Creek. The distance played games with her confidence. She started to doubt that he could actually love her and wonder if he'd gradually stop calling when time and distance dulled the memory of her.

At dinner with her friend, Deanna, Tess tried to explain why she wasn't sure what to do.

Deanna stared at her incredulously. "You mean to tell me you had a hot fling with a sexy guy from Alaska, he told you he loved you and wants you to move there and you're not sure what to do?"

Deanna took a swig of beer and brushed her bangs out of her eyes. Deanna had been a friend since childhood. They'd grown up in New Bern together. While Tess had attended college in Maryland, Deanna had gone to college in Florida for, as she put it, sunshine, surfers and scuba diving. She'd gone on to get a doctorate in biology and ended up in Greenville after she got a faculty position at East Carolina University. On top of being one of the most intelligent people Tess knew, Deanna was a rock solid friend and beautiful. She had straight glossy hair of a rich brown color with bright gray eyes. She wore little makeup, save for red lipstick that stood out in contrast to her dark hair. She was average height with an athletic build. She was outspoken and blunt with her friends and somewhat reserved with strangers. She claimed she was too busy for relationships, but she was usually dating someone, albeit casually.

Deanna became impatient at Tess's lack of response. "What? Nothing to say? I'll miss you, you're one of my best friends, but don't be stupid. Greenville's a nice place to be, but let's face it: it's not like you have some amazing reason to stay. You're a rock star fundraiser, but not because of where you live. You've worked your butt off and have contacts from here to D.C. You can take your work with you. Your parents are close by and that's great, but they'll come visit you. Have some adventure girl, go," she said firmly.

"Deanna! It's not that easy to just get up and go. Plus, I only knew Nathan for a few weeks. What if I move all the way out there and it blows up in my face?"

Deanna gave her a long look. "Then you'll have a great story. Tess, listen. I watched you disappear into that shitty relationship with Chad. I tried to be a good friend and just be there for you. Now that it's over, let me just say it. Thank fucking god. Take a chance. I'll help you pack," she said matter-of-factly. She took another swig of beer and a few bites of the steak she'd ordered.

"You're as bad as my mom. Not to mention that you haven't even met Nathan," Tess said.

Deanna shrugged. "No, I haven't met him, but I have a good feeling."

When Tess rolled her eyes, Deanna chuckled. "Look, if you're mom likes him, he's got to be a good guy. She's pretty protective and damn opinionated. I don't always agree with your mom, but if she's telling you to get your butt to Alaska, then we're on the same page on this one. I also think you need to shake your life up a bit."

Tess bit back a laugh. Deanna was nothing if not direct. She took a sip of wine before replying. "You know Mom, she's all about happily ever after. She thinks Nathan is perfect for me. Plus, she's been worried ever since the whole thing blew up with Chad."

"Sometimes a blow up is a good thing and that was," Deanna said emphatically. "Let me say it another way. Hot guy. Nice. Loves you. Alaska. Go for it!"

Tess gave up and laughed. Deanna wasn't the friend to let her dawdle. She challenged her. Tess just had to figure out if she was up for the challenge.

* * *

TESS SMOOTHED the front her lightweight black slacks and adjusted the collar on the silky cream blouse she wore. She was at a dinner fundraiser for the local hospital. She's been the lead organizer for the dinner, so she was in full 'on' mode tonight and dressed the part, sleek and professional. She touched up her light pink lipstick, and left the restroom, the kitten heels of her black pumps tapping the floor. She entered a crush of people in the ballroom at the convention hotel. Tess had worked on this fundraiser for a solid six months and her work had paid off. The dinner was five hundred dollars per attendee with a collection of donated artwork up for auction at the end of the dinner. The dinner had sold out before Tess had left for the family trip to Alaska. Since her return, she'd managed to procure additional artwork to auction.

As she threaded her way through the crowd, she felt a tug on her elbow. Turning, she found herself looking into Chad's brown eyes. Startled, she carefully slipped her elbow out of his grasp, aware that they were surrounded by people and conscious of the need to avoid making social waves. She had no idea why Chad was here, but she wasn't about to let that be known. Plastering a polite smile on her face, she greeted him. "Hi Chad." She stepped back as much as she could in the tight crowd. Chad stepped closer just as she backed away, erasing what little distance she'd created.

"Hey Tess, so good to see you," Chad replied, slipping his hand through the crook of her arm. He smoothly began moving, pulling her along with him.

"Chad, what are you doing here?" Tess asked, her voice low.

"I wanted to see you, and I knew you'd be here," he said simply.

She glanced up at his profile. His expression was flat. His blonde hair was carefully gelled in place. He wore a black suit. She knew he'd spent much more time than most men would checking himself in the mirror time and again. Events like this were candy for Chad. He viewed them as a chance to see and be seen. Tess resisted the urge to wrest her arm free of his clasp. He held her arm firmly, walking her over to the edge of the ballroom by an alcove that led to the kitchen.

Tess quickly turned, giving her arm enough of a yank that she freed it and could step away from him. "Look, I told you I didn't want to see you and I meant it," she said, her voice rising with annoyance. She carefully took a deep breath, reminding herself she needed to stay calm.

Chad didn't respond—it was as if she hadn't spoken. He was looking over the ballroom. She considered walking away, but guessed that he'd follow. The prickle of unease she'd felt after he'd called her returned with force. He finally turned to her.

"Here's the thing Tess. Some issues came up at work. I need you to help me out."

Tess looked at him, incredulous. "You need me to help you out? Why would you think I'd do that and why me?"

"I need your connections." Chad held her gaze and shrugged. "I tried to do this the nice way, but you're playing hardball, so I will too. I figure you'll help me because the last you want is me talking about how you had a meltdown after your miscarriage and our break up. Won't take much, just a little gossip. All I need is for you to attend a few dinners with me and make nice with the higher ups at the hospital."

Tess's mind whirred in confusion and anger. She knew if she kept pushing, Chad would be less likely to tell her what was going on. She was furious, so angry she could barely look at him. She stared blindly out over the ballroom. Much as she wished she could convince herself he was bluffing about what he would do if she didn't help him, she knew he would. If she'd learned one thing about Chad, it was that his primary focus was himself. He did what he needed to do to keep his image intact. Whatever had happened, he needed to create the impression that they were on good terms and as he'd so bluntly put it, to use her connections. It made her sick to do that. Her professional connections were nurtured and legitimate. She hated that he'd try to capitalize on that.

Much as she wanted to just walk away, Tess knew that might lead to a scene, and Chad had a strained quality to him. Keeping her eyes focused on the crowd, she spoke through tight lips. "You're an asshole. Did I forget to tell you that when we broke up?" she asked, a bite to her tone. "I don't want to help you. Isn't there someone else you can ask? You're the one who's so damn proud of your social connections."

"Don't have time to find another option. Play nice with me tonight and the next dinner is after the hospital's annual golf tournament. It's not like you don't know that, you organize it every year."

Tess nodded tightly. "I'll play nice for tonight because

you know damn well I can't make a scene here. I'll think about the golf tournament. You can't threaten me like this Chad," she said angrily, her heart beating rapidly, a crushing sense of shame washing over her that he'd put her in this position and that she'd stayed with him long enough to give him this kind of ammunition. She fought to keep her composure. She figured she could stall on the golf tournament dinner and maybe find out what was behind this and then put a stop to it.

Chad nodded abruptly and started to walk away, not before he leaned over a placed a kiss on her cheek. His lips felt dry and cold. Nausea rose inside her at his touch. "I'll be making the rounds. I'll come find you here and there," he said, before finally walking away.

Tess stepped quickly to the door to the kitchen and slipped through it. The kitchen was in full swing, chefs, line cooks, waiters and waitresses all in motion. No one noticed her. She briskly walked to the back where there was a private bathroom. Closing the door, she breathed a sigh of relief in the quiet room. Dampening a tissue, she carefully wiped her hot and flushed face. Leaning her hips against the sink, she waited in the quiet until her heartbeat slowed, the muted sounds of the crowd filtering through the door.

* * *

A FEW DAYS LATER, Tess carefully scanned her computer screen, reviewing some numbers her brother had sent her. After her run in with Chad the other night, she'd called Simon and asked for his help. Among his other talents, Simon was a forensic accountant with the ability to ferret out irregularities and dive down rabbit holes to the end of a trail of numbers. He was very, very good at discovering when money was being shifted where it shouldn't be. Given that the accounting firm Chad worked for managed the hospital's accounts, Tess had a suspicion something had gone awry and Chad was responsible.

When she'd first started dating Chad, Simon had known of him through shared professional connections in the accounting world. He'd later told her that he'd been worried from the start since Chad had a reputation for playing the field and seeking out women solely based on their social connections. While Tess didn't view herself that way, she was well-connected in the professional world of eastern North Carolina and up to Washington, D.C. due to her reputation for being an excellent fundraiser. She bridged many fields in her work. Simon had worried that Chad was only after her for her connections but had hoped for the best on her behalf. When she called about what happened at the fundraiser, after Simon finished swearing, he promised her he'd find out what was behind Chad's threat.

Tess had made it through the rest of the fundraiser the other night on sheer will, fixing a polite smile on her face and gritting her way through her encounters with Chad. He'd clearly wanted to make it seem as if they were back together by seeking her out repeatedly, making small talk with anyone near her, often resting his hand on her back and forcing her to tolerate a few more kisses on her cheek.

Tess figured she had a solid two weeks before the golf tournament dinner to find out what lay behind Chad's maneuvers. If she could get to the bottom of it, she could get out from under his threat. She'd avoided Nathan's call last night just because hearing his voice hurt right now. Chad's reappearance in her life tore the scabs off the wounds she'd thought had finally healed. Chad elicited those old familiar feelings of doubts about her judgment in men, her attractiveness, and that lingering sense of shame about not seeing Chad for who he was and being stupid enough to stay with him even when it became more and more obvious that he was a complete jerk. She hated that

Chad would publicize her miscarriage and make it seem as if he'd been the one to end their relationship, rather than the other way around. Not that she thought she needed to hide what happened, but she didn't want to have to deal with the type of insidious gossip that Chad would spread.

Nathan had left her another message after she'd ignored his first call. For a moment, she let herself picture him: those blue eyes in his masculine, sculpted face, those dark curls, always half mussed and those dimples every time he smiled. She could use one of his smiles today. For a moment, she pictured Chad and couldn't believe she'd ever thought him attractive. While he was attractive in an objective sense, his looks were superficial. Blonde hair, brown eyes, cultivated tan and athletic build – athletic only because he spent long hours at the gym, not because he came by the build naturally. Tess laughed to herself, considering whether Nathan had ever been to a gym. She seriously doubted it. Nathan's lanky, muscled build came from an active life.

Her cell phone vibrated on her desk. A quick glance and she saw it was Simon. "Hey Simon. Just got your email."

"Thought I'd just call and explain."

"Go for it."

"Long story short, looks like someone at the accounting firm where Chad works has been siphoning off money into an account that definitely doesn't belong to the hospital," Simon said.

"Seriously?!"

Tess heard Simon sigh. "Seriously, Tess. My guess is Chad. The account name is encrypted, so I can't see that data. I'm thinking we ask dad to check with his buddy, Norm Waters, at First Citizens Bank because that's where the account is held. Once we can identify that the account belongs to Chad, I say we turn him in."

Norm Waters was a longtime friend of their father's.

They'd met in college and had been friends since then. Norm had lived in various towns around North Carolina as he moved his way up the chain in the bank, eventually landing in New Bern as the president of the local branch. Tess knew he'd be happy to help, but that meant asking her father, which meant her mother would find out, which meant lots of questions. She sighed.

"There's no other way to get the name on the account?" Tess asked Simon.

"I know the last thing you want is to involve dad because that means involving mom. Without some help from the bank, I'm not sure how we can get that name. I may be good at chasing down hidden accounts, but I'm not a computer encryption expert."

"I know…you've done more than enough already. I just hate getting mom and dad involved. Maybe I should just let it go. I'm sure I just have to get through a few more public functions and that should be enough."

"Tess, get a clue here. If Chad has been funneling money to a side account from the hospital and someone there is on his trail, he's got to cover his tracks and make himself look real good to keep people distracted. This won't go away."

Tess heard the thread of irritation in Simon's voice. He'd been overprotective ever since she'd broken up with Chad. It wouldn't sit well with him if she just let this go. She knew he was right, she was just so infuriated with Chad. To think she'd once thought she might marry a man who'd been illegally stealing funds from a non-profit hospital.

"I know you're right, Simon. I don't have to like it though. Should I call dad about Norm or should you?"

Simon chuckled. "That's not the question. It's who's gonna tell mom first. If it's me, she's just gonna be annoyed you didn't call her the minute the hospital fundraiser was over."

"Have I mentioned that I hate it when you're right?" Tess asked.

"Many times. Hope it helps that I don't want to be right about this. Chad is an ass and I'm pissed as hell that he's dragged you into this. Much as I'd like to beat the crap out of him, let's play these cards right and make sure he's held accountable."

For the first time in days, Tess felt a release of the pressure she'd been under. She knew Simon would make sure Chad was held accountable. What she didn't know was what Chad would do.

"Alright, I'll call mom. I'm due for a dinner with her anyway. It'll be better if I tell her in person. Once I've talked to her, I'll talk to dad and ask him to call Norm." Tess paused and took a breath. "Thanks Simon. I knew you'd help, but I didn't know what we were looking for. I still can't believe I didn't see Chad for who he was."

"Happy to help. And more than happy to make sure Chad gets to squirm on this one. Stop beating yourself up over him anyway. It's not like I have the best judgment in women," Simon said wryly.

Tess thought of Simon's ex-wife for a moment. Meredith had been Simon's college sweetheart. She was blonde and beautiful, always perfectly put together. She was also from a wealthy business family in South Carolina and the southern version of a high-society socialite. To this day, Tess wasn't sure what Simon had seen in her, but he'd fallen for her superficial act. Once they'd married, Tess had watched Simon bend over backwards trying to keep Meredith happy, when keeping her happy was clearly impossible. Tess figured they would have divorced soon if Meredith hadn't gotten pregnant. Not long after Jordan had been born, Meredith's casual drinking became much more than that. When Jordan was two years old, Simon had filed for divorce. Meredith hadn't even attempted to get custody and only rarely visited Jordan after moving back to her hometown in South Carolina. Simon had barely dated since the divorce, focusing his energy on being a damn good single father.

"Speaking of your judgment in men, when are you going back to Alaska to visit Nathan?" Simon asked, interrupting her train of thought.

"I have no idea," Tess replied.

"Well, on the subject of men, Nathan is solid. Ran into Deanna the other day and she told me that she's worried you're about to let him pass you by."

"I should have known she'd say something! And she doesn't even know Nathan! My god, Simon, could you give me a chance to sort this mess out with Chad before I have to worry about Nathan?"

"Deanna talked to mom who thinks Nathan fell from heaven just for you, not to mention that she thinks you need to do something other than work. And Chad, I don't see what he has to do with Nathan. You broke up with him over a year ago. Nathan's a good guy and it'd be stupid to not give him a shot."

Tess became flustered and was relieved they were on the phone, or Simon would see her blush. "Simon...I know Nathan's a good guy. It's just complicated because we live about four thousand miles apart. I mean, how are mom and dad going to feel if I move away? If that even happens..."

"Are you kidding? Mom'll be over the moon if you actually give Nathan a chance and move there. Mom and dad don't care where you live as long as you're happy. As for dad, he'll have a reason to visit and fish to his heart's content. If you're worrying about mom and dad, forget it. You're just using that as an excuse."

Tess shifted in her chair. She wasn't about to admit it to Simon, but he might have a point. "Just give me a little time to figure this out. It's not like I was planning to move away.

I love my work and it's taken me years to get established here."

Simon cut in. "And most of your work can be done from a distance. Except for local functions, which is just part of your business these days, you do most of your work from a distance already."

"You're repeating Deanna now," Tess countered. "I won't pretend I can't take some of my work with me, but face it, moving clear across the country will affect my work."

Simon sighed. "Just what Deanna was worried about. She said you'd come up with all kinds of reasons why going back to Alaska wasn't a good idea. Just think about it, okay? In the meantime, talk to mom ASAP, so we can get the name of the account holder from Norm."

Tess quickly agreed and hung up the phone. She looked around her office, her eyes scanning across the award plaques mounted on her walls for various fundraising campaigns and notes of appreciation. She'd worked her tail off to get where she was, which was one of the reasons why she was incensed that Chad would try to take advantage of her connections, nor how it would help. If he was embezzling, it didn't matter how many connections he had. The view from her office was of a flat, grassy field, flanked by loblolly pines. She thought of the view in Diamond Creek, the deep blue of Kachemak Bay, the stark mountains towering around the bay, Mount Augustine, a lonely sentry in the water, and the fields of fireweed that Nathan had shown her. Her heart clenched at the thought of Nathan and Diamond Creek. She couldn't let herself think about what it would be like to be there.

Nathan listened to Tess's voice mail message again and wondered why she didn't answer. For the past week, she'd been sporadic at answering his calls and sounded off when they did talk. He'd made a few attempts to ask her what was going on, but she brushed him off. He left another message for her and slipped his phone into his pocket. Walking to the windows in the living room, he stared out over the bay. The brief season that passed for fall was well on its way. The fireweed had faded, the wispy white seeds drifting around on the wind. It was late afternoon and the sun was already setting. The endless days of summer were rapidly shortening. The spruce trees in the field behind their house were stark green against the blanched grass. Red, yellow and orange danced low on the ground, the leaves of flowers and shrubs turning as they fell. The wind was up with the water in the bay dotted with whitecaps. In another few weeks, he and his brothers would be getting both boats ready to be stored for the winter.

Nathan turned away from the view and resisted the urge to call Tess, yet again. Jared had left earlier to meet with

Susie to go over some accounting details. The house was quiet. Restless, Nathan began to get ready to head to the harbor when his phone rang.

An unfamiliar number flashed on the screen, although he recognized the area code from North Carolina.

"Hello?" Nathan said, curious as to who would be calling.

"Hey Nathan, it's Simon."

"Oh, surprised to hear from you," he replied, questions immediately filling his mind as to why Tess's brother would be calling him.

"I'm sure you are. Look, I'll get right to the point. I'm worried about Tess and even though she'll probably hate me for it, thought I'd call you."

"Is Tess okay?" Nathan asked, alarm rising inside.

"Yeah, she's okay. It's just that an ex of hers is making life a little difficult for her. I don't usually get involved in her personal life, but I trust you. Even though Tess might not admit it, I think you mean a lot to her." Simon paused, the silence on the phone stretching.

"Simon, I appreciate your call, but I'm not sure what I can do."

"Don't know myself. Not sure if Tess told you anything about her ex, Chad, but he was a total ass to her. Now he's threatening to spread rumors about their breakup—basically make things uncomfortable for her in her business. Took her a while to get over what happened between them, which is why I was damned happy to see her with you. First time in a while where she seemed like her old self. Since he showed up at one of her fundraisers and dragged her into this mess…well, she hasn't looked good. I called you, hoping maybe you'd get in touch with her."

Nathan felt flushed, hot with quick rush of anger. He'd love to get his hands on Tess's ex. While Tess hadn't told him anything about her ex, he would've guessed someone had treated her badly—it explained how guarded and distrustful she'd been. He wished she'd mentioned what was going on. Concern for her and how she was doing was hot on the heels of his anger. He wanted nothing more than to be right there with her, to pull her close and let her know it would be okay. But he wasn't there, and he wasn't so sure she wanted him there, which devastated him. Much as he'd been trying to honor her need for time, it was driving him crazy.

"Man, wish I could tell you a call from me would help, but we were talking every day for a bit and since last week, now it's a lot harder to get her on the phone."

Simon swore softly. "Dammit. So she's avoiding you then. No surprise there. Tess thinks she can handle everything herself."

"You know what? I'll fly out there soon as I can get a ticket," Nathan said.

Simon sounded as surprised as Nathan was by his quick offer. "Really? Well that might shake her up enough to get out of this funk."

"Let's keep it a surprise though. Can you pick me up at the airport?"

"No problem."

"Will you help me beat the shit out of this lousy ex of hers?" Nathan asked, his anger barely held in check, close to boiling over.

Simon gave a sharp laugh. "Would love to, but I'm working on another angle."

Simon quickly filled Nathan on a sketch of his suspicions. Nathan hung up a few minutes later. He was relieved to know what had been bothering Tess but worried about her.

By evening, Nathan had gotten his travel set up and talked with Jared and Luke about being away for a few weeks. Both had teased him, but they'd also been completely supportive. Given that he would be out of town for a few guiding trips and some of the winter preparation, they could've given him some grief about his timing, but they didn't. Which was one of the reasons he loved his brothers. Much as they'd tease him and make his life hell, when it mattered, they supported him.

* * *

A MERE TWO DAYS LATER, Nathan looked around as Simon drove along the interstate in North Carolina, headed from the Raleigh-Durham airport east towards New Bern where Simon and Tess's parents lived. Tess had previously explained that she lived just over a half hour north of her family in Greenville. The highway stretched ahead, almost completely flat. The air was soft and humid, permeated with an earthy green scent. It was early morning. Nathan had flown through the night, changing planes in Chicago not long after midnight, promptly falling asleep for the remainder of the trip from Chicago to North Carolina. Tall pine trees flanked the highway with occasional patches of flowers at exit areas and fields between the trees of various crops, including corn, cotton, and soybeans. Nathan had only been on the East coast twice before, once on a college trip to Washington D.C. and another on a trip to New York City with his brothers and parents. Both times had been in the summer, and he recalled the sweltering heat and constant air conditioning in every building. Growing up in the Pacific Northwest was a contrast with coolers summers and much less humidity, even though part of the area was rainforest. The rainforests of the Northwest, while damp and green, were much cooler than the Southeast. He couldn't believe it was over eighty degrees in September.

He was glad for the time with Simon. While he'd gotten to know him somewhat during Tess's family visit to Alaska,

Nathan had been focused on Tess. Simon elaborated on what he'd learned about Chad's scheme.

"Since Tess talked to our parents, our dad's friend, Norm, from the bank has confirmed my suspicion—the account is under the name of a side business that is registered under Chad's name," Simon explained.

"So what now?" Nathan asked.

"Norm is working with the main office for the bank to freeze the account before we go the DA's office with what we know. He wants that in place before Chad has a chance to try to empty the account."

"Won't Chad notice something up?"

"Our plan is to be in touch with the DA the same day the bank freezes the account, that way there won't be time for Chad to get suspicious."

"Can't help but ask if you're worried about what Chad might do once this whole thing blows up in his face," Nathan said.

Simon shrugged. "Course I am. Tess is freaked out because she's worried he's gonna make good on spreading gossip about her once he realizes what's happened. I keep telling her that no one will believe him once he's charged for embezzlement."

"What exactly is this asshole threatening to say?"

When Simon didn't answer immediately, Nathan looked over to see Simon looking uncomfortable. "Can't be that bad," Nathan said.

"It's not," Simon replied. "Mostly bullshit, but Tess is pretty private and has worked hard to establish a good reputation as a fundraiser. She's all worried that Chad's going to tarnish that. As for the details…that's up to her to tell you."

* * *

AFTER A QUICK STOP at Simon's office and then his house, Nathan entered Tess's address into the GPS in Simon's truck. Simon had refused to let him rent a car and insisted Nathan take his truck. Simon had driven off in his sedan with a wave after he'd quickly pulled Nathan's single duffel bag from the trunk of his sedan and plunked it on the passenger seat of the truck. Nathan chuckled to himself as he looked around the truck. Simon referred to it as old, but it was in immaculate condition and maybe a few years old. Nathan had realized Simon was a man of great sense the second they'd pulled up at Simon's home and Nathan saw the black Toyota truck.

Nathan surveyed the area before he drove away. Simon lived down a quiet road, the homes spread out amongst towering pine trees, mixed with hardwoods. Simon's home was at the end of a gravel driveway, situated on a flat lot, mixed with trees, shrubs and an expanse of grass in the back that ended at the shore of a river. Trees draped with moss flanked either side of the lawn on the way to the river. The grass gave way to a small sandy beach. Simon's home blended into the landscape, a single story ranch style home with cedar siding and a porch that wrapped around the house. While quite different from Alaska, the landscape was lovely, its beauty soft and understated.

A quick glance at the GPS and Nathan saw he had a forty-minute drive to Tess's place. He felt a little ragged from the long flight, although thankfully he'd slept through most of it. Aside from getting the update from Simon on the status of the situation with Tess's ex, Nathan had refrained from asking questions about what Simon might think about how Nathan should approach Tess. He'd come to the conclusion that his only option was to just blow through it. He knew she'd be surprised to see him, but he was banking on what lie between them to shake the doubts out of her—at least, for a few minutes.

As he drove, Nathan considered what else he'd learned about Tess from Simon. In the short time they'd shared in Alaska, Tess had mentioned that she was a fundraiser, but they hadn't talked much more about her work. Clearly proud of his sister, Simon had informed him that Tess was quite well-known in the area as one of the go-to fundraisers for non-profits and businesses involved in various causes. It gave Nathan more of a glimpse into what made her tick. He could see how that prickly side of her would work as an advantage when turned to a cause for which she was impassioned. She'd be a hell of an advocate with the intelligence and wit to strategize well. Considering how her ex was trying to take advantage of her connections would hit Tess where it hurt, which notched up Nathan's anger towards him.

Nathan managed to get to Tess's condo in Greenville under the forty minute mark. Though he was entirely unfamiliar with the area, the drive was straightforward. As he pulled into the condominium complex, he glanced around and saw that the landscape was similar to where Simon lived. Her condo was tucked in the back corner of the complex. While Simon couldn't be certain Tess would be home, he guessed she would be as it was a Saturday morning. Even with the two plus hour drive from the airport to New Bern and the drive here, it still wasn't eleven in the morning yet. Nathan saw the red Toyota Prius that Simon had described and parked beside it. He yawned and wished for a moment that he'd thought to stop for coffee somewhere. With the travel and four-hour time difference, he was more tired than he wanted to be.

Nathan didn't allow himself to think and quickly strode to Tess's door. After a quick knock, he had to wait a long moment, his heart beating so fast he could hear it.

Tess swung the door open, her mouth dropping. Nathan took a long look at her. Those honeyed curls that he'd grown to love were a rumpled mess. That perfectly pink bow-shaped mouth was plump and inviting. She wore a fitted pink T-shirt with lightweight black cotton pants that clung to her curves. Her ginger eyes were wide and starting to fill with tears before Nathan broke out of his stare and stepped through the door, tugging her into his arms.

"Hey there," he murmured into her curls. "Missed you, so I thought I'd stop by."

He felt her vibrate with a giggle. She tilted her head up, eyes bright with tears. "You thought you'd just stop by, huh?"

Nathan smiled down at her, his heart so full in his chest, he thought it might burst. "Exactly. Hope it's okay."

Tess nodded firmly. He leaned down and captured her lips in a kiss. Her mouth opened to his immediately. In seconds, what started as a greeting spiraled into a heat that built so fast, Nathan lost all sense of where he was. He immediately missed the feel of her lips when Tess broke the kiss. All he wanted was to pull her close and memorize every inch of her, with his hands, his mouth, his body...and his heart.

With a shake of his head, his gaze cleared. Tess's ginger eyes came into view, clouded with passion, humor and that subtle guarded quality he was accustomed to seeing in her.

She slid her hands down his arms and tugged him inside. "Door's wide open, you know," she said with a wink. "Why don't you come inside, sit down and tell me how the hell you pulled off this surprise?"

Much as Nathan wanted to drag Tess back into his arms and forget everything but the feel of her lips and what came next, he was tired enough that he allowed himself to be led into her condo. He took in the open kitchen and living room area with its view of a shaded lawn and scattered pine trees. A small circular table was situated between the kitchen and living room. An open laptop with a mug of coffee sat on the table. Glancing around, Nathan found the space warm and welcoming with its soft colors and comfy looking furniture. He imagined napping on the couch among its plethora of throw pillows, which cued him to how tired he was.

Tess waved him to the living room while she got him a cup of coffee. "It's safe to say you surprised me," she said as she walked towards him on the couch and handed him a cup of coffee. "Just a dash of cream, right?"

Nathan nodded and took a welcome sip. "Damn, this is perfect." He savored the flavor and the dose of caffeine, along with the odd comfort of having this kind of moment with Tess. Hard as he'd fallen for her in Alaska, all of their time together had been in the bubble of her vacation, which didn't offer moments of the usual daily activities. Having coffee in the place she lived carried a sense of newness and comfort.

Tess had fetched her own cup of coffee and joined him on the sofa, tucking a bright blue pillow on her crossed knees, angling to face him. "So?" she asked.

"So what?" he countered.

She rolled her eyes. "Let's see...you didn't say a word about this trip and just showed up here out of the blue. I don't even know how you got my address. I'm thrilled to see you, but a little startled."

Nathan pondered for a moment whether he should tell her that Simon called and decided it was best. She'd find out one way or another, so it was easier to cut through it. "Simon called me a few days ago. Said he was worried about you. He seemed to think maybe a call from me would cheer you up. But when I pointed out we'd been talking pretty regular until the last week or so..."

Tess's eyebrows arced up into two peaks, irritation flashing across her face. "Simon called you? Oh my god, he had no right to do that! What did he say?"

For a second, Nathan questioned whether he should tell her what Simon said, but he didn't think it would help to avoid it. Taking a deep breath, he explained. "Simon told me what's going on with your ex, Tess. He just got worried. Don't get pissed at him. He didn't put me up to coming out here, or even ask. That was all my idea. I miss you like hell. You've been avoiding my calls and then Simon tells me what this Chad guy is pulling. Decided to just come out here. I don't want you thinking I'll forget about everything with us just because you blow off a few calls. Plus, I can be another distraction for Chad while Simon puts his plan in motion." Nathan paused, trying to gauge Tess's reaction. Her face was guarded, but she didn't look too angry. Another breath and he plowed forward. "I don't know what happened between you and Chad. You don't deserve whatever the hell he did before and what he's doing now. You matter to me, so I wasn't gonna sit tight in Alaska while I worried about you."

Tess bit her lower lip and twirled a soft golden curl in one hand. "I don't want you getting involved in this mess with Chad. Simon has it all sorted out."

"That's not why I'm here Tess. Sounds like Simon has it under control. I'm here because I was worried and I wanted to see you. I may not have known you that long, but it took damn near all I had to get you to go on a date with me, much less be open to more than that. You think I'm gonna stand by while this jerk messes with your life again? I don't know the backstory with Chad. Simon was pretty quiet on that. But I could've guessed someone had done a number on you. I had no idea if it would be okay with you that I just showed up like this, but I decided it was worth the risk to make sure you knew that I was still here."

Tess's eyes welled with tears again. She knuckled them away. "I hate it when I cry. I don't know why I am," she said ruefully, taking a shaky breath.

Nathan was surprised to find he wasn't the least bit

bothered by her tears. He hated seeing them, but the sight of a woman crying usually made him squirm because he didn't want to deal with the emotion. With Tess, he just wanted her to feel better. Not knowing what to say, he simply laid his hand on her knee.

As he pondered what to say, there was a knock at the door. Tess swung her head to look at the door. "What? I don't usually get unannounced visitors and now I have two," she said bemusedly. She gave his hand a quick squeeze and got up to answer the door.

Nathan heard another woman's voice and in seconds, Tess returned to the living room, a medium-height woman with dark straight hair and bright red lipstick following behind. The woman was dressed in workout clothes; black fitted spandex leggings with a matching top and running shoes. She smiled widely at Nathan, walking straight to where he was seated.

"Deanna," the woman said, reaching out to shake his hand. "I hear you're Nathan. *Sooo* nice to meet you."

"Nice to meet you too," Nathan replied, shaking Deanna's hand and looking to Tess.

"Deanna's an old friend, one of the best," Tess said. She gestured for Deanna to take a seat in a chair that was situated on the other side of the coffee table, facing the couch.

Deanna sat down and gave Nathan an appraising look.

"Ignore her," Tess said firmly. "She thinks it's her job to assess any man that I may be involved with." She turned to Deanna. "Don't be like that. Nathan just surprised me with a visit. Be nice," she said emphatically.

Deanna rolled her eyes, which were a soft gray. "Really, Tess? I think it's completely awesome that Nathan flew out here to see you. I'm just happy to meet him."

Nathan decided immediately that he liked Deanna and had the sense she'd be on his side when it came to persuading Tess to give him a chance to be something other than a vacation fling. "And I'm happy to meet you," he said with a smile.

"Tess," Deanna said, turning toward Tess. "You forgot to tell me Nathan had dimples."

"That's where we're starting?" Tess said with a roll of her eyes. She sat down beside Nathan and picked up her coffee, taking a sip.

Deanna shrugged. "I'm just saying that dimples make for an even better smile." Deanna turned her gaze back to Nathan. "So, how long do you plan to stay? Please tell me you came to sweep Tess off her feet and take her back to Alaska with you."

Tess choked on her coffee, a blush staining her cheeks. "Deanna!"

Nathan liked Deanna more every time she opened her mouth. Much as he wanted to wholeheartedly agree with her that he should take Tess back to Alaska with him, he was already well-versed with how Tess handled pressure. With Deanna, he could take a back seat and just might get what he wanted anyway.

He bit back a smile and shrugged. "Not sure how long I plan to stay. Just happy to be here."

Deanna's eyes took on a calculating gleam. "And we're happy to have you here. I'll let you play your cards close… for now," she said with a wink.

Tess's glare at Deanna was tempered with a half-smile. "You just can't help yourself, can you?" she asked, her question directed to Deanna.

Deanna just shrugged. "Not when I have an opinion. In this case, I do. He's great," she said, gesturing to Nathan. "Alaska sounds amazing. What else is there to say?"

Tess rolled her eyes and turned to Nathan. "I'm sorry. Deanna likes to boss me around, and she's not shy about making her opinion known." She turned back to Deanna. "He just walked in the door! I know how long it takes to fly here from Alaska, so he has to be exhausted. How about you use your manners and give him a break?"

Deanna smiled politely. "Nathan, how was your trip?" she asked, her tone sugary sweet.

He couldn't help but laugh. "Just fine."

"See, I used my manners," Deanna said, glancing at Tess.

Tess merely shook her head and took another sip of coffee.

Deanna's gaze sobered. "Simon filled me in this morning. How come you didn't mention what was going on with Chad?"

Tess took a deep breath. "Simon seems to be filling everyone in," she said sardonically. "I haven't mentioned it because I didn't see the point."

Deanna was silent, holding Tess's gaze for a long moment. "I know you like to keep things to yourself, but maybe you should realize that you have people that want to help. I wouldn't have brought it up just now, but Simon told me Nathan was here and that he'd told him about it too. Trying to pretend like nothing is happening won't help. I'm sure you're worried about rumors, but did you forget that between me, your parents, Simon, my parents and all of our friends, we can stir up plenty of trouble for Chad without it ever getting back to you?"

Tess shifted her position, took a sip of coffee, and looked away from Deanna. Nathan wasn't sure what to say or do. While he cared a hell of a lot about Tess, he didn't have the history with her that Deanna did. It was obvious the situation was uncomfortable for her and that she preferred not to discuss it. But, he was with Deanna on this one. Keeping it to herself only worked to Chad's advantage. Much as he wanted to point that out, he kept quiet, sensing that if he spoke up, it would only increase Tess's defensiveness.

Deanna caught his eye and gave the slightest shake of her head. Despite only knowing her for maybe five minutes, it was clear that Deanna read the direction of his thoughts. Nathan didn't nod, but lifted his eyebrows. He was happy to let her bear the brunt of Tess's frustration for now.

Tess sighed and turned back, her eyes capturing his for a moment and then focusing on Deanna. " I know Dee. I know you want to help, along with my family and yours. The whole thing just sucks. I can't believe Chad has put me in this position."

"Damn right it sucks! As for Chad, given what Simon's found, I can absolutely believe Chad has put you in this position. He's trying to buy some time by playing nice in the circles that matter. You're his ticket there and he knows it," Deanna said. She looked toward Nathan. "I'm hoping with you around, you can throw a wrench in Chad's plans."

"Deanna! What are you talking about? Could we leave Nathan out of this?" Tess asked.

"Kind of hard to do that when he's here. Tonight's the golf tournament dinner. Did you forget that? Simon said Chad mentioned this was one of the events he expected you to attend. Bring Nathan with you," Deanna said.

Tess slapped her hand against her knee. "Oh my god, I forgot about tonight." Her shoulders slumped. She turned to Nathan, her ginger eyes weary and wary at once. "I have to go to this dinner. Even if Chad hadn't asked me to be there, I have to anyway. I organize this tournament every year and attend the awards dinner."

"So I'll go with you. Deanna's right. Having someone with you will make it harder for Chad," Nathan said.

Deanna nodded emphatically.

Tess looked between them. "I don't want you any more involved in this mess with Chad than you need to be."

Before Nathan could reply, Deanna spoke. "You're already freaked out that Chad is going to spread bullshit rumors about you. Having Nathan with you just complicates that for Chad. Plus, you keep forgetting that most people know Chad is a jerk."

Tess sighed deeply, setting her mug on the coffee table and putting her face in her hands. Nathan glanced to Deanna. She tilted her head towards Tess. Nathan reached over and rubbed Tess's back. His hand rose and fell with the several deep breaths that she took. Tess finally lifted her head, glancing between him and Deanna.

"I give up. Between Simon and you two, I either succumb to the process or end up ticked off at all three of you. I'm too tired for that," Tess said. "You can come tonight, but we're going to have to find you something to wear and you'd better follow my lead. She may be bossy..." Tess gestured toward Deanna "...but I can be too."

Nathan experienced a moment of relief. He'd started to worry that Deanna might be pushing a little too hard. "Whatever you say. Trust me, I know how bossy you can be," he said with a chuckle. "And what do I need to wear?"

Tess lifted her eyebrows. "It's black tie. You have to wear a suit." She eyed him appraisingly. "Wish you wore Simon's size, but you're too tall."

"Damn glad you're here," Deanna said, gracing Nathan with a broad smile. "As for you," she continued, addressing Tess, "if you need to be pissed at someone for interfering, pick me, not Nathan."

Tess shot her a glare, immediately followed with a rueful smile. "I might be a little pissed, but it's too late to avoid your interference now."

Deanna stayed for a while longer after that, conversation turning to her long list of questions about Alaska. At some point, Nathan realized he was having trouble staying awake. Even with the coffee, the travel and emotion were catching up to him. He distantly heard Deanna commenting that she'd call later.

* * *

NATHAN HEARD the sound of a shower and assumed Jared was up. He rolled over, his elbow hitting something hard. Jarred awake, he opened his eyes and realized he wasn't in his bed and it definitely wasn't Jared in the shower. He was on Tess's soft green couch with a fleece blanket tangled around his legs. He had no memory of Deanna leaving. Shifting his position, he grabbed one of the loose throw pillows and tucked it behind his back, propping himself to a semi-seated position. His mug of coffee was still on the coffee table. Grabbing it, he took a sip, which was barely lukewarm. He figured he must have been asleep for at least an hour or so. A few more sips, and he kicked the blanket off and stood.

Tess had left the bathroom door open. As he walked toward it, he looked into what he assumed to be her bedroom, which held a queen-size bed with a lightweight quilt and more pillows than he could count. Between the couch and her bed, it was clear Tess loved her pillows. Her bedroom was decorated in the same shades as the rest of the apartment – soft earthy tones with flashes of bright colors. Before stepping into the bathroom, he stripped off his clothes and tossed them on her bed.

Peeking his head around the edge of the shower curtain, Nathan found Tess's back to him as she soaped her hair. He quietly stepped in and slipped his arms around her, reveling in the feel of her wet skin against his. He leaned down and nuzzled her neck.

Tess jumped and squealed. "Nathan! You startled me!"

He spoke into her neck. "Mmmhmm. Couldn't resist joining you."

She leaned her head back against his shoulder and angled her face towards his. Lifting his lips from her neck, he met her gaze. Her ginger eyes were darkened, her lashes spiked with water. She bit her lip and smiled.

"You were sound asleep a few minutes ago," Tess said.

"I'm awake now," he replied, sliding his hands up to cup her generous breasts. "Missed you like crazy. Diamond Creek hasn't been the same without you." He toyed with her nipples, enjoying the feel of them pebbling in his hands.

Tess sucked in her breath. "I missed you too..." Her eyelids fell as she gasped when he slipped one hand down through her curls and into the warmth between her legs. He carefully parted her folds, which were slick and heated, sliding a finger inside her, delving slowly.

"Nathan...thought...maybe we should talk first..." Tess said, her words breaking.

"You just can't wait to talk, can you? How about this? Let's just enjoy being near each other for the first time in way too long. Talking is not going to change the fact that *this*..." he slid another finger inside her channel and lightly pinched a nipple with his other hand "...feels *soooo* damn good."

Tess's hips bucked against his hand. "Okay...you win. But promise we can talk later," she said, her hips grinding in soft circles.

"Promise," Nathan replied, his voice muffled against her neck. The feel of her bare bottom shifting against his cock had him so hard, so thoroughly aroused, his precarious hold on thought was weak. He let go into the feeling. Kissing and licking his way along her neck, Nathan slowly turned Tess in his arms. Facing her with the feel of her luscious breasts against his chest, he could barely focus. Hooking his hands under her knees, he lifted her slick body, still soapy, up against the tiled shower wall. He took her lips in a deep kiss, delving deep into her open mouth, their tongues tangling wildly. The sounds Tess made ratcheted up the madness he felt. He wanted to go slow, to take this time to show her how much he missed her, but he couldn't. He pulled back and looked in her eyes. In a rare moment, her gaze was unguarded and wide open, her eyes dark with passion and intent. She reached down to stroke his cock, holding it for a moment before guiding him to her entrance. He thrust deep the moment she removed her hand and curled it around his neck. Still holding her gaze, Nathan slowly pulled out and plunged back inside, establishing a slow and deep rhythm.

In moments, Tess arched against the shower wall, her climax pulsing around him. Nathan drove once more into the cradle of her hips and threw his head back with the burst of his own climax. As he shuddered, he held her firmly. When the fog cleared, he tilted his forehead forward until it rested against hers. Eyes a mere inch from hers, he spoke against her lips. "We can talk now."

Tess giggled, the puff of her breath soft against his lips. "How about we talk after I rinse this shampoo out of my hair?" She gestured to her soapy curls, laughter in her eyes.

A half hour later, Nathan sat at her kitchen table, feeling much better after his nap and the interlude in the shower. A fresh change of clothes, a little food, and he felt like himself again. Tess had insisted on making sandwiches and was bustling around the kitchen cleaning up.

"So we have to go find a suit and tie for you. We need to be ready to leave here for the dinner by five thirty or so. That only gives us a few hours to go shopping," Tess said, briskly wiping the counter.

Nathan thought he'd be happy to sit here all day, just enjoying the fact that he was in the same place as Tess.

"Nathan, are you with me?" Tess asked, waving a kitchen towel in his direction.

"What? I'm right here."

"You're just sitting there, kind of smiling. You didn't say anything when I asked about shopping."

"Oh, whatever. Just take me where you think I should go and I'll get what you say."

Tess started laughing, her shoulders shaking as she leaned against the kitchen counter.

"Was it that funny?" Nathan asked. "I was being serious. You said it's black tie, so I'll just get a suit. You pick it out. I could care less about that kind of thing."

Tess kept laughing, tears rolling down her cheeks. She tried several times to stop, taking gulps of air, straightening her shoulders. Each time, she only laughed harder. Finally though, she brought it under control. As she did, Nathan saw that tears were still rolling down her cheeks. She kept her gaze averted.

"Tess? You okay?" he asked, standing to walk toward her.

As he reached her side, he saw a tremor in one of her hands that rested on the counter and heard the catch in her breath.

"Tess?" he asked again, his voice soft.

She shook her head sharply and looked up. Her eyes held uncertainty and vulnerability. Sensing that she needed some semblance of space, Nathan held still at her side. Much as he wanted to step closer and wrap her in his arms, he didn't think that was what she wanted right now.

"I'm okay," she finally replied, her voice soft. Her breathing slowed and while her eyes were damp, no more tears came. Taking a slow breath, she looked away and then back at him. "Sorry about that. There's just been a lot going on for me. You showing up...it's amazing, it really is...but I guess I got overwhelmed on top of everything else."

Nathan nodded. "No need to apologize. Do you want to talk about it?"

A rueful smile graced her face. "I said I wanted to talk, didn't I?" She shrugged, a small laugh escaping. "Maybe we should just take care of finding you a suit for now. I'm not sure I'm up for talking." She held his gaze for a long moment. "I'm really glad you're here. I just wasn't expecting it. And…well, I don't like this situation with Chad and hate that you're involved now."

"Tess, I wouldn't be here if I didn't care about you," Nathan said.

Tess nodded. "That's not about you. As you saw with Deanna, I kind of hate having anyone involved in this. I'm kind of private."

"Really?" he asked sardonically. "I'd never have guessed."

Tess giggled and rolled her eyes. She pushed her hips away from the counter and strode toward the entryway, stepping into a pair of clogs. Glancing back to Nathan, she asked, "Need anything before we go?"

Nathan looked around and spied his tennis shoes by the coffee table. "Just my shoes."

CHAPTER 14

*T*ess paused in front of the mirror. Her honey curls were in their usual disarray, but she'd let go of trying to make them behave. Not to mention that Nathan kept mussing them every time he kissed her. A blush warmed her. While she was bedeviled with doubts about what to do about him and annoyed with the interference of Simon and Deanna, her heart hummed at his presence, and she had to admit she was overjoyed that he'd flown all the way here to see her. Though she hadn't wanted to think it, tiny doubts kept popping up since she'd flown home—worry that Nathan couldn't really love her, worry that he'd forget about her when she was gone. Now that he was here, she could maybe believe that someone as amazing as he was really did love her and couldn't forget about her.

Nathan stuck his head through her bedroom door. After a measured look, he gave a low whistle. "*You* are beautiful," he said with a wink as he stepped into the room.

Her blush deepened while her heart pounded at the sight of him. Nathan looked too handsome for his own good in a dark navy suit. As promised, he'd gone along with her suggestions when they shopped for his evening attire. With the help of the friendly salesman, they'd selected the dark navy over black as it brought out the blue of his eyes. Nathan had been a good sport while the salesman had him try on several options.

Nathan paused just in front of her and leaned over, placing a lingering kiss on the side of her neck. Her breath caught and a heated chill raced through her body. Stepping back, he ran his hand across her hip, his caress warm through the silk dress she wore. "Don't think about colors much, but the way green looks on you has made it my favorite."

Tess couldn't hold back a giggle. She wore a deep green silk wrap dress that wound around her curves dipping artfully between her breasts and accenting her hips, draping at an angle across the front of her calves. Knowing that she'd be standing and moving through the crowd throughout the evening, she wore her most comfortable pair of black dress shoes with low kitten heels. A hammered silver bracelet on one arm with a matching choker and earrings accented her outfit. Her eyes were shaded with smoky gray, and she'd added a touch of pink gloss to her lips.

She tried to quell the anxiety she felt. Chad likely assumed she would attend tonight's function alone. Part of her was relieved Nathan would be with her, while another part of her was fraught with worry for how Chad would react. Much as she'd hoped for Simon and the bank to have started the ball rolling before tonight, that hadn't happened. Chad had left her a message on her work phone – because she refused to give him her personal cell number – reminding her that he expected to see her tonight.

"Tess?" Nathan asked.

Tess realized she must have spaced out and looked up at

Nathan. His blue eyes looked into hers. "You're worrying," he said flatly. "Don't."

Tess bit her lip. "It's not that simple."

He held her gaze for a long moment. "Okay, I get why you're worried. But you can't do a damn thing about what Chad might do. You already couldn't. Try to stop worrying so much. Let's enjoy tonight. I haven't gone out like this since I moved away from Seattle. Getting to take you out looking like *that...*" his eyes traveled up and down her body in a heated gaze "...is way more fun than any date I can remember."

Tess couldn't hold back her smile, although the way Nathan looked at her flustered her. On the one hand, she'd never felt so desired. On the other, she half couldn't believe it. With a quick shake of her head, she stepped right up to Nathan and reached behind his neck to pull him down for a quick kiss before stepping past him to walk toward the door.

"Let's do this," she said firmly.

As they stepped through the door, the hand Nathan had placed in her lower back slid down to caress her bottom through the green silk. "We might have a problem," he said.

"What?" she asked, turning to glance at him.

"Can't keep my hands off you in that dress. Not sure I can be socially appropriate with the way I feel," he said with a wink.

Tess thought she might melt on the spot, her heart swelled. She had to force herself to remember they had somewhere to be when what she wanted to do was shove him right back inside and forget everything else.

* * *

TESS CLASPED Nathan's hand in hers as she threaded through the crowd, leading the way toward their table. The ballroom at the convention center was already filled. The annual hospital golf tournament was popular. The awards dinner was simply an excuse for the attendees to see and be seen yet again. Once they'd arrived, any worry that she'd had about Nathan being with her dissolved when she realized how relieved she felt not to be alone this evening. Much as she'd been pushing the thoughts out of her head, she'd dreaded coming here ever since Chad had approached her. With Nathan at her side, it would be impossible for Chad to try to make it appear they were together again. Anxious as she was about what Chad may do or say, she would have worried about that with or without Nathan at her side.

The first hour or so passed uneventfully. Tess enjoyed introducing Nathan and found him surprisingly adept at navigating the social niceties required at such an event. Aside from being handsome as hell and frequently drawing looks of admiration from many of the women they encountered, Nathan was smooth and gracious in his social interactions. At one point, when Tess threw him an inquiring glance as they paused together, Nathan gave her a rueful smile.

"Surprised I can handle myself?" he asked wryly.

Tess thought for a moment before answering. "I guess so. Doesn't seem quite your personality."

Nathan shrugged. "Not my first choice, but I know the ropes. We probably didn't talk about it much, but my dad was pretty well known in Seattle society. He used to run an aerospace engineering business. He made good money and then sold it. I attended plenty of events like this for his business. Might not be my personality, but then I wouldn't say it was yours either. Just means we can play the game when we need to."

Tess contemplated his answer. "I guess it isn't my personality. It's part of what I do, but it's not the reason I do it. I like that my work matters. I may just be the one that sets the stage, but the money I help raise goes to things that matter. That means a lot to me. And it also means…this," she said gesturing toward the crowded room.

Nathan followed her gesture and turned back to her, his eyes steady on hers, a small smile at the corners of his mouth. "I like seeing this side of you. It doesn't surprise me one bit to hear that you're amazing at it…" he paused, his gaze shuttering as he stepped closer. Tess felt a hand on her arm. She turned to find Chad stepping to her side from behind. Instantly, nausea welled and anxiety blossomed.

"Tess, you got here early," Chad said smoothly, not appearing to have noticed Nathan. Chad leaned down and gave her a kiss on her cheek.

Tess felt Nathan slide his arm around her waist. Chad gave her a questioning glance.

Trying to quell the sick feeling she felt, Tess called upon the manners that had been drilled into her. "Chad, this is Nathan," she said. "He came with me tonight."

Chad's gaze was flat, his eyes calculating. He nodded tightly. "I'm Chad." Markedly, he didn't reach to shake Nathan's hand, but then Nathan didn't extend his hand either.

Nathan nodded. "As Tess said, I'm Nathan."

Tess forced a polite smile during a long moment of silence. After looking out across the crowd, Chad turned to look at Tess.

"Didn't know you were coming with anyone tonight," he stated, a sharp edge to his tone.

Tess toyed with one of her earrings and tried to keep her breathing slow. Nathan's voice caused her to jump a little.

"Tess and I met when she was on vacation in Alaska. Decided to surprise her with a visit. Just happened to be this weekend," Nathan said, his hand squeezing her hip.

Chad nodded, his expression remaining flat. "How long will you be here?" he asked.

Nathan smiled widely and leaned over to kiss the side of Tess's neck—a blatant move to make a point. Tess couldn't help the heated shiver that raced through her at his kiss. He caught her eyes as he lifted his head and winked. "Depends," Nathan replied, looking back to Chad.

Chad was silent for a moment, his jaw clenched. He turned to Tess. "I expect your date here won't interfere with our work."

Tess choked back a laugh. Her anxiety was turning her giddy. Hearing Chad describe what he was doing as 'work' was ridiculous. As she pondered what to say, Chad continued, directing his words to Nathan. "I handle the accounts for the hospital, so we coordinate on projects when she handles fundraising for us. She needs to take some time tonight to work the crowd with me."

Chad's arrogance floored Tess. What was funny a moment ago was infuriating. But—she knew damn well she needed to do what she could *not* to make Chad suspicious. With Simon and the bank close to making a move, it was best if Chad thought she was going along with his plan. She swallowed her anger and forced a smile.

"Nathan knows I'm here on business," she said.

Tess sensed Nathan's tension, but yet again, his smooth social skills masked whatever he might be feeling. Nathan looked down at her, his eyes silently conveying his anger along with the understanding that he knew they had to get through this charade for now. Looking back to Chad, Nathan said, "Oh yeah, Tess made sure I knew part of tonight was business for her." He surreptitiously caressed her bottom through the thin green silk of her dress as his hand slid away from her waist. "How 'bout you two take care of business for a bit while I get us some drinks?"

Tess immediately missed the warmth and strength of

Nathan's arm around her waist. Much as she wanted to do anything but, she smiled politely towards Chad and stepped to his side. She carefully avoided getting close enough for him to touch her. With Nathan present, Chad seemed inclined to allow her the distance. Glancing back to Nathan, she saw that he'd locked his gaze back on Chad, his eyes dark. When Tess cleared her throat, Nathan's eyes shifted to her. "See you in say, fifteen minutes?"

Tess nodded. "Sounds good."

Nathan lifted his chin and nodded. "Meet you at our table. I'll make sure to find a glass of Pinot Noir, seeing as that's your favorite."

Tess knew Nathan said that to make his familiarity of her known to Chad. She bit back a smile. There would have been times when his blatant territorial marking would have irritated her. Now wasn't one of those times. Nathan's possessiveness would buoy her through this first round of social charades with Chad.

The next fifteen minutes weren't quite as hellish as Tess would have expected had she been here alone and absent the knowledge of Simon's behind the scenes work to pull the cover off of Chad. As well as she knew most of this crowd, all she had to do was keep her manners turned on high and work the Southern charm that had been steeped into her. The painful part was coming face to face with how wrong she'd been about Chad. Watching him work the crowd illuminated how shallow and superficial he was. The excuses she'd made for him in the two years they'd been together seemed flimsy now. She'd told herself over and over that Chad only came across the way he did because of his insecurities, that he was a good guy underneath that. Witnessing him tonight, every lie she'd told herself about him cracked under the brittle façade.

Tess made small talk as she stood with Chad in a group that included some of the biggest donors for the golf tournament. As Chad schmoozed with the owner of a regional car dealership, Tess felt a tap on her shoulder. Glancing over, she saw the wife of the same car dealer tilt her head slightly, gesturing for Tess to step back from the center of the group.

Gauging that Chad was occupied in his current conversation, Tess took a few steps away to stand beside Theresa Stephens. Theresa's husband, John Stephens, headed up a business that ran car dealerships in most of eastern North Carolina, while Theresa was a respected pediatrician and an excellent contact when Tess needed to get fundraising campaigns started. Theresa had short blonde hair in a sleek cut that hugged her scalp. She was petite with dark brown eyes that held a twinkle and dressed in bright colors. This evening she wore a wine colored sheath paired with dangly gold bracelets and matching earrings. She radiated intelligence and warmth. Theresa was committed to a number of charitable causes, particularly those related to public health. Tess had known Theresa and John for years and considered them personal friends, in addition to their professional relationship.

As Tess stepped to Theresa's side, she saw Theresa carefully look around before turning to Tess.

"Tess, hon, since we're in a crowd here, I'm going to get right to it. For one, what are you doing here with Chad?" Theresa asked, her voice low and her tone matter-of-fact.

The wheels in Tess's mind spun. Tess contemplated how to answer what she was doing with Chad, and while she couldn't tell the whole story, she didn't want anyone to think she was back together with Chad. "I'm not here *with* him. We're not back together or anything. I guess..." Tess's voice trailed off as she tried to figure out how to explain.

Theresa gave her a pointed look and leaned closer, keeping her voice low. "If you're not back together - and let

me just say I'm more than a little relieved to hear you're not
- then why are you traipsing around with him?"

Tess knew it would be obvious to Theresa if Tess tried to
make it seem like she was friendly with Chad, so she abandoned that and gave her the partial truth. "It's complicated,
Theresa. I can't really explain it here. I'm trying not to make
waves and Chad wanted me to work the crowd with
him, so…"

Theresa nodded firmly. "Right. He's trying to use you to
grease the social wheels for him. Figures," she said
pointedly.

Tess looked toward Chad, he was still deep in conversation with John who was nodding politely but looked distant.
Chad, of course, didn't seem to notice that John wasn't too
interested in their conversation. She looked back into
Theresa's warm brown eyes. With a twist of her lips, she
replied, "Yeah, that's one way to put it. What do you know,
Theresa? Maybe you could fill in a few blanks for me."

Theresa leaned in again, her voice dropping further. "I
don't have all the details. John's heard rumors that some
irregularities came up in the accounts that Chad manages. It
started with the hospital, but now the accounting firm is
auditing all of Chad's accounts. Sounds like Chad may have
caught wind of the concerns at the hospital, but he has no
idea the firm is auditing everything. I was worried you were
back together with him when I saw you two a few minutes
ago. Thank god you're not."

Tess took a slow breath. Knowing that it looked like
Chad was illegally funneling money from hospital accounts
had been bad enough, but to hear that it was possible he'd
done this with other accounts made her feel even sicker.
Another breath and she turned back to Theresa. "Simon
looked into the hospital thing, but I had no idea there were
others. That's the only reason I'm playing nice with Chad
right now. Simon and the bank are working on a plan to

freeze the account that Chad has been using to funnel money from the hospital and notify the DA's office at the same time. But dear god, if Chad is pulling this with multiple accounts, I need to talk to Simon. Maybe he can get in touch with the firm where Chad works."

Theresa's eyes took on a determined glint. She took a sip of the wine she held and glanced toward Chad and John. "I feel better. You're not clueless and Simon's on it. I agree, call Simon ASAP. They need to coordinate anything with the firm. As for you, this must be hell," she said, gesturing toward Chad and around the crowd.

"That's one way to put it. I'm just trying to play nice. I should let you know though…" she paused and couldn't hold back her smile "…I actually came with someone else tonight. He knows what's up with Chad."

Theresa's eyebrows arched. "Really? Do tell."

Tess blushed. "It's a guy I met in Alaska, Nathan Winters. The whole thing took me off guard. Things were pretty intense, but I chalked it up to a vacation fling. Then he surprised me with a visit. Simon called him." Tess paused and shook her head. "I won't pretend it doesn't annoy me to have Simon interfere, but I'm glad Nathan's here. Chad isn't too pleased about it because he can't pretend we're together, but whatever."

Theresa smiled broadly and slipped her hand through in the crook of Tess's elbow, giving Tess's arm a squeeze. "Oh hon, you deserve someone good. And if he flew all the way from Alaska to visit you, then I want to meet him. Where is he?"

Tess nodded her head in the direction of their table. "He's waiting at our table. How about I walk you over to meet him? That'll get me out of this round with Chad."

Theresa winked. "Let's do it." She called to John. "Honey, Tess is taking me to meet someone." When Theresa spoke, Chad looked over and she addressed him. "I'll walk Tess back to her date, Chad. Nice to see you," Theresa said brightly, quickly turning and tugging Tess along with her.

Moments later, Tess stood at Nathan's side, his arm once again warm around her waist. The tension she'd been holding in her body unwound with the relief at being back by Nathan's side and away from Chad. Nathan was charming Theresa who comfortably flirted with him and teased Tess. Theresa quickly solicited a waiter to relocate her and John's seating to the same table.

Once they were seated, Theresa shifted from teasing to serious. "So Nathan, aside from being tickled to meet you, I'm so glad you're here with Tess. Promise me you'll stay until this mess with Chad has blown over."

"Theresa!" Tess exclaimed. "We have no idea how long that's going to take. You can't ask Nathan to promise something he can't. He has a life in Alaska, you know."

Theresa turned her sharp gaze to Tess. "Of course he has a life in Alaska! But Nathan said his trip was open-ended. I'm glad he's here with you tonight to force Chad to take a step back from this charade he's putting you through. I want you to have back up however you can get it, and I don't care if it embarrasses you." Theresa softened her words with a smile and reached over to squeeze Tess's hand. "Not to mention that he's handsome as all get out, and I love seeing you two together."

Tess swallowed against the tightness in her throat. She knew Theresa cared, and she was beyond relieved that Nathan was with her tonight. She just didn't know what to do with how *right* it felt to have Nathan here. Masking her discomfort, she took a sip of wine.

Nathan chuckled. "Well, I appreciate your support, Theresa. I'll have to play it by ear, although if Tess will have me, I'll stay as long as I can. I'm just hoping that Chad has to face the music sooner rather than later. *Not* because I want to leave sooner, but because I hate watching what this does to Tess." He slid his arm around the back of Tess's chair and squeezed her shoulder.

The rest of the evening passed far more smoothly than Tess had anticipated. Theresa assigned herself as Tess's personal companion, tagging along with her the next time Chad took advantage of a break in the events to have her circulate the crowd with him. Given that Theresa had been a frequent presence at events that Tess coordinated and she was about as well connected as anyone in the room, Chad seemed pleased to have her nearby. Tess did wonder if her teeth were going to crack during one of Chad's schmooze sessions with the Chief Financial Officer at the hospital, but she survived. Catching Theresa's sly smile helped her relax.

As the evening wound up, Nathan walked her out of the dining area, his hand on her back. Tess was exhausted. With her nerves in high gear all evening, she felt like an over-wrought wind up toy. When Nathan stepped away to fetch her jacket from the coatroom, Chad came to her side. He kept a polite distance between them but gave her a hard glance before looking away when he spoke.

"So I'm hoping to join you at the dinner next weekend. I'd prefer if you didn't bring a date," Chad said, staring out into the lobby area.

Tess forced herself to take a slow breath. Once again, Chad had caught her off guard. She should have known not to allow herself to relax until she knew for certain he'd left.

"You mean, the bimonthly dinner hosted by the hospital board?" Tess asked, somewhat stunned that Chad thought it would be kosher for him to attend. While the dinners were open to the public, they were generally smaller affairs, less formal and less public.

"Exactly. Haven't been to one in a while and it'll be a good chance for me to show my face," Chad replied, his voice tight.

Before Tess could reply, she felt her jacket being settled

on her shoulders. Nathan ran his hands down both of her arms and casually stepped to her side, sliding an arm around her shoulders.

"I'll be joining Tess at the dinner. If you were wondering," Nathan said, his words directed at Chad, his voice measured. Tess glanced at him quickly. A muscle ticked in his jaw. She wanted to thank him for interjecting and making it clear to Chad that he would be with her—no matter how Chad tried to manipulate it otherwise. She glanced between Nathan and Chad. The contrast between them was stark. Chad appeared a faint imitation of what Nathan was—not in looks per se, but in how he wanted to be seen: masculine, in control, dominant. Nathan was all of those things and it had probably never crossed his mind to *try* to be any of that. He was also far less interested in what anyone thought of him.

Chad had yet to turn and look at Nathan. When he finally did, his eyes barely connected with Nathan's gaze. He looked to Tess. "Well, I guess your date here will be at the board dinner. Fine by me. Just remember it's business too."

Tess nodded tightly and smiled, wondering if her face would actually crack from the fake smiles she'd plastered on for Chad's benefit. "I never forget that it's business too."

Chad had looked away again. He simply nodded and walked off. Tess watched him until he exited through the lobby doors. She took a deep breath, releasing it in a long sigh. Nathan slid a hand up and massaged the back of her neck, the mere touch of his strong, warm hand releasing hours of built up tension.

"Okay, he's an ass. That's about all I have to say," Nathan said.

"I know. I'm sorry you had to go through this. You see why I didn't want you in the middle. It's bad enough that I have to be," she said.

During the long pause, doubts bombarded Tess. She was

mortified enough that she'd ever dated Chad. Having Nathan meet him and be witness to the kind of man Chad was only heightened her embarrassment. Nathan's hand stilled on her neck.

"You're doing it again," he said.

Tess looked up at him to find him smiling down at her, his eyes warm. "Doing what?"

"Worrying about things you shouldn't worry about."

"I can't help it. I feel awful about this whole thing with Chad and now you're in the middle. Tonight couldn't have been any fun for you," she said with a huff.

"Don't get me wrong. Chad *is* an ass. And I had to keep reminding myself that Simon is going to make sure he gets held accountable. But aside from that…" Nathan paused and turned to face Tess, tugging her hands into his. He held her gaze, the blue of his eyes darkening. "Everything else was fun. I got to look at you all night, even when Chad was dragging you around. Pretty cool to see what you do. Everyone respects the hell out of you. Theresa seems to think you're the most amazing woman in the universe. I didn't have the heart to tell her she didn't need to sell you to me."

He leaned forward and gave Tess a soft kiss, lingering about as long as was proper in the middle of the crowded lobby at the convention center. When he pulled away, she bit her lip, a blush warming her face.

"So stop worrying about me. The only thing that bothers me about being in the middle of this is seeing what it's doing to you."

Tess closed her eyes and, for once, let her worries go, dropping them like pebbles on the ground. Opening her eyes, she smiled ruefully. "I'll stop worrying about you. Only because you asked."

Nathan chuckled. "Let's go."

CHAPTER 15

$\mathcal{A}$ few days later, Tess slowly came awake. Curled on her side, Nathan was spooned behind her, one arm thrown across her hip, the weight warm and heavy. Rays of sun fell on the bed. Tess sighed, wanting to stay right where she was as long as she could…except for the minor annoyance that she might wet the bed if she didn't get up soon. She giggled to herself as she carefully slid out of Nathan's embrace. Once awake, Tess found herself too restless to crawl back in bed. Leaving Nathan to sleep, she showered and started making breakfast.

Not much later, Nathan came out to the kitchen, wearing only his boxers. Tess took a good look at his muscled chest and giggled at his black curls, sticking out every which way.

"Smells good," he said, his voice gravelly from sleep.

Tess quickly poured him a cup of coffee and put it in front of him when he sat down at the table. Nathan tugged her close, resting his head on her hip. She ran her fingers through his curls.

"Feelin' damn lucky this morning. I wake up, you have coffee ready and if my nose is right, you're cooking bacon."

Tess felt his smile against her hip. "Your nose is right. Decided I should cook for you this morning. I love to cook."

Nathan lifted his head and gave her waist a squeeze before picking up his coffee for a sip. "Oh god, that's good. Just what I need. If your food is half as good as your coffee, it will be amazing. You make a damn good cup of coffee. Strong—just the way I like it."

Tess dropped a kiss on his forehead and went to check on the bacon. She started cooking the scrambled eggs she had prepped before Nathan got up. She had added chopped spinach, red peppers and garlic to the eggs. As she flipped the bacon, there was a knock on the door. Before she had a chance to get there, Nathan had sauntered over and answered.

"Dear god, you should *not* be allowed to go without a shirt!"

Tess couldn't help but giggle at Deanna's exclamation. She turned to look over her shoulder to see Deanna walking through the door as Nathan held it open. Deanna looked as if she had just been to the gym. She wore purple spandex leggings, running shoes and a fitted black spandex top. Her dark brown hair was pulled back in a ponytail. Her usual red lipstick was absent.

Deanna came over and planted a kiss on Tess's cheek. "You really shouldn't let anyone see him like that. It's too tempting for other women. I can handle it, but not everyone can."

Tess laughed. "I'll do my best." She glanced over at Nathan who just rolled his eyes and shrugged. "I wasn't thinking when I answered the door," he said with a chuckle. He headed for the bedroom. In seconds, she could hear the shower running.

Tess turned back to Deanna. "Coffee?"

Deanna sat down at the small table adjacent to the kitchen. "Yes please."

"Didn't know you were coming by," Tess said as she brought a cup of coffee over to Deanna.

"I forgot Nathan was here, or I would have called. Just wasn't thinking. Hope it's okay that I came by."

"Of course it is! Just because Nathan's here doesn't mean you can't come over."

Deanna gave Tess a pointed look over the rim of her coffee mug. "I know that. You just might have better things to do." She lowered her voice. "I knew he was cute. But *damn*, his body is to die for. I was already on the 'Tess should move to Alaska bandwagon,' but now I'll think you're crazy if you don't."

Tess blushed. "Trust me, I know how cute Nathan is. I just kinda can't believe he's interested in me."

Deanna set her coffee down and tilted her head. "You're cute as hell with a hot little body. Even before Chad, you were oblivious to how cute you were. He just made it worse. Turn that voice *off*. Just accept that you're worthy for once."

Tess gave her head a hard shake. "I'll work on that. But you know, I don't just like Nathan for his body. He's so... well...nice. Much as I can hardly stand everyone knowing about this thing with Chad and especially not Nathan, he's been amazing about it. He was great at the fundraiser the other night."

Deanna nodded. "I know it's not just his body. I just can't help but comment on the obvious. Trust me, after Chad who—I hate saying it—could be called handsome, I wouldn't support you being with anyone who wasn't awesome in the ways that matter. Nathan fits the bill."

Tess noticed that the bacon was done, so she turned the burner off and stirred the scrambled eggs. "Do you want breakfast while you're here?" she asked Deanna, glancing over her shoulder.

"If it includes bacon, yes. I try to eat healthy, but damn if I can live without bacon. Just the smell is divine," Deanna replied. "Speaking of Nathan, ran into Theresa at the grocery store. She's ready to plan your wedding. She might be worse than your mother."

"Wouldn't surprise me," Tess said, keeping her tone casual though her thoughts were anything but. Ever practical, she didn't know what to make of how quickly her otherwise rational friends were insisting she just throw caution to the wind with Nathan. It ran against her grain. "She was at the fundraiser the other night and sat with us. Thank god she was there. She gave me some breathing room when I had to work the crowd with Chad," Tess continued, shifting the topic away from Nathan.

Deanna curled her lip. "Ugh. Chad makes me sick. Theresa told me what John had heard about the accounting firm auditing all of the accounts Chad handles. Has Simon gotten in touch with them?"

Tess nodded. "I called him on the way home and filled him in. He was in touch first thing Monday morning. Haven't heard anything else from him though. I'm getting impatient. I want this over and done with." Satisfied that the scrambled eggs were ready, Tess pulled plates out and started serving the food.

"We all want this done and over with," Nathan said as he returned from the bedroom. He was showered and dressed in lightweight shorts and a royal blue cotton shirt. His curls were damp. "Simon's right though. The better their case against Chad, the cleaner it will be once he knows they're investigating."

Tess felt him come up behind her as he planted a soft kiss on the back of her neck. "I know it's better if they take the time they need," she said, handing a plate to Nathan. "I just hate that I have to keep playing charades with him in the meantime."

After setting one plate in front of Deanna, Nathan carried the remaining two full plates to the table and tugged Tess away from the sink. "You're not going to start cleaning up now. I'll do it later," he said firmly. With a soft caress on her bottom, he turned her toward the table. Tess couldn't hide the blush that came with a smile at his touch.

Deanna nodded approvingly at Nathan. "I like you. You treat Tess right. Please don't stop or I'll have to kick your ass." She picked up a piece of bacon and ate it with relish.

Tess wrinkled her nose at Deanna, as she sat down. "She will not kick your ass," Tess said to Nathan as she bit into a piece of bacon. "Oh god...this is *so* good."

Nathan laughed softly. "If I stop treating you right, I'd deserve it. I get it."

Deanna looked to Tess, tilting her head toward Nathan, her eyes practically demanding that Tess grab Nathan and hold on with both hands. "See, he gets it." When Tess didn't take the bait, the teasing look in Deanna's eyes faded as she continued. "So do we have a timeframe on when Simon, the bank and now the accounting firm are going to move on Chad?"

Tess shook her head. "Wish we did. Simon says it's better if they have time to take a look at everything. They don't want to give Chad a chance to clean up his trail. I tried to get a timeline out of Simon, but he said it would be at least until next week. Which means..." Tess paused and looked at Nathan "...that I have to get through the hospital board's dinner this coming weekend. It's on Chad's radar, so he wants me to be there."

"I'm going too though," Nathan added.

Deanna smiled widely. "Oh goodie. I'm so glad you're here. Maybe I'll go. Would you want me to?" she asked, directing her question at Tess.

Tess was surprised because these kinds of functions

were not Deanna's favorite thing to do. With a shrug, she replied, "If you want to. You don't have to though."

Deanna gave her a long look. "I know I don't *have* to. I may not always go to these things, but I have to attend faculty dinners all the time. I actually want to go now that I think about. It'll be fun to watch Chad try to deal with me and Nathan," she said with a sharp laugh.

Nathan gave her an approving glance. "Damn fine plan. We'll tag team him."

Tess looked between them and burst out laughing. "This oughta be good."

* * *

SEVERAL HOURS LATER, Nathan pulled up in front of Simon's house. They'd driven to New Bern so Nathan could return Simon's truck and to visit Tess's parents. Celine had called the day after Nathan arrived and insisted that if Tess didn't bring him down to visit them, they'd come up there. Much as Tess wanted to keep Nathan to herself and wanted to avoid her mother's obvious glee at his visit, she knew it would be better to visit sooner rather than later. She hadn't seen her parents since the night she'd met her mother for dinner to talk to her about what was going on with Chad. Celine had called Tess's father to come meet them that same night to fill him in so he could talk to his friend at the bank. Tess was braced for more questions about the status of that situation.

With Simon at work, Tess used her spare key to open the garage, so Nathan could park the truck. It felt odd to drive around her hometown with Nathan in the car. She took a circuitous route through town, heading to the downtown historical district on the way to the far side of New Bern. Her parents lived on the outer edge of New Bern toward the coast on the banks of the Neuse River, the widest river in the continental United States. Perhaps not as famous as the Mississippi River, but wider and beautiful. New Bern had water flanking it on three sides. The Neuse ran through town with the smaller Trent River bisecting town in another direction. The Neuse River fed into the Atlantic Ocean, which was roughly thirty minutes east. Simon's home was on the Trent River. Tess gave Nathan a mini primer on New Bern's history. It was the original capital of North Carolina before the state voted to relocate the capital to a more central location in Raleigh. New Bern had one of the best-maintained historical Governor's Palaces in the country – Tryon Palace. Among many others, George Washington had stayed there once. New Bern had an extensive historical district with many colonial homes dating back to before the Revolutionary War.

As they drove past the old homes, Nathan asked Tess to pause repeatedly while he read various signs about the history of different homes and places. "Nothing quite like this out West, you know," he said. "Even in Seattle, things were settled much later. As for Alaska, a house is considered old if it's been there more than fifty years. I don't know if I've ever seen homes that were built during the 1700's."

They had stopped by the Neuse River where they could see the grounds of Tryon Palace. Tess started driving again and kept her speed slow as she turned down the street that ran past the front of the palace. As she looked around, she contemplated how different it was here than Alaska. New Bern was lovely, especially this part of town. The views along the rivers were beautiful, but a different kind of beauty than Alaska. Even in a town like Diamond Creek, which had been settled in the late 1800's and was fairly progressive and even ahead of the curve as far as arts and restaurants went, Alaska felt wild, fresh and crackling with vitality. The beauty of New Bern was much softer and cultured. Neither was better or more, just different.

She glanced over at Nathan to see his gaze carefully surveying everything around them. "I'm thinking we need to spend an afternoon here, so we can walk around," she said with a smile.

Nathan turned to her. "Would love it! I love old houses. That's one thing I wish we had in Alaska and it just won't happen. You can't make history after the fact."

"No you can't," Tess replied wryly. "I have some work to do this week, but I can get most of it done in the mornings. Why don't we pick a day to spend here? We can take a tour of Tryon Palace and walk around town. There's plenty of shopping and some good restaurants."

"I'm in. By the way, I know you didn't expect me to visit like this. Just say the word, and I'll stay out of your way for work. You haven't even mentioned it…" Nathan paused, his gaze lingering when she stopped at a red light. Tess blushed at the heat in his eyes. "Not to mention that I haven't been too focused on things like work since I've been here," he continued with a sly smile. His eyes sobered. "But seriously, I know you have a job, so just let me know your schedule."

Tess started driving when the light turned green. "My job's pretty flexible. Some weeks I work a lot more than others. It all depends on what projects I'm working on. You caught me at a good time because I just finished up on the planning phases of some bigger projects. The easy part is showing up at the events themselves. Minus the fact that I'm stuck dealing with Chad's charade right now. Otherwise, I have an office, but I often work from home, one of the perks of working for myself. I can take care of most of what I need to do by just working around whatever we do. As long as you don't mind watching TV or something like that when I'm working at home."

"No problem. This'll be a nice break for me. I don't get to be lazy too much in Alaska."

"No you don't. You and your brothers work your tails

off fishing. Hope they don't mind that you're gone right now," Tess said.

Nathan shrugged. "They don't. They're good like that. They'll give me shit about falling for you, but they're totally supportive. Timing was pretty good for me to go. We had done most of the winter prep already. Jared and Luke have a few guiding trips to do, but other than that, we're headed into the quiet season. By late fall, the tourist crowd thins. We don't do any winter fishing, so our only cash flow comes from plowing."

Tess turned down her parents' driveway, a long, winding gravel drive that sloped down a hill. The drive was flanked by tall pines. Their house was built into the hillside along the river. The house was a two-story brick colonial style home, a modernized version with tall windows that ran floor to ceiling in every room. Celine swung the front door open before they even got out of the car.

Tess closed the car door and called out to her mother. "Hey Mom!"

Celine waved. "Hi dear!" She wore a white gauzy blouse with a lavender skirt that twirled with each step she took as she walked down the brick walkway to meet them.

"Nathan! So good to see you," Celine said, reaching her hands out to clasp Nathan's. She tugged him close to give him a kiss on the cheek. "I forgot how handsome you are," she exclaimed, pinching one of Nathan's cheeks.

Tess couldn't hold back a laugh when Nathan actually blushed. Her mother turned to her and gave her a quick hug. "Sweetie, so good to see you. Thank you for bringing Nathan down to see us." Celine turned and led the way into the house, asking Nathan what he wanted to drink and insisting they plan to stay for dinner.

Celine led them into the sunroom at the back of the house, which faced the river and was filled with plants. The room was furnished with a wheat-colored overstuffed couch with a pair of matching chairs, along with a few dark wood rocking chairs. Tess's father was reading in one of the comfy chairs, his feet resting on the coffee table. This room was where the family spent most of their time and held a sense of comfort for Tess. With the soft furnishings, plants, and the sense of openness created by the windows on all sides, it felt like being in a comfortable garden, sun filtering into the room through the trees outside.

"Michael, good to see you," Nathan said, reaching to shake her father's hand when her father set down his book and stood up to greet them.

"You too, Nathan," Michael replied, giving Nathan a friendly pat on the shoulder. "Think you'll like it here. I was thinking I could take you out fishing one of the days you're here. Won't be quite like Alaska, but fishing's fishing."

Nathan smiled and nodded. "That it is. I like fishing no matter where it is. I'd love that." He turned and looked towards the river. "Wow, the view here is amazing."

Tess followed his gaze to take in the view she'd known for as long as she could remember. Her parents had moved to this house when Tess was but a toddler, so for her, this was all she knew. Her parents' home sat on three acres and was fairly private. The nearby houses could be seen through the trees, but weren't very close. The backyard was a mix of pines and hardwoods that gave way to an open lawn, then sand and the river. They were close to the mouth of the Neuse River here with the river over a mile wide in this area. A cluster of cypress trees stood to one side growing in the edge of the water, moss draped on the branches.

Celine had left the room to get them drinks and returned with a tray that held a pitcher of sweetened iced tea and water. After they were all seated and through the preliminary social chatter, Celine turned her gaze to Tess, focused and direct. "Have you heard from Simon about the situation with Chad?"

Tess sighed and set her tea down on the coffee table. "Mom, don't you think I'd let you know right away if there was any news?"

Celine rolled her eyes and harrumphed. "Oh, you'd let us know at some point but perhaps not right away."

Michael interjected, "We're just worried about you. I'm sure your mother's worrying drives you crazy, but cut her some slack. We hate seeing this happen."

"I know. I don't mean to seem impatient. The whole thing is just frustrating." Tess turned to her mother. "Mom, I promise I will call you right away when I have any news. Don't forget that Simon will be one step ahead of me anyways. He's doing all the hard stuff. I just have to play charades with Chad at whatever events he decides to show his face. Fortunately, he seems to have limited it to anything to do with the hospital, which is mostly what's been on my schedule. The week after next, I have a fundraiser for a runaway teen shelter up in Richmond. I can't imagine he'd want to go to that. I'm hoping this is done and over by then."

Celine nodded firmly. "It has to be. Simon said the accounting firm doesn't want to drag their feet in case that gives Chad time to cover his tracks." With a shake of her head, she changed topics, turning to Nathan. "I'm just so glad you're here. We can return your hospitality. We were thinking we could take y'all out to dinner this evening. I thought about cooking, but I thought maybe it would be better if you could try some Southern seafood. Have you ever had shrimp and grits?"

Tess was relieved to have her mother move on. While she would try to curb her frustration with their worrying, it was vexing to have to talk about the mess with Chad so often. Each conversation only refreshed her sense of embarrassment at not seeing him for who he was when they first started dating.

Nathan and her parents chatted about the differences in seafood between East coast and West coast with her father happily moving onto a discussion about where he could take Nathan fishing. Hours later, Tess and Nathan drove across the river, the sky a rich pink as the sun fell behind the trees that ran along the river.

"A sunset over the water is beautiful no matter where you are," Nathan said as he looked out over the water.

Tess glanced over quickly as she drove. "I know. I'm glad you've gotten a chance to visit here. It's so different from Alaska but beautiful too."

Nathan settled his hand on her knee, warmth seeping into her skin. "I'm glad I got a chance to see where you grew up." He squeezed her knee. "And I'm just damn glad to see you again."

Tess blushed *again*. Reticent as she was to let herself go into her feelings for Nathan, she found the words tumbling out before she thought about them. "Me too. I missed you."

"That's good because I missed you too. Simon tipped my hand when he called, but I wanted to come out here one way or another," Nathan replied, tracing circles on her knee as she drove.

The drive passed in a blur with Tess contemplating their safety as she pulled up in front of her condo, what with Nathan teasing her into a tizzy with soft caresses on her leg, his hand stealthily unbuttoning her blouse and unhooking her bra to play with her nipples. Tess tore her seatbelt off and dragged Nathan into the house, holding her blouse together with one hand. The door slammed behind them, Tess turned to push Nathan against it.

Sliding one hand behind his neck, she tugged his head down for a kiss. His lips came against hers forcefully. Their kiss was greedy, messy and not enough. Close to an hour of taunting foreplay in the car had left her flushed, wet and ready. She pulled her lips a fraction away from his. "You don't play fair," she said, her lips moving against his, the friction only notching the heat between them even higher.

She felt his smile against her mouth. He shrugged, his eyes laughing. "Not my fault that you're so damn cute I can't help myself." He placed a palm on her chest and pushed her back a step, tugging her blouse open and pushing her bra out of the way. He cupped her breasts with both hands, his touch soft. For a moment, he just held her breasts. Tess's breath broke, heat and moisture building between her legs. He leaned forward and suckled one and then the other nipple, pulling back to blow softly. Her nipples pebbled, almost sore from the tension. The only sound was their fractured breathing. Nathan's voice made her jump. "You are so damn beautiful," he whispered, lifting his head to look in her eyes.

Tess resisted the urge to turn away from the intimacy in his gaze. Pushing away from the door, Nathan closed the small gap between them and brought his lips to hers again. She sighed into his mouth, their tongues stroking into each other. He slowly started walking into the living room until she bumped into the side of the couch. Breaking their kiss, Nathan turned her around, nibbling on the back of her neck and stroking her breasts. With one hand, he tugged her pants down, her panties coming with them. Tess kicked them off. Through the haze of desire, she dimply heard the sound of his zipper coming down. He tilted her forward over the armrest of the couch, reaching a hand down between her legs, his fingers dipping into her slick moisture.

Tess gasped his name. Seconds later, she felt his shaft slide in from behind as he held her by the hips. As he sank into her slowly, she sighed with relief. He established a slow rhythm, stroking in and out in a measured pace. Already overwrought with desire, she spiraled into a frenzy. She pushed her hips back to meet his thrusts, gasping in relief each time he drove deep. His hands stroked her bottom, cupping it as he pounded into her. The heat built with Tess teetering on the edge of climax for long moments.

"Nathan…" she gasped, her voice breaking. "Now…come with me now," she begged.

He slipped a hand around front, delving into her folds for a mere second before her climax burst upon her, breaking in long spasms. He continued to stroke into her as her muscles clenched around him. She felt him begin to pulse as he came into her, arching back with one last plunge. Leaning forward, he curled around her, slipping his arms around her waist and deftly turning them to roll onto the couch. Tess landed in a languid pile on top of him. She laid still, her head resting on his chest. He still wore his shirt. Unbuttoning a few buttons, she slipped her hand inside. His heart beat against her palm, the rhythm slowing as their breath slowed in tandem.

Tess soaked in the feeling—just allowing herself to *be* in the moment. She didn't know if she'd ever felt better. It felt so good to be with Nathan, it was slightly terrifying. She pushed against her fear and ignored it, nuzzling closer to Nathan. He stroked his hand through her curls, absently untangling them.

Eventually, she lifted her head and looked at Nathan. When he opened his eyes, she thought she could just look at those blue eyes all day every day and never tire of it. They'd left one lamp on earlier, so the light was faint. The angles of his face were sharper in the dim light. His lips quirked in a small smile as he lifted a hand to brush hair out of her eyes. "I do love your hair," he said, twirling a curl around his finger.

Tess chuckled, reaching up to stroke his curls. "That's convenient because I love yours too."

His chest rumbled against hers with a soft laugh. His eyes sobered. "Your hair isn't all I love though…"

Tess bit her lip. "And neither is yours…" she replied, pushing away the urge to play it cool. Nathan held her gaze for a long moment, his eyes saying far more than words ever could. Tess could barely tolerate the intimacy. Her heart started to race again, this time not out of passion. In another moment, she broke away and pushed up to a seated position, straddling him. She wrinkled her nose and smiled down at him. "I think we need a shower."

Nathan returned the smile, reaching a hand up to cup one of her breasts. "We might not *need* a shower, but any excuse to get naked with you works for me."

Tess giggled and carefully lifted a leg up to climb off of Nathan. She grabbed his hand and tugged him up. "Follow me."

CHAPTER 16

*T*ess walked at Nathan's side, his hand resting on her waist as they entered the hospital conference room. The catered board dinners were held in the hospital's large formal conference room. Usually forty to fifty people attended. It was a smaller scale opportunity to mingle with the power brokers at the hospital. Tess had gotten a call from Chad yesterday, confirming that she'd be at the dinner. He'd asked again if Nathan would be there and remained silent when Tess said Nathan would. While Chad wouldn't say it out loud, Tess knew he'd been hoping he could manufacture the impression they were back together, which infuriated her.

Tess's heart rate kicked up a notch when they entered the already crowded room. Just the thought of getting through the farce with Chad brought a wave of anxiety. Nathan slid his hand up her back in a slow path, coming to rest curled around her shoulder. His touch soothed her. She released the breath she hadn't even noticed she was holding and glanced at him. Just as he had the other evening, he'd transformed from the rugged outdoorsy man she'd gotten to know into a polished version of that. His curls were somewhat under control, just looking at them prompted a giggle. Nathan glanced down at her.

"What?" he asked, a dimple winking with his small smile.

Tess couldn't hold back another giggle. Between her anxiety about tonight and the overwhelming feelings Nathan elicited, she was almost giddy. She bit her lip and pulled herself together. "Just you. You're so spiffy."

Nathan gave her a look of affront, although his laughing eyes gave him away. He shifted his shoulders under his blue button down shirt. Tonight wasn't formal but was certainly more formal than Nathan's usual evenings out in Alaska. He wore a deep blue button down shirt with black slacks, both selected by the same salesman that had helped him with his suit last weekend. The salesman appeared to consider Nathan a challenge, wanting to make Nathan look as good as possible while retaining the rugged, devil-may-care attitude that he carried. Nathan had been smug about the salesman's suggestion that he forgo a tie for this evening's dinner. Tess couldn't help but notice that the blue of his shirt only brought out his eyes even more. Just looking into his laughing blue eyes brought wet heat between her legs. The pulse of desire his mere presence elicited ran on high idle at all times. The slightest provocation and her body was off to the races.

Nathan held her gaze, his eyes saying everything they couldn't act on. His shoulders rose and fell with a purposeful breath. "*You* are so beautiful. Have I mentioned that yet today?"

Tess thought back to this afternoon...the memory of Nathan's lips closing around her taut nipple, his fingers slipping into her slick channel, and the moment when he sank home inside of her, his eyes meeting hers through the blur of passion, his navy gaze reading into her soul and returning the gift. The sound of glasses clinking brought her back to the moment. With a quick shake of her head, she absentmindedly fiddled with the collar of her shirt. She wore a fitted wrap skirt, a bright berry shade, with wedge heeled black sandals. She'd paired this with a gauzy white blouse that fell in loose folds, the top cinching just above her breasts with a small bow. Nathan had already teased the bow apart in the car on the way over. Blushing, she'd admonished him and insisted he must behave during the dinner tonight as she'd tied it again.

Looking back toward Nathan, Tess realized she hadn't answered him, lost in the memory of this afternoon. A blush washed over her, *again.* "You might have mentioned it but feel free to repeat yourself," she belatedly replied.

"You're beautiful. I've decided that I wouldn't mind attending these things with you more often since I get to see you looking like that," Nathan said with a teasing smile.

A shiver ran through Tess. The thought of Nathan being a part of her world on a more regular basis was so....*right...* that she didn't know what to do with it. She thought about what Simon had said—that her work could be done anywhere. While Tess had her own doubts about moving away from North Carolina, she couldn't imagine Nathan living anywhere other than Diamond Creek. Nor did she want him to even consider it. While she'd miss the easy access to her family, Tess knew, if she let herself think about it, living in Alaska would be phenomenal. It would take some planning but Simon was right; she could bring her work with her.

She turned to Nathan, biting her lip. "You're looking pretty good yourself," she said, another giggle bubbling up. Just as she started to speak, she saw Chad across the room. Looking up at Nathan, she asked, "Have I mentioned how much I appreciate that you're here tonight?"

Without her saying a word about Chad's presence, Nathan scanned the room. "Ahh." He brought his eyes back to her, his hand sliding down her back, the warmth creating a trail of comfort. "Just remember, this is almost over. Plus…" Nathan's eyes brightened "Deanna's coming. It'll be fun. She'll make Chad squirm, just because she's here."

Relief bloomed. It wasn't Nathan's reminder that Deanna would be here, but that he cared enough to do what he could to help her relax. She'd never experienced someone who so naturally cared for her well-being and did so without making sure it was noticed. In every action, small and large, Nathan showed that how she felt mattered to him. While the grand gesture of flying all the way across the country on a surprise visit was enough to sweep her off her feet, Tess was just as touched by his willingness to tolerate shopping for dress clothes, his easy patience with her parents, that he unloaded the dishwasher without being asked, and that he tucked the covers around her when he lay beside her at night.

"Tess! I wasn't sure you'd be here tonight," Theresa said, her voice breaking through Tess's meandering thoughts about Nathan. Tess looked past Nathan who was turning toward Theresa to see Theresa and John approaching. Theresa was dressed sharply in fitted black slacks, a basic white blouse with a high collar and black flats. John wore what Tess considered the men's Southern dress uniform – khaki slacks, light blue button down shirt, and brown loafers.

"Theresa, how are you?" Tess asked, leaning forward to clasp Theresa's hands in hers.

Theresa smiled warmly, leaning to kiss Tess on the cheek. "Quite well, dear. I don't think I need to ask how you're doing seeing as Nathan is still here," Theresa said with a sly smile.

Tess blushed and shook her head. "I'm just fine." Tess turned to John and Nathan. Though it had been mere seconds, she saw that they both looked serious. "What?" she asked.

Theresa stepped back to John's side. "You didn't just dive right in, did you?"

John nodded. "I did, honey. Thought they needed to know." He turned to Tess. "Hello there. I know Theresa would have preferred we wait to tell you, but seeing as Chad is already here, I didn't want to miss any private moment that we had."

Tess looked between John and Theresa, her gaze skittering to Nathan who looked serious, but not particularly worried. "Well, could you fill me in since we still have that private moment?" she asked.

Theresa shook her head at John before turning to Tess. "John got a call from Simon on the way over here. Simon said he tried to call you but just got your voice mail, so he called John since he knew we'd see you tonight." Theresa paused and looked to John.

John glanced around before speaking. "The long and short of it is that Simon says the accounting firm fired Chad this afternoon and the DA filed charges of embezzlement. Not much else to report..." John paused when Tess choked back a laugh.

"Sorry John," Tess said. "It's hard to think that isn't much to report. I know we were expecting this, but dear god, why is Chad here tonight if this happened today?" she asked, incredulous that Chad would appear publicly at the event of one of his former primary accounts after being fired the same day.

John nodded while Theresa just shook her head and rolled her eyes. John continued, "I was hoping Chad wouldn't dare show his face here tonight, but the one thing Simon didn't know was if HR at the accounting firm gave Chad any info on the court charges. They didn't have to and may have decided they just didn't want to go there with him. If that's the case, Chad may not even know he's facing charges. He might think that losing his job is all he's got to deal with. Seeing as he's here tonight, my guess is he doesn't know about the charges."

Tess remained quiet for a moment. "Well, he's here, so we're stuck dealing with him." She glanced toward Nathan who slipped his arm around her waist.

"Don't worry. Between me and the rest of us, you won't be stuck with him alone." Nathan glanced toward Theresa and John. "I trust you're with me on this."

Theresa nodded emphatically. "Absolutely. He won't get a minute alone with you, and he won't even notice that we're making sure that doesn't happen."

John smiled ruefully at Tess. "Sorry you got caught in the middle of this. We're here for you however you need us."

Nathan softly squeezed her waist, leaning over to press a kiss on her cheek. "And don't forget Deanna will be here too."

Tess's heart swelled. As private as she was, it was hard for her not to be embarrassed at the situation. Yet, Nathan's solid support, along with that of her family and friends was helping her in ways she couldn't have imagined. The two years with Chad had somewhat isolated her from the support of others. It's not that her family and friends weren't there for her. It was just that much as they tried to mask it, Tess knew none of them cared much for Chad. Instead of realizing that made them worry for her, she'd interpreted it as a failure on her part and withdrawn further into her own shell.

Tess felt Nathan tense while Theresa and John both assumed bland polite expressions. Before she could turn, she heard Chad's voice. "Hi there Tess. Good to see you," he said, stepping smoothly to her side with a stiff smile.

Just as Tess opened her mouth to respond, another voice cut in.

"Well, hello there!" Deanna exclaimed, stepping into the small cluster. Her voice was bright and cheery. Her glossy dark hair hung straight down her back. She wore gray slacks with a red blouse and black flats. Her lipstick matched her blouse. Her forceful presence bolstered Tess.

Chad stiffened beside Tess. He'd never liked Deanna and had complained about her to Tess when they'd been together. He thought she was too bossy. In hindsight, Tess surmised that Chad had picked up on the fact that Deanna saw him for what he was.

Nathan smiled broadly at Deanna. "Hey there. Nice to see you here," he said with a wink.

Between Nathan, Deanna and Theresa, the social banter picked up. Deanna drew others to her, and the circle around them quickly expanded. At one point, Chad leaned toward her. "Tess," he said, his voice barely audible. "I need to talk to you..."

Theresa immediately drew her attention, her voice bright and impossible to ignore. "Tess, do you think I should persuade John to go to Alaska? Nathan was just telling us about it. I'd love to hear about your trip."

Surrounded by others, it was impossible for Chad to try to pull Tess aside, so he merely stayed quiet in the group as the conversation about Alaska continued around him. The time passed quickly. Much as Tess wished otherwise, Chad lingered near her side despite the presence of Nathan and her friends. At one point, Nathan left her side to go to the restroom. Chad stepped closer to her.

"So you think if you just keep him nearby that I'll forget you promised to mingle with me tonight?" Chad asked, his tone laced with anger.

Tess looked up at him, trying to ignore the unease he triggered. "Chad, I'm not avoiding that. In case you haven't noticed, we're mingling right now," she said, gesturing around them. "I'm not sure what you thought, but this is how these dinners are. It's not quite the event you may have expected."

Chad didn't even bother to look around, just kept his eyes locked on her. "You know, Tess, things haven't gone so well for me lately. I've decided to move on from the firm. If you have any contacts at Coastal Alliance, I'd appreciate an introduction."

Tess was startled and then realized she should have expected this. Chad looked at everything as a narrative to spin. Rather than questioning himself and learning from the situation, he was moving on, trying to make it sound like he chose to leave, not that he got fired. Coastal Alliance was the firm that Simon used to work for before he started his own business. Through Simon, Tess had plenty of contacts there. Although she knew damn well that by the time Monday rolled around, any chance Chad had of getting a job anywhere in the accounting world would be long gone. She just had to stall for now. But she was uncomfortable about blatantly lying, even to Chad, even with everything he'd done.

She kept her answer vague. "Oh I don't know, Chad. Can't say that I'd know who to introduce you to there."

Chad looked at her sharply. "Really Tess? Simon worked there. I know damn well you have connections. Don't play me on this. I meant what I said. Your friends might not care, but I have no problem spreading those rumors about you. None of it will help your reputation."

Nathan's voice came over Tess's shoulder just as he returned to her side and slipped his arm around her waist. "The hell you'll be spreading rumors," Nathan said, his voice low, anger vibrating through.

Chad's eyes shifted to Nathan. "This is none of your business."

"Sounds to me like you're planning to talk trash about

Tess. You've made it my business if that's the case," Nathan replied.

Nathan's eyes were dark, his gaze locked onto Chad. Tess felt like she was watching two dogs circle each other. Chad may have been trying to convince himself otherwise, but Nathan was clearly the superior alpha, dominant on multiple levels.

Tess subtly elbowed Nathan's side. Much as she appreciated his presence, she didn't want to inflame Chad's anger. Though she'd ignored it when they were together, Chad tended to be childish when angry. Given his situation, she figured Chad was feeling cornered. The chances of him making a bad situation worse and dragging her through it increased on pace with his anger.

Chad didn't respond to Nathan. He gave Tess an appraising look. "Seems like your friend here doesn't understand that we had an agreement."

Tess's throat tightened. She wanted to just walk out and forget tonight. But she knew damn well that would lead to all sorts of questions from everyone in the room that didn't know what was going on with Chad. She took a deep breath, trying to gather her thoughts.

"We don't have an understanding Chad," she finally said, her words startling her.

"Oh really? That's not what I remember," Chad said, an edge of warning to his tone.

"Chad, you can't force this," Tess said, relieved to finally just say what she wanted.

Chad glanced away, a muscle ticking in his jaw. He turned back quickly, eyes raking over Tess. "Maybe I can't, but I can make sure you'll wish you had helped me." Chad looked to Nathan. "Not sure Tess mentioned it to you, but we were engaged once. In case you haven't figured it out yet, there's a damn good reason I dumped her. Only kept her around because her connections made it worth my while."

Nathan stiffened at her side. "Bullshit. Tess wised up and ditched you, not the other way around."

Chad rolled his eyes. "That's the story Tess likes to tell," he said, raising his voice. Tess cringed when she noticed most people in the room turning their direction. Theresa, John, and Deanna swung in unison, all stepping closer. Chad ignored them and continued. "Tess freaked out when I broke up with her. Called me all the time, crying about her miscarriage and whining about how we were meant to be."

Tess wanted to hide her face and run. Chad had done precisely as he'd threatened. To make matters worse, he'd done so quite publicly. The conference room was large, but small enough that Chad's raised voice could easily be heard. While her thoughts whirred through options and she stared blindly at the floor, she didn't notice Nathan's hand had slipped off her waist.

There was a sudden jolt of motion. Tess glanced up as Nathan's fist connected with Chad's face. Chad turned away just as Nathan's fist landed, the blow striking his cheekbone. Chad righted himself after Nathan's punch, his face red. For once, he seemed to have forgotten he was in a crowd. He threw a punch at Nathan with Nathan quickly dodging, leaving Chad's fist to thump against his shoulder.

Nathan twisted to face Chad, pulling his fist back again, this time connecting squarely with Chad's nose. Blood gushed from Chad's nose as he again attempted to punch Nathan. Nathan was faster, stepping neatly out of the way. The next few seconds passed in sickening slow motion as Tess watched Nathan efficiently dispatch Chad. Every eye in the room was focused on them, those nearby gathered closer, yet no one moved to help Chad. Though Tess had known in her gut that Chad wasn't that well-liked when they were together, she had somehow convinced herself otherwise. The complete lack of response from some of his colleagues and acquaintances as Nathan made quick work of Chad drove home the point that Chad didn't have many friends to call upon, if any. This reminded Tess why he'd been interested in her to begin with—he'd badly needed the social currency she offered. A few moments later, Chad lay sprawled on the floor, blood smeared across his face.

Nathan calmly adjusted his sleeves as he looked down at Chad. "Next time you want to talk shit about Tess, you might want to think twice."

Chad came to his feet unsteadily, vainly attempting to come off as cool and collected. He swiped a napkin off the nearby table. Wiping the blood off his face, he looked back to Nathan and shrugged. "Sure, you'd like to think I'm talking shit," he said with a sneer. "You may think you know Tess, but just wait until she bores you to tears. Fuckin' relief to walk away from her."

Nathan's breath was audible, his pulse visible at his temple. Tess put her hand on his arm, feeling the vibration of his restraint. "Oh no, no you don't. There's a damn good reason you came running back for her and you know it. She's brilliant, gorgeous and has the one thing you'll never get—respect," Nathan said through his teeth.

He looked away from Chad into her eyes and for a moment, the crowd around them faded. His blue eyes were dark with anger and a mix of pride and concern. His arm relaxed beneath her hand. Tess flamed from her blush, a part of her savoring how protective Nathan was warring with how mortified she felt.

Chad glanced at her, his eyes cold and flat. "Well, hope you got what you wanted." He took a quick look around before stalking out of the room.

* * *

TESS LEANED against the bathroom stall door and sighed, her arms wrapped tightly around her waist. After Chad had left the boardroom, Nathan, Deanna and Theresa had tried to talk to her, all insisting that Chad had only made a fool of himself, not her. Tess had fled, needing a few moments to herself. She felt physically sick, her cheeks still hot from the humiliation of those long moments in the boardroom. She fought back tears, her throat tight. She knew intellectually that she had nothing to be ashamed of and knew that Nathan and her friends were mostly right. Yet she was utterly humiliated that the entire room of people, most of them professional acquaintances, now knew she'd had a miscarriage and were witness to just what an idiot she'd been to stay with Chad. Not to mention the way Chad made her sound. She knew that he looked like a complete jerk and that it was unlikely anyone would believe him, but she was mortified nonetheless.

Tess heard the outer door to the bathroom open and hoped it wasn't anyone that she knew. Footsteps came to a stop in front of the stall.

"Tess, I know you're in there, so just come on out," Deanna said.

Tess took a long breath. "Could I have just a few minutes to myself?"

"You already did. I'm fending Nathan off as it is."

Tess sighed and let her arms fall before stepping out of the stall. Deanna was leaning against the marble counter that held a run of sinks. She took a long look at Tess, her eyes searching and worried, yet with that ever-present touch of determination.

"Well, you haven't been crying. That's good news," Deanna said with a wry smile.

Tess smiled ruefully, feeling tired inside. "Nope, no crying, close but not quite." She took a shaky breath. "I just didn't want what just happened to happen. The last thing I need is everyone knowing my personal business and Chad making me look like an idiot. Not to mention that it wasn't exactly helpful for Nathan to get all protective and start a fight."

Deanna tiled her head to the side, rolling her eyes. "Okay, I totally get it that you didn't want your private laundry aired. But the only one who looks like an idiot is Chad. He's up against the wall and he knows it. As soon as its public that he's on the hook for embezzlement, anyone left who has a halfway decent opinion of him won't anymore." Deanna pushed away from the sink and stepped in front of Tess, reaching to straighten an errant curl.

"As for Nathan, he may have thrown the first punch, but Chad is the one that set that fight in motion. I know I wasn't the only one in that room that enjoyed seeing Chad take a few punches," Deanna said, a sly smile on her face.

A small laugh escaped as Tess looked back at Deanna. "I'm sure you weren't. And Nathan...I don't know Deanna. I appreciate that he was pissed at Chad, but a public fight isn't exactly what I needed. I was hoping *not* to draw attention and that did the opposite."

Deanna pursed her lips. "Don't you dare think about letting this get in between you and Nathan."

Tess sighed. "Dee, I know you want me to ride off into the sunset with Nathan..." Deanna's emphatic nod brought another laugh out of Tess before she continued "...but it's not that simple. It never was. Yes, he's amazing and we have tons of chemistry, but the only option for us to be more than a fling or a long distance relationship is for me to move to Alaska. I'm not sure about uprooting my whole life just yet."

Deanna gave her a considering look and nodded. "I could've predicted you'd say that. I know how you deal with pressure so I'll leave it be for now. Let me just say this— don't be stupid."

The bathroom door swung open again. Theresa entered, her shoes tapping on the floor. She immediately walked to Tess and gave her a swift hug. "Don't you worry about this. John and I have already made the rounds to clue in anyone who didn't hear the rumors about Chad. I've also made your excuses for you. So get out of here before Nathan beats the door down," Theresa said firmly.

Tess had all kinds of things she wanted to say, but her nerves were worn. Looking between Deanna and Theresa, a small smile bloomed in her heart. Regardless of how she felt about the fiasco of tonight, she had amazing friends. They were her anchor tonight and would be when the dust from this settled. Without them, she didn't know what she would do, especially after a night like tonight. And that just stacked on top of every other doubt she had about moving away. With a sharp shake, she forced her thoughts away from that. She just needed to get through tonight. "Thank you both. I certainly didn't want...*that*...to happen," she began, waving her hand in the direction of the boardroom. "But I'm glad you were both here to smooth things over. I'll get out of here now and worry about straightening things out later."

Tess squared her shoulders as she stepped out of the bathroom. Nathan leaned against the wall directly across the hall. Although he'd clearly dominated Chad, Tess felt a wash of protectiveness when she saw the bruise forming on his knuckles and a red area on one cheek. As Tess stepped toward him, Nathan pushed away from the wall and enveloped her in his arms. Tears welled. Tess forced herself to breathe slowly, hoping she wouldn't fall apart in the hallway.

Nathan held her close and pressed his lips against her hair. His voice was muffled when he spoke in a whisper. "You're probably pissed with me and that's fine. I get it. Just wanted to make sure you knew that before we walked out of here."

Mere moments ago, Tess had been pissed off—with Nathan, but Chad most of all. Just the fact that Nathan knew that and could say right off that he understood dissipated her anger. With her cheek pressed against his shoulder, she said, "It's okay. I'm just upset that the whole situation blew up. But that's not your fault."

Tess leaned her head away, a curl catching on Nathan's collar. She brushed it away and looked into his blue eyes—eyes filled with worry. "I didn't want that fight to happen and certainly not in the middle of tonight's dinner. But I'll figure out how to deal with all of it. For now, let's get out of here." She grabbed his hand and led the way out.

CHAPTER 17

Nathan woke the following morning in Tess's room, bright sun splashed across the bed. Half-awake, he rolled over, sleepily thinking he'd be curling around Tess. Finding the bed empty save for him, he rolled onto his back again, kicking the covers off of his feet. As he came slowly awake, his mind replayed the events last night. Just as he had last night after Tess had fallen asleep, he berated himself for losing control and punching Chad. That thought alternated with the fact that Chad damn well deserved to get the shit beat out of him. It was just that Nathan couldn't remember the last time he'd had a fight—his only recollection was from high school when a tussle broke out during a basketball game. And he felt horrible that it had happened in such a public place. Tess had tried to be a good sport about it, but it was pretty clear she was struggling. Nathan wanted to shake her and remind her that while he may have lost his temper, Chad was the one who pushed her into this corner.

There'd been a moment in the hallway at the hospital when he'd thought Tess would be okay. That had passed.

The ride home had been quiet. She'd been distant when they'd gotten back to her condo. In the time he'd been visiting, they'd made love every night. Last night, she hadn't pushed him away when he'd tried to be affectionate, but he'd sensed a wall of reserve. Moving beyond cuddling didn't feel like an option. He'd lain awake by her side, spooned behind her while she fell asleep. Lying still now, he heard the drip of the coffee maker.

With a mental shake, Nathan rolled to his side, swinging his feet to the floor and standing. Clad in only his boxers, he walked out of the bedroom to find Tess seated at the small table that lay between the kitchen and living room area. Her laptop was open and she appeared engrossed in reading. She didn't turn toward him as he entered the room.

"Morning," he said, leaning over to kiss the side of her neck.

Nathan hadn't realized he was banking on Tess turning her head so he could give her a thorough good morning kiss. He became aware of his unconscious expectation when she didn't turn to him. His chest tightened. He felt robbed—the easy affection that they'd had was gone—nothing, not even anger. She kept reading and mumbled a greeting. Not sure what else to do, he stepped past her and went into the kitchen to pour a cup of coffee.

After a few fortifying sips of coffee and several more moments of silence, Nathan decided he'd had enough. "Look, I said it last night. I get it if you're pissed at me. But the silent treatment isn't working for me. Give me a shot here. Don't just shut me out."

Tess kept looking at her computer screen, but her eyes stopped scanning. She abruptly stood and walked into the kitchen, topping off her coffee. Returning to the table, she sat, finally bringing her eyes to meet Nathan's. Her hand clenched tightly around the coffee mug. It took all Nathan had not to say something right away, but he sensed that she needed to speak first.

While he waited, his eyes took in the sight of her—her tousled curls that he loved so in the morning, her ginger eyes, and plump pink lips. He'd fallen and fallen hard for Tess in Alaska and coming to her world had only deepened those feelings for him. He just wanted for whatever they had to be more than a passing chance. He wanted to wake up to her every day, to that mix of feistiness and vulnerability that clashed within her. He ached to touch her, to just hold her close and suffuse her with the depth of what he felt for her.

Tess took an anxious sip of her coffee, her shoulders rising and falling with a deep breath. "I appreciate that you get why I might be pissed. And honestly, I know that none of this would have happened if it weren't for Chad. But..." She paused, biting her lower lip. "I don't think you realize how embarrassing it was for you to start that fight where you did. The only thing that keeps my career solid is my ability to stay on good terms with the people who contract with me and whatever social world they navigate to raise money. Sure, there are plenty of people that will overlook what happened. But most of my work isn't for people that are close to me the way Theresa and John are. I'm just trying to figure out how to smooth things over. It would have been bad enough for people to link me to Chad with what he's facing, and now everyone in the room and then some knows I had a miscarriage and will remember that my boyfriend hauled off and punched Chad in the middle of what should have been a polite social event. It's not like we were at a bar."

Nathan was momentarily stuck when Tess called him her boyfriend—he was so damn pleased to have her describe him that way, he didn't respond right away. A few seconds ticked by when the rest of what she said sunk in.

"Tess, I know I fucked up. I'm sorry. I just lost it when he threatened you and started putting you down. I know me punching him didn't help anything. I don't suppose you'll believe me, but it's not exactly my style to fight. I know that what happened makes things worse for your business. It's just…you matter *a lot* to me. I couldn't even think straight."

Tess blushed at his words, but her hand was still clenched around the coffee cup. "Nathan, I get it. I just don't know what to do. I need some time to think and figure this out."

Nathan's stomach felt hollow. He didn't know what she meant by needing time and was afraid she was about to tell him to book that return ticket to Alaska. While he missed Diamond Creek, his brothers and friends, he sure as hell didn't want to return with things like this with Tess. In his fantasy, she'd be flying back with him. His feelings for her were so strong, he was even willing to consider moving to where she wanted. *That* floored him. His life in Alaska defined him in so many ways. He loved it so much that if someone had told him, even after he first met Tess, that a woman might lead him somewhere else he'd have firmly believed that was impossible. But now—he loved Tess, much more than he loved Alaska, and it was far more than lust that would burn out.

He swallowed and forced himself to wait. While he didn't yet know Tess in all the ways he wanted, the way he would when they'd been together for years, he knew that pressure was not a strategy that worked for her. If he wanted Tess and wanted her to come to him with her heart wide open, it had to be on her terms.

Nathan looked over at her to see a tear roll down one cheek. Tess knuckled it away with a sigh. "Tess…" he said, starting to reach over.

She held a hand up. "Don't. Just give me some space." She took a slow breath, gathering herself. When she looked over again, Nathan sensed that his gut was right. He didn't know how it would play out, but Tess wasn't ready to hop on a plane with him and certainly not ready to ask him to move here to stay with her. Yet again, he recalled the moment his fist connected with Chad's face and wished he'd been able to stop and think.

Tess held his gaze, her eyes confused and worried. "I love that you came out here. I love that you're so protective of me. But…I need some time to make sense of everything and decide what I'm going to do. You're not saying it, but I get the feeling you're hoping I'll move to Alaska. I just don't know if I'm ready to make that decision."

Nathan forced himself to stop and think before he spoke. Part of him wanted to downplay his hopes, but he didn't think that would help. Telling Tess how he felt wasn't pressure. It was just the truth. Looking into her ginger eyes, he told her what was in his heart. "I'm hoping that you'll give us a chance. That's all I'm hoping. The details don't really matter. I won't pretend that I wouldn't love it if you moved to Alaska, but I love you. I told you that before you left Diamond Creek. If you'd give us a chance if I moved here, I wouldn't have to think about it. It would happen. If you said we should move to New York City or Timbuktu, I'd be there. Just tell me when and where. Where you want to be is where I want to be."

Tess's eyes opened wide, her mouth parting. She held still for a long moment. "Nathan…you don't have to promise me you'll move wherever I want you to. Diamond Creek is part of you. I can't imagine you living anywhere else."

Nathan shrugged. "Sure, Diamond Creek is important to me. But you're more important than a place. I'll give you the space you're asking for because I don't want you coming to me out of obligation. I'd just ask that you keep in mind that I love you…*really* love you…and that we have something between us that doesn't just happen. I'm more sorry than you can imagine about last night. But I'm not dumb enough to think that's all this is about. I know you've had your doubts. Hell, I didn't expect this when I was trying to sweet-talk you into going to dinner with me in Diamond Creek." He paused, a small smile crossing his face. "I'm damn glad I didn't give up, but I knew from the start that you had your reservations. Makes me want to kick Chad's ass all over again because far as I can tell, he had a hand in making you doubt yourself and relationships."

When Tess started to protest, Nathan waved a hand. "I'm not trying to analyze you. I'm just saying he was a jerk and you didn't deserve it." He took a long look at Tess and reached for her free hand, cupping it in both of his. "Give me a day or so to get my trip booked and then you can have your space. But, could we maybe plan a timeframe here? Like I could plan another trip in a few weeks or you could come out there?"

A mix of emotions danced across her face – sadness, joy, fear, anger. She nibbled on her lower lip, making Nathan want to pull her close for a kiss. She finally met his eyes, her gaze resigned and uncertain. "I'm not sure I want you to leave, but I'm not sure I can think clearly with you here."

Much as it caused a visceral flash of pain in his heart, his chest tightening, his stomach clenching, he nodded. "Okay." After a long moment of silence, he lifted her hand and placed a soft kiss in the center of her palm. "Know this…I love you."

Another tear rolled down Tess's cheek. This time, Nathan didn't hesitate to reach up and wipe it away, cupping her cheek for a moment. "About my question, a timeframe?"

Tess shook her head abruptly, appearing to jolt herself out of her thoughts. "Oh! Yes, that's a good idea. How about we say I come to Diamond Creek in a month? You came here this time, it's only fair for me to come to you."

A flame of hope sparked in Nathan's heart. He nodded with alacrity. "Works for me. Want to book the trip when I set up my return trip?"

He didn't want to say it aloud, but he was worried she would change her mind. A small smile stole over her face when she nodded. The heaviness in his heart eased, hope buoying it.

* * *

A WEEK LATER, Nathan stood on the deck of Iris, their commercial fishing boat, looking out across the bay. It was late afternoon with the sun already starting to dip in the sky. It would eventually slip behind the mountains that were still dark and green, void of snow. Termination dust – the first snow to dust the mountains – would fall any day now. Every fall, it felt like winter raced toward them as the days rapidly shortened. The contrast from the endless summer days only heightened the feeling.

Nathan took a full breath of air, savoring the crisp, salty scent. He wore a lightweight blue down jacket over jeans to ward off the bite in the air. His mind wandered to Tess, which it did every few minutes. He wished she were here to enjoy fall in Diamond Creek. He loved the taut sense of being outdoors in the fall. This window of time between summer and fall was a blink but filled with life. Walks on the beach were bracing, and hikes through the local spruce forest were dappled with splashes of color scattered along the ground. Fall here happened mostly at your feet, as most of the trees were evergreens with a few birch and cotton-wood thrown in the mix. The berry bushes and other flora and fauna changed in rich shades of red, orange and purple.

But, Tess wasn't here, not just yet. She'd been good to

her word and they talked every day. But the phone didn't give him all the details of her expression, which shared so much. After she'd asked for some space, he'd flown back to Alaska a mere two days later. Oddly, the reserve that she'd cloaked around her the night after his fight with Chad and the following morning had dissolved after they'd talked and Nathan had offered to fly home. That reinforced what he'd quickly come to know about her—pressure only made things worse. As soon as the imagined pressured of him staying there had disappeared, she had relaxed back into the way she'd been—warm, affectionate and with enough passion to singe him.

Nathan turned away from the mountains and quickly stepped into the boat cabin. He'd stopped by to check the moorings since there had been a pounding storm last night. The wind had thrashed against the house well into this morning. Wind up on the hill meant much stronger wind over the water and by the shore, even in the protected harbor of Otter Cove. The lines had loosened a bit, but had held fairly well. In another week or so, they'd be pulling the boat out of the harbor for winter storage. Their smaller guide boat would stay in the water a little longer. Right up until December, they occasionally took trips for fun, along with a few for business.

He locked up and headed back to the harbor lot. Moments later, he was driving past the post office when his cell phone vibrated in his shirt pocket, the ring interrupting the local news on his car radio through the Bluetooth system. He tapped the answer button on his car console. "Nathan here," he said.

"Hey man, what's up?" Jared asked.

"Just leaving the harbor. Lines were a little loose, but all's good. What are you up to?"

Nathan could hear the sound of papers shuffling and a muffled voice in the background. He shook his head and smiled to himself. Jared was constantly working and was obsessive about details. He often pored over accounts, orders and more even when it wasn't necessary. Nathan was happy to admit that he didn't see how complicated it could be since their fishing business was pretty straightforward, but Jared would immediately start explaining to him why the details mattered when it came to maintenance, repairs, cost for supplies, insurance and more. Nathan and Luke would nod politely and thank Jared profusely for his contribution to their business. And privately heave sighs of relief because Jared wanted to do what they didn't—the minutiae.

Jared said something garbled.

"Dude, can't hear you," Nathan said.

"Oh sorry. Just answering Susie. To answer your question, I came by Susie's office to go over some accounting stuff," Jared replied.

"I'm assuming you'd tell Luke and me if we needed to worry about anything in that corner."

Jared chuckled. "Hell yeah, you'd hear about it. Nothing to worry about. We've had a great year so far. Winter plow jobs will be icing on the cake."

Nathan figured Jared was again talking to Susie because all he heard was a mumble of words for a moment and then Jared's voice became clear again. "Susie wants to know if we want to meet for an early dinner at Sally's."

Before Nathan could respond, Jared started laughing. "What now?" Nathan asked.

"Oh just that I don't think I can say no. Susie says she knows I don't have anywhere to be…" There was another pause, and Nathan could hear Susie laughing. "She says that you have to come too and update her on your visit with Tess."

Nathan shook his head, laughing as he did. "Tell her I'll be there. When are you two headed that way?" he asked.

"In a few minutes. I have to get gas, but then I'll be right there," Jared said.

"Okay, see you in a few," Nathan replied before tapping to end the call.

When he arrived at Sally's a few minutes later, he took a look around as he walked in. Sally's was in an old renovated barn with two sides to the restaurant. One side held the bar and tables scattered in front of a small stage for live music. Booths lined all walls. The kitchen was in the center of the barn with the other side holding the quieter sit down area with large tables for families. The old hayloft was above the restaurant side and held additional seating for full nights, which were common year round. Sally's was a local favorite and had been around for decades. The original owner, Sally James, had passed away many years ago, but the two owners since kept the name. Aside from its local stature, Sally's was a hub for good music, often booking small-scale bands from all over the country, hosting comedy shows and all sorts of functions and fundraisers. It was almost always busy and filled to capacity on weekends. Diamond Creek was small but social and active.

Nathan used to spend a lot more time at Sally's than he had in the last year or so. He still came in every few weeks, but he used to be here at least several times a week. While he hadn't yet met Tess when he'd eased off his late nights and casual dating patterns, Nathan was glad he already had when he met her. He didn't know if he would have noticed her in the way he did if he'd carried his old mindset. Oh, he'd have noticed she was cute and sexy as hell, he just might have moved right on when faced with her reserve. Now, he knew he'd have lost the chance at something amazing. Yet again, he cringed internally as he considered that he needed to let Tess have this time so she would come to him on her terms.

Nathan forced his thoughts away from Tess, waved at a

few friends and snagged a booth over on the restaurant side. He ordered a beer and was perusing the menu when Susie sat down across from him. Looking over at her, he automatically smiled. Susie was warm, friendly and funny. She was petite and curvy with wild brown curls and kind brown eyes that almost always carried a spark of mischief.

"Hey you!" Susie exclaimed. "When were you gonna come see me and fill me in on what's going on with Tess?" she asked and then continued, clearly not expecting his answer just yet. "I consider her a friend, you know. She may have only been here a few weeks, but we got to know her. She's a sweetheart. Did you convince her to get her butt out here?"

Nathan opened his mouth to reply but was cut off by Jared who slid into the booth beside Susie. "Do tell," Jared said with a wink at Susie. "He's been keeping this on the lowdown. All we know is that he's hoping Tess will visit soon. But there's more to the story because he gets cranky every time I ask about it. Even Hannah tried to pry some details out of him but got nothing."

Nathan took a sip of beer. Irritation flared. He knew they were only asking because they cared, even if caring meant that they gave him shit about it. But he didn't have the heart to tell them he may have blown it by losing his temper and slugging Chad.

"Well?" Susie asked, her eyes wide and expectant.

With a sigh, he set his beer down. "Just like Jared said. I'm hoping she'll be out for a visit in a few weeks."

"Oh that is soooo not all there is to tell. If things were going great, you'd say so. I pretty much had it decided that you two were meant for each other, so you have to give me a little more info here. Maybe I'll call Tess," Susie said.

"Oh god, don't go calling Tess," Nathan said. He looked back and forth between Jared and Susie. "Promise me you won't bug Tess about this when she does visit."

Susie huffed and nodded while Jared rolled his eyes.

"Seriously? You know I wouldn't say anything," Jared said.

"Okay, here's the quick and dirty version..." Nathan started and gave them a sketch of the situation with Chad and how that had prompted Simon to call Nathan to begin with because he'd been worried about Tess.

"So her ex is a total asshat, we all have at least one of those in our past. Could you get to the part about why you seem not so sure Tess will visit?" Susie asked impatiently, circling her hand as she did.

Conversation paused when the waitress arrived to take their order. They elected to share a pizza with Susie insisting on extra pepperoni. "I'm starving and I need the protein," she said. "And don't you dare imply I shouldn't eat whatever the hell I want. I'll take that as a passive aggressive way of telling me I need to lose weight."

Nathan almost choked on his beer when he saw the look of affront on Jared's face.

"Since when have any of us ever commented on what you eat?" Jared asked.

Susie shrugged. "Well, old Mrs. Simmons—you know her, she works at Dr. Stevens' office. She told me young ladies—not that I'm all that young—were supposed to eat smaller portions in public. She happened to be at one of the galleries on the First Friday Art Night and saw me help myself to the buffet. God knows why she was there. I hate that kind of crap."

Nathan watched a barely discernible flush rise of Jared's neck and tucked that away for future reference. Luke had once mentioned that he wondered if Jared had the hots for Susie. He and Nathan had agreed that the likelihood of Jared admitting that and acting on it was next to nil. Nathan thought that was too bad because although there wasn't the slightest spark for Nathan with regard to Susie, she was smart, cute, sexy and a damn good friend. She was also one of the few women he'd met that wouldn't just kowtow to Jared, which would be good for Jared.

"Well since you hate that crap, I'd suggest you ignore it," Nathan said when it became apparent Jared wasn't going to respond. He was relieved to have Jared slightly thrown since it took the heat off of him.

Susie, of course, immediately beamed her focus back where she wanted it. "So ex is an asshat, et cetera. Tell us what else matters."

Nathan sighed and chuckled, giving in to the inevitable. Susie would get her answers one way or another. "Yup, ex boyfriend is an asshat..." Nathan explained, relaying the events that led up to the fight. "When he wouldn't back down and actually started talking trash, right in the middle of the boardroom with everyone there, I couldn't think straight and hauled off and punched him..." Nathan paused for a fortifying swig of beer.

"You punched him in the middle of the boardroom?" Jared asked.

Nathan gave him a flat look. "Uh, yeah," he said succinctly. "That's where we were. And to be honest, I punched him more than once. Just enough to knock him down, but...it was an event, to say the least."

Susie clapped her hands in glee. "Oh my god! He totally deserved it. You were avenging Tess's honor, that's so romantic!"

"Maybe it was romantic, but I'm guessing Tess didn't exactly love that it happened where it did." Jared said wryly.

Nathan nodded. "Bingo."

Susie scrunched up her face. "So maybe Tess was upset about that part, but she's got some sense. She had to see that maybe it was a bit public, but Chad deserved it, and you just did what you did because you love her."

Nathan shrugged. "I think she knew all that, but... She

didn't talk much about it here, but she runs her own fundraising business. The dinner was work related. So she's worried about cleaning up that mess. I kinda blew it."

Jared gave him a questioning look.

Nathan explained further. "Tess had some doubts about this whole 'us' thing anyway. Can't say I blame her. I didn't expect to fall for her the way I have. It's definitely not convenient that we're on opposite sides of the country. Either I move there, or she pulls up stakes on her work, along with the rest of her life. I don't know what's gonna happen. She just said she needed some space and couldn't think straight if I was there. She's supposed to fly out here in a few weeks, but that's all I could get for now."

Susie harrumphed and leaned back when the waitress arrived with their pizza. As soon as the waitress stepped away, Susie returned to the topic. "Well between now and when Tess gets here, she'll come to her senses. If not, she just might hear about it from me."

Nathan shook his head. "For god's sake, no pressure. Tess doesn't do pressure well. She just pushes back."

Jared glanced over a Susie as he slid a slice of pizza onto his plate. "I'm sure it'll kill you, but maybe take Nathan's word for it."

Susie gave Jared a soft punch on his shoulder. "I might listen to Nathan for his sake, but not because you said so."

Jared chuckled and took a bite of pizza as Susie turned her focus to Nathan again. "Don't be stupid and forget to tell her how you feel. She might want space, but that's not an invitation to act like she doesn't matter."

Nathan found himself nodding obediently before he burst out laughing. "What is it with you? You boss everyone around and we all go along with it."

Susie's return smile was broad, her eyes impish. "Hey, I'm the one that set the ball in motion for Hannah and Luke and look how that turned out. Not to mention that you had your own opinion about what Luke should do when he got all wishy-washy. You might want to remember your own advice."

Nathan recalled that he'd told Susie he thought Luke was about to lose something amazing because he was too afraid to make sure Hannah knew how he felt. He just didn't know how to follow his own advice with Tess four thousand plus miles away.

CHAPTER 18

Tess stood in line at the coffee shop. It had been just over a week since Nathan left, or rather since she'd asked him to leave. Slipping her phone out of her purse, she opened her calendar and counted the days until her flight to Diamond Creek—twenty-two days left. She'd begun to think she'd been stubborn and stupid to ask him to go. Instead of feeling clear-headed and logical, as if she could make a decision about her life in a rational way, she missed him fiercely, her thoughts drifting to how it felt to wake up beside him in the morning, so many moments when he took her breath away, and his eyes...those blue, blue eyes.

As much as Tess had worried about the fallout from Nathan's fight with Chad, her business contacts had been surprisingly supportive. In the intervening week, Chad had been formally charged and arrested for embezzlement. All of his assets were frozen. His parents had bailed him out, although the court had ordered him to wear an ankle monitor because some of the emails on his computer indicated he might have been planning to fly to

Mexico. Once the news about Chad was out, she received a number of calls that she needn't worry that what happened would affect her business. Tess had discovered that she'd cared far less than she thought she would've. Since returning home to her empty condo after dropping Nathan off at the airport, she had shifted from fretting about her business and the situation with Chad to wondering if she'd just blown up the best thing that had ever happened to her.

While it hadn't been clear to her a few weeks ago, one thing had come into sharp focus since Nathan left: she simply wanted to be with him. She stood at the edge of a decision—a decision that held a possibility she'd given up—the possibility of love and passion. And it was terrifying. Every time she considered it, she couldn't imagine Nathan living anywhere but Diamond Creek. Nor did she think it would be fair to ask that of him. That meant she'd have to be the one with the courage to leave behind the safe and familiar. In doing so, she'd make herself vulnerable in a way she'd sworn never to do again. The link between her and Nathan was so potent that it was be crushing if she threw caution to the wind, embraced the chance that their connection could blossom into something solid and long-term…and it fell apart.

Tess was startled by a tap on her shoulder, turning to find Deanna. "Hey! What brings you here?" Tess asked.

"Coffee," Deanna said, a hint of sarcasm in her tone. "I've been standing behind you for a solid minute, and you didn't even notice. Let me guess, obsessing about Nathan? Do yourself a favor and stop trying to think your way out of this one."

Tess rolled her eyes. "Just spaced out. That's all," she replied, not ready to fess up and admit Deanna hit on precisely what she was obsessing over. "Good to see you. Want to sit with me for a bit once we get coffee?"

Deanna nodded and then nudged Tess's shoulder. "You're up next."

"Oh!" Tess turned and stepped to the counter, quickly ordering and getting Deanna's drink while she was at it.

Once they were seated, Tess took a welcome swallow of her latte. "Oh, that's good. I've been behind the ball all morning."

"So when did you say you were flying to Alaska?" Deanna asked, avoiding any preliminaries.

"I told you the other day, in a few weeks. Why?" Tess countered.

"Because Simon says you've been down again and you look like it. I think it was dumb for you to make Nathan leave. Sure, the whole fight scene at the hospital board dinner wasn't the best move, but I was damn happy to see Chad get the lumps he deserved. So now you need to stop dilly-dallying and admit that Nathan's worth it and move to Alaska," Deanna said matter-of-factly.

Tess felt herself bristle inside. Deanna knew she didn't like to be pressured, so why she was doing this, Tess didn't know. "Dee…" Tess said, an edge of warning to her tone.

"What? Is now when you remind me that you hate being pressured? Honestly, I don't know anyone who likes it. And we've known each other for way too long now. I usually lay low when it comes to stuff like this. But that's what I did when you started dating Chad and that was a huge mistake. Wished I'd spoken up sooner. So I've decided I'm not gonna sit back and watch you let Nathan go. You don't have to listen to me, but at least I won't wish I'd said something before it was too late."

Tess took another sip of coffee, stalling for a moment. Deanna knew her so well, and she trusted Deanna's opinion. In a way, she was relieved. She needed Deanna's blessing on this, and she needed something to help jolt her out of her indecision. She glanced around the restaurant before bringing her eyes back to Deanna. "Fair enough. Huge mistake is a good way to describe Chad. I may not listen right off, but I trust your opinion. And don't go telling everyone about this, but I'm seriously thinking about moving to Diamond Creek…"

Deanna held her hand up for a high-five. "That's my girl! Thinking about it is enough for now. Say the word and I'll help however I can. Packing, whatever you need."

"Give me a little time here. I said I was *thinking* about it. It's not like I can make it happen overnight. I've got to make plans, figure out what to do about my condo lease and office lease, sort out just what I'm going to do with my business…" Tess began before Deanna cut her off.

"Since I'm all about stating the obvious today. Sure there's plenty of practical crap to deal with if you actually move to Alaska. That will fall into place because it has to. As for whether or not you'll move…I've known you long enough to know that if you're ready to admit you're thinking about something…it's not a matter of if, but when. My vote is make it sooner rather than later," Deanna said before draining the rest of her latte in a long gulp.

Tess's heart cheered, drowning out her rational brain for the moment. While she wasn't ready to let her heart run the show just yet, just saying out loud that she was thinking about moving to Diamond Creek almost made her dance for joy. Deanna's confidence buoyed her.

Deanna opened her purse to pull out a tube of bright red lipstick. Quickly applying a fresh coat to her lips, she glanced back over at Tess. "What can I do to help you make this decision?" she asked, mischief in her eyes.

Tess sighed and shook her head. "Maybe you do know me well, but it's not easy to uproot my entire life and move away from my family and friends. And *you* happen to be one of my best friends, so you're part of this equation."

Deanna's expression sobered. "Look, I'm not trying to

make light of this. I get it. Moving anywhere is a big deal and a pain in the ass to boot. I just think the stuff you're worried about will be okay. You'll miss your family and they'll visit plenty. I'll miss the hell out of you, but I'll visit too and see you every time you're here. End game is that Nathan is worth it. Move."

Tess couldn't help but laugh. Deanna tended to make bold decisions quickly. Much as she wanted to tell Deanna to butt out, Tess knew that she needed someone to cast light into the dark corners of her mind that harbored doubts. Rather than engaging in a debate, she merely promised Deanna she'd let her know as soon as she made her decision. Fortified with coffee, she headed back to her office and promptly sank into a few hours of futile efforts to stay focused on work. Nathan's dark blue eyes, his dimpled smile, and the feel of his touch circled into her thoughts again and again.

* * *

A FEW DAYS LATER, Tess walked briskly toward her office. When she stepped inside, she was startled to find Chad leaning against her desk. In a brief glance, she saw that he was perfectly put together – dark blonde hair slicked back, pressed khakis and button down navy shirt. What struck her was the expression in his eyes—they held uncertainty and wariness. Tess was immediately on guard and purposefully left the door to her office wide open.

"What are you doing here Chad?" she asked.

"Coming to see you. Thought maybe we could talk," Chad said, a thread of hesitance in his tone. "Your boyfriend still around?" he asked.

Tess ignored his question about Nathan. "Chad, I don't know what you think we could have to discuss. You have enough to worry about with your legal situation. If there's anyone you should talk to, it's your attorney, not me."

Chad's lips flattened. "Tess, I'm not stupid. I know I have to face the music. I was hoping you'd be willing to testify as a character witness for me. I know maybe I shouldn't have done what I did a few weeks ago. But we were almost married at one point. If anyone can testify that I'm a decent guy, it's you. They have a pretty good electronic trail on me, so my attorney suggests that my best bet to get a good plea deal is to line up some character witnesses and show that I have a history of good deeds – you know, my donations to charity and whatnot."

Once again, Tess found herself shocked by Chad. And once again—realized she should have known better. Chad sincerely didn't understand how unhappy she'd been during most of their relationship because he just wasn't capable of it. His emotional lens was so narrow and focused on himself that he couldn't see beyond that. His alleged charitable donations were laughable. During their relationship, Tess had continued her yearly donations to select charities. She never had a ton of money to give but always gave what she could. Once they were engaged, she'd started adding Chad's name to her donations. He'd initially complained about the waste of money and then discovered that he enjoyed the good press.

Much as Tess wanted to remind Chad of the many reasons why she walked out on him, she knew it would be a waste of breath. He didn't have enough insight about himself to comprehend. The very fact that he had the nerve to come to her office and ask for her to be a character witness illuminated just how oblivious he was, not to mention how few people he could turn to for support.

Tess looked at Chad for a long moment, regret for the time she'd wasted on him competing with sympathy for his situation. He faced a hard time ahead, a time when he wouldn't be able to rely on his façade and salesman persona to erase the damning trail he'd created. She looked him straight in the eye when she finally responded. "Chad, I can't testify for you and I won't…" Tess paused, considering whether to explain. A sense of freedom rose inside when she realized she didn't owe him an explanation. She stepped to the open door of her office and gestured for Chad to exit. "I'm sorry for what you're going through, but you'll have to ask elsewhere for a character witness."

Chad pushed away from the desk, his eyes shifting from uncertain to angry. "Thanks for nothing then. Can't believe you won't even bother to help me out a little." He strode through the door before turning to glance back at her. Just as he did, Tess heard Simon's voice.

"What the hell are you doing here?" Simon demanded. He stepped past Chad through the door to stand beside Tess keeping his eyes trained on Chad.

As Tess could have predicted, Chad didn't look the least bit chagrined at Simon's question. Although any halfway decent person would likely be embarrassed to be facing the charges Chad was, his defenses were so well-constructed, confrontation merely caused him to double-down.

"Came to see Tess. Are you her keeper now?" Chad asked snidely.

Simon threw Tess an exasperated look before replying. "Tess doesn't need a keeper. But you also shouldn't be here and you damn well know it. You're in a heap of trouble and on monitored release from what I understood, so if I were you, I'd steer clear of creating more problems. Leave Tess alone," Simon said flatly.

Chad gave her a disgusted look. "Between your brother and your boyfriend, seems like you need all kinds of back up."

Tess shook her head. "Chad, just go. And don't come back."

Chad turned away without another word. Apparently, he thought better of pursuing the verbal confrontation with Simon. Simon walked to the office windows. Tess followed him over, and together they watched Chad get in his car and leave.

Simon went to close her office door once Chad drove away. "What the hell did he want?" Simon asked, his tone sharp, gaze annoyed.

"Geez, Simon, it's not like I invited him here."

Simon's eyes softened, the annoyance fading quickly. "I know, I know. Just couldn't believe he had the nerve to show up here. But seriously, what did he want?"

"You'll love it. He wanted to know if I'd agree to be a character witness for him."

A sharp burst of laughter came from Simon. "You gotta be kidding me! He's clueless. Man, am I glad you broke up with him long before his whole scheme came to light."

Tess smiled ruefully. "Me too. If I could have a do-over, I'd have figured out what a jerk he was much faster than I did." She shrugged. "Oh well, if there's one thing I can't do, it's change the past. What brings you here?"

"Oh right. I was up for a work meeting and stopped by to see if you wanted to come to New Bern tomorrow to have dinner with mom and dad. Thought we could take them out for dinner the night before their anniversary."

"Sure. I'd love to. What time should I head down?"

They quickly settled on a time before Simon got ready to leave. Just as he walked to the door, he turned back. "Heard from Nathan lately?" he asked.

Tess felt a prickle of irritation that she quickly quashed. She knew Simon meant well, but it was near to driving her crazy that everyone wanted an update on Nathan when she was busy trying to decide what the hell to do.

She summoned her patience. "Talk to him every day. He's doing great," she replied.

"Don't get annoyed with me. I just want to see you happy. Ten seconds with Chad should show you how awesome Nathan is," Simon said. "While you're busy getting annoyed with people who care about you, just think about Chad for a second. That might refresh your memory about why we like Nathan. You know I'm right, which is why you're cranky about it." Simon winked and tugged the door shut behind him.

* * *

Driving to New Bern the following afternoon, Tess watched the familiar scenery roll by. She loved eastern North Carolina, being here felt like slipping on a comfortable pair of slippers. The soft, humid air, the scent of pine needles scattered underfoot, and the subtle hint of the ocean. The roads here were mapped in her mind, she could travel without thought. Being near her parents and her brother meant a lot to her. And yet, she didn't feel the crackle and spark she'd felt in Alaska. Not to mention that the ache of missing Nathan grew more acute by the day. Texts and calls didn't fill the void left by his absence.

When she pulled up a half an hour early, she found that her parents weren't home and Simon hadn't arrived yet. She'd left work early after speed session this morning of entering final data from the fundraisers she'd done recently and making a few calls on upcoming contracts for the holidays. Rather than waiting inside, she walked around the back of the house down the sloping lawn to the river.

Tess sat in down in a swing bench situated just where the grass met the sand. A soft breeze came off the water. Years ago, her parents had a dock that had been blown to bits during a hurricane. The dock pilings remained, worn and weathered. Today, a seagull sat atop one piling. Pelicans flew low across the water in a line. She had always loved pelicans as a child—she'd thought them to be dinosaur birds with their massive beaks and full throats. Being by the river was like a step out of time—peaceful, the earthy, rich scents of the river laced with the ocean pervading her senses. Soaking in the quiet, Tess thought back to her encounter with Chad yesterday. She considered that Nathan had offered to move wherever she wanted if she'd give them a chance. The contrast between Nathan's consideration of her feelings and Chad's was stark. So stark in fact, it made her uncomfortable to think about it.

"Tess!"

Tess turned when she heard her mother's voice. Celine stood between the open French doors on the sunroom that faced the river. The flowing red dress she wore waved softly in the breeze. Tess waved and took a long look out over the river before standing to walk up the slope to the house. Her mother enveloped her in a warm hug. As Celine stepped back, she clasped Tess's arms with her hands. "How are you darlin'? Your father's been worried and so have I. I know all this press about Chad is the last thing you wanted."

Celine stepped back, the cluster of silver bracelets that she wore on one arm clinking against each other. Tess's was quiet for a moment when she realized she'd been about to automatically agree with her mother. All her worry about Chad publicly humiliating her and being associated with the legal fiasco he'd created just wasn't there. She just didn't care about any of it, not even a little.

Tess looked up, into her mother's warm eyes, so like her own. A glimmer of relief and happiness started to hum in her heart, her lips following its tune with a smile. "Mom…" she began with a shrug. "I could care less about any of it."

Celine's eyes widened, her brows rising in question.

Laughter bubbled out of Tess. "I honestly don't care. In fact, much as I want to see you and dad tonight, I'm ready to head home so I can change my flight to Alaska to next week and start packing. I'm moving to Diamond Creek," she said decisively. For once, she let her heart lead the way, her doubts evaporated and a sense of elation filled her.

Celine squealed and tugged Tess back into another hug. She clapped her hands together, tears welling in her eyes when she released Tess. "Oh honey! This is the best news I've heard from you in a long time!" She slipped a hand through Tess's elbow and led her inside. "Why don't you use your father's computer to change your reservation? Let's just take care of that right away."

Instead of feeling the accustomed flash of irritation that she would at her mother's bossy manner, Tess was happy to comply. This was her decision, not anyone else's. It felt so right that she didn't care what anyone else thought.

Celine stepped ahead of Tess, freeing her arm. The flared edge of her red dress swung with her gait as she walked quickly into the living room, calling to Tess's father. "Michael! Tess is moving to Alaska! Isn't that wonderful? She needs to borrow your laptop for a few minutes."

Tess entered the living room in her mother's wake. Michael enjoyed reading the news online. He merely shook his head and chuckled as Celine lifted the laptop out of his hands.

Michael turned to look in Tess's direction. "Hey Tess! Got your mom pretty excited here." Michael stood from his customary reading chair, pushing the ottoman out of the way as he did. When Tess reached his side, her father wrapped her in a bear hug. Tess returned the hug and stepped away with a laugh as her mother asked which website she needed to change her flight.

"Give me a sec, Mom."

Her father tilted his head to the side and winked, his smile crinkling his eyes. "So sounds like you're goin' for it then? You know your mother damn near talked my ear off about how wonderful Nathan was, so it's a good thing you're decidin' to take a chance on 'im.'"

Tess felt a wash of emotion. All her worry about moving away and her parents just wanted her to have what she wanted. She nodded firmly. "Yup, I'm going for it. I figured that if I missed Nathan as much as I do that it'd be stupid to not give this a shot. Not to mention that Diamond Creek is amazing."

Michael's small broadened. "Amazing is one way to put it. Don't you worry, we'll be out there plenty. Some of the best fishing in the world is there, you'll just give me a good excuse. As for Nathan—far as I can tell, he's a keeper. Never been one to tell you who you should be with, but now that you've made your decision, I'll say that much." Her father tugged her into a side hug, rubbing her shoulder.

"I know you'll be there plenty, Dad. That's half the reason I got over myself and decided to go for it. I'll miss being so close to you and mom, but much as you love fishing and travel, I'm guessing I might even get more quality time with you," she said with a small laugh.

"Tess," her mother called.

Her father released her. "Better get over there. You know your mom. She's like a dog with a bone when she's got something in mind."

Tess went to her mother's side and quickly logged into her account, picking a flight a mere week away. Simon arrived while she was still on the computer, immediately high-fiving her after being updated by their mother. In short order, they went out to dinner, Tess making sure to enjoy shrimp and grits, figuring she'd better stock up the Southern seafood specialties now.

Hours later, Tess set the remote on the coffee table and glanced at her phone screen. Nathan had texted earlier to say he and his brothers had headed to Anchorage for a shopping run and he might not be able to call tonight. Her level of disappointment was completely out of proportion. To think she'd been struggling over this decision.

The only struggle she had now was whether to tell Nathan or surprise him. She grabbed her phone and tapped her contacts open. A moment later, Hannah answered.

CHAPTER 19

Nathan swung his truck into the small lookout area where he'd brought Tess when she'd finally agreed to have dinner with him. He was on his way to Luke and Hannah's place for dinner. The sky was gray, the air chilly and damp. Looking out over the bay, he wished Tess were here with him. He missed her warmth, the way her eyes tipped up when she smiled, those luscious curves…just *her*. The fireweed that had filled the view when she was here in late summer was long gone now. The once fiery fuchsia flowers were blanched petals scattered in the field. The flicker of fall in Alaska was almost past. The bright reds, oranges, and yellows that hugged the ground were faded to brown. The only color left was the green of the spruce, which held true no matter the season. Once the snow fell, the evergreen trees would appear an even deeper shade of green in contrast to the bright white.

The view seemed muted, the mountains dark against the gray of the water. Termination dust, the first snow, was expected any day now and would brighten the dark mountains. The next few months on the way to winter solstice tended to feel long as the days shortened rapidly. Nathan couldn't say he enjoyed the short days of winter, but he did enjoy the quiet. Winter was a marked contrast to the insanity of summer in Alaska. Summer brought work that he loved, but at a frenetic pace. By the time November rolled around, he could breathe and relax into a few months of quiet, slow paced days.

Facing winter this year left him melancholy, a feeling to which he wasn't accustomed. He still couldn't suss out where Tess stood. They talked every day, along with plenty of texts, some random, some steamy. As far as he knew, she was still planning to fly out to visit in another two weeks. But that was all he knew. While she hadn't started shutting him out, as she had before, he sensed something was afoot. It was a harrowing distraction—not knowing, wanting Tess here, *with him*, so fiercely that if Tess ended up deciding not to give them a chance...He couldn't even think about it.

Nathan took a last look out over the bay before putting his truck in gear. The setting sun flashed in his rear view mirror as he pulled away, the light arcing brightly through the truck cab. When he parked at Luke and Hannah's house a few minutes later, their dog Jessie came racing up to greet him the second he opened the door. Hannah stepped onto the deck and waved from the kitchen door.

"Hey there," Nathan called out as he gave Jessie a quick pet and followed her to the house. He reached Hannah's side on the deck as Jessie's tail disappeared inside.

"Jessie knows how to make someone feel welcome," Nathan said with a chuckle as Hannah tugged him in for a quick hug.

"That she does. We can't really compete with her," Hannah said. She stepped away and gestured Nathan into the house.

He took off his boots while Hannah hung his coat. She looked as if she'd just come in from the cold. Her cheeks were flushed and her glossy brown hair windblown. She wore jeans and what looked to be one of Luke's shirts over a fitted cotton tank top.

"How you been?" Nathan asked.

Hannah headed for the refrigerator. "Oh fine. We just got in from stacking wood. Beer or wine?" she asked, gesturing from the wine on the kitchen counter to beer in the fridge.

"Beer," he replied. "Where's Luke?"

Hannah poured a beer into a pint glass for Nathan, setting the glass in front of him where he'd seated himself at the counter. "He's upstairs putting John down for a nap. We spent most of the day running errands and picked up a load of wood this afternoon. Between that and then watching us stack wood from his car seat, John's fussy and ready for a nap," Hannah said with a small laugh as she poured herself a glass of red wine.

Nathan nodded. "Nobody said kids were easy, but John seems pretty easy-going most of the time." He reached down to stroke Jessie when she rubbed her head against his leg. Her tail thumped softly against the legs of a stool to one side.

Luke answered as he entered the kitchen. "Most of the time. But when he's cranky, he's cranky. Not the best sleeper when we're out and about. How you doing bro?" Luke asked, giving Nathan's shoulder a quick squeeze as he walked past him to kiss Hannah on the cheek. Luke helped himself to a sip of her wine. Hannah merely shook her head and poured him his own glass, giving him a pointed look when she handed it over.

"What? Can't share your wine?" Luke asked wryly.

"Not when I need it as much as I do right now." She glanced to Nathan. "Last night was rough. John was up every few hours, which means we were too. Between that and today, I could use a few glasses of wine to take the edge off."

"You know, you could have canceled tonight. Jared and I can fend for ourselves," Nathan said. He caught a glance between Luke and Hannah. It was so brief that he couldn't be sure, but something was up. He started to ask and thought better of it.

The next half hour passed quickly. Jared joined them shortly. Luke was in and out from the deck, grilling halibut while Hannah tossed a salad. Nathan noshed on the array of cheese and crackers that Hannah set on the counter. When Luke returned with a large quantity of grilled halibut, Nathan said, "Dude, we eat a lot, but not that much."

Luke ignored him and set the halibut on the counter. Just as he did, a knock came at the kitchen door.

Susie's voice burst into the room. Nathan took a long swallow of beer and turned to greet her only to see Tess standing at Susie's side. He promptly choked on his beer.

The shock at seeing Tess spun his world on its axis. The worry and uncertainty he'd been trying to push away dissolved into euphoria. Tess stood at Susie's side, a tentative smile on her face. After wiping the beer off of his chin, Nathan walked straight to Tess and wrapped her in a bear hug.

Susie started clapping. "Yippee! See Tess, I told you he'd love it."

Nathan pulled back, holding Tess by both arms and looking deep into her ginger eyes. "Damn, it's good to see you."

Tess simply nodded, her eyes bright with tears. Nathan glanced around the room. Luke had a knowing smile on his face while Hannah and Jared seemed the only two in the room allowing the moment to unfold without their interference. Hannah just continued chopping vegetables, although she called out a greeting to Tess. Jared remained where he was on a stool by the counter. Beyond a quick grin, he remained quiet. Susie, on the other hand, bounced up and down and squealed.

Nathan glanced Susie's way quickly. "I hate admitting you're right, but I will. *Love* this surprise. Whose plan was it?' he asked.

Susie pointed to Tess. Nathan looked back into Tess's eyes. She shrugged and smiled. "It was. Since you surprised me, thought I'd surprise you. I had a little help though. Hannah and Luke agreed to host this dinner tonight and picked me up at the airport. I've been waiting at Susie's until they called to tell me you were here."

Luke winked and nodded with satisfaction. "Had our bases covered."

Nathan brought his gaze back to Tess. Everyone else faded from his consciousness. Tess encompassed his awareness—the tilt of her eyes, her full pink mouth, and tousled honey curls. He tugged her close again, almost groaning at the feel of her lush breasts against his body. Breathing deeply, he inhaled the scent of wood smoke and crisp cool air under laid with the scent he'd come to know as Tess—a sharp hint of vanilla.

He didn't know how much time passed as he held Tess close, so relieved to have her physically here with him. The reality of where they were hit him when Susie remarked, "Oh dear god. You know it's pretty boring for the rest of us to be polite while you all but tear Tess's clothes off."

Nathan realized one of his hands had wandered its way down to caress Tess's bottom while the other was headed down her shoulder about to curl around one of her luscious breasts. With a chuckle, he pulled back, turning to Tess's side, keeping her tucked close.

"Sorry 'bout that," he said, addressing the room. "Just damn glad to see Tess."

Nathan glanced down at Tess, seeing the blush staining

her cheeks. He shrugged, this time his smile just for her. He lowered his voice. "Feel free to surprise me like this every day," he said. Just looking into her eyes kicked his heart rate up a notch again.

Luke cleared his throat, quite obviously, as he stepped up to Nathan's side. "Thought you might appreciate a drink," Luke said, handing Tess a glass of wine. "Susie seems to think your preference is red wine."

Tess took the proffered glass. "Thank you. Red wine is perfect," she replied.

"Well now that you've remembered where you are, why don't you join us?" Susie asked slyly, waving from the kitchen table across the room.

Hannah shook her head as she glanced in Susie's direction and looked over towards Nathan and Tess. "Feel free to take a seat. We're about ready to eat," she said, lifting a bowl of salad with one hand. After delivering it to the table, Hannah and Luke bustled about getting plates out. Hannah went to check on John while Luke started serving the grilled halibut steaks.

Dinner passed quickly, Nathan encompassed in a cloud of elation and lust—solely derived from the presence of Tess. After dinner was over, Luke brought a still sleepy John down while they dawdled over a dessert of strawberry rhubarb pie. Nathan took his turn holding John to give Luke and Hannah a chance to eat undisturbed by the sleepy bundle that John was. Nathan took a sip of coffee, shifting John from one arm to the other, savoring the moment. As he looked around the table surrounded those who mattered most to him, he hoped Tess would realize how natural it was for her to be here. If she weren't here, her absence would be a glaring void for him.

Tess was deep in conversation with Susie, their two sets of curls leaned towards each other. "Trust me, you'll be able to keep busy here. I'm happy to make some introductions for you. As it stands, you can easily get some business from Anchorage…"

"What's that Susie?" Nathan asked, his interest piqued.

Susie looked up past Tess and grinned. "We're talking about Tess's options to keep herself busy with work in Alaska. That's what," she said pointedly. With a grin, she continued, "We've named her business here—Meant to Be. Get it? Whatever Tess is raising money for is meant to be. What do you think?"

Nathan's chest swelled. He hoped that meant what he thought—that Tess was seriously considering a move to Diamond Creek. He'd meant it when he'd told her he'd move wherever she would be if she'd give them a chance. But that didn't change the fact that he'd love to stay here in the place he knew was home. Susie cleared her throat. He belatedly realized he hadn't answered her. "It's perfect."

Tess turned to him. "We haven't had a chance to talk, but I'm hoping to move here. For now, it's a visit, but I need to figure out how to get my business started here. As you can see, Susie has all kinds of ideas," Tess said, a smile in her eyes.

Nathan shifted John again, curling his free arm around Tess's shoulder and leaning over to drop a kiss on her cheek. He looked across Tess's head to Susie. "Plan away," he said. "For once, I'm completely in favor of your bossiness."

Jared chuckled. "Watch what you wish for. Next thing you know, Susie'll be planning your daily schedule."

"I don't see why that should be a problem. In fact, maybe you should let me plan your life. You might have more fun," Susie said pointedly, sticking her tongue out at Jared.

Jared flushed and rolled his eyes. As he stood and started gathering plates, carrying them to the dishwasher, Susie and Luke continued the banter about who was bossier – Susie or Jared.

Tess nudged Nathan with her elbow. "Hope you don't

mind that I talked to everyone else about this before you," she said, her voice low.

"If what you're talking about involves you moving here, feel free to tell the whole world before you tell me. Just promise me that you won't back out. Didn't know what to expect from your visit, but this is as good as it gets," he said.

Tess giggled, her cheeks flushed. "I figured you'd be okay with this surprise. How much longer will we be here?" she asked, her eyes filled with heat.

Nathan glanced down at John who was sound asleep on his shoulder. "Just give me a chance to pass this little guy on and we'll get going. Don't think it's right for me to think what I am with John right here," he said ruefully.

* * *

As much as Nathan wanted to make their exit quickly, that's not how it happened. It was a good hour later before he was finally driving away, Tess seated beside him in the truck. Tess shivered. "Cold?" he asked, automatically reaching to turn up the heat.

"Just a little. It gets cold fast here once the sun goes down," she said.

"Definitely colder than what you're used to. Hope you brought some warmer clothes than what you had this summer."

Her curls bounced as she nodded. "When I talked to Hannah about surprising you, she reminded me it would be a bit colder than it was this summer. I would have guessed that, but I'll have to get used to it."

Nathan smiled, thrilled beyond belief to realize that she planned to get used to it. He reached across the console between the truck seats and rested his hand on her thigh, giving it a gentle squeeze. Now that they were finally alone, he could hardly think straight, his thoughts hazy with lust and love. He approached a stop sign where he would turn to head up the hill to the home he and Jared shared. Without a thought, he kept going straight after the stop, heading for the boat harbor in Otter Cove instead. He wanted Tess to himself for the rest of tonight.

Tugging his cell phone out of his pocket, he called Jared. "Hey man, spending the night on Iris tonight."

Jared chuckled. "Good plan. See you two tomorrow."

Nathan glanced over at Tess as he slipped the phone back in his pocket. "I want some privacy with you. Iris is our big boat, in case you forgot." At Tess's nod. "No worry because we've got heat on her. We'll have the cabin to ourselves."

He could have sworn she blushed, but it was impossible to tell in the dark. When they pulled up at the harbor, he practically dragged Tess down the docks onto Iris. Once they got inside the cabin, he moved quickly around, turning on a few lights and getting the small propane heater running. He stood from checking the heater to find Tess standing at the front of the cabin looking out over the harbor into the bay.

Coming to her side, he followed her gaze. The harbor glittered with lights from the docks and a few occupied boats. An almost full moon hung low over the mountains, its reflection rippling in the water.

"It's so beautiful at night," Tess said softly. She turned and looked up at him.

Nathan reached a hand under her chin, lifting it slowly. Bringing his lips to hers, he felt like he was coming home. It had been a mere two weeks since he'd flown away from North Carolina and yet the feel of her lips against his was like water to a parched man. He stepped closer, bringing her flush against his body, his arousal straining against his jeans.

In seconds, Nathan thought he might burst into flame. The heat between them was scalding. Their tongues stroked and tangled. Tess nipped at his lips, his neck and his ear. She tore his shirt open while he tugged her sweater over her head, her breasts spilling into his hands when he unhooked her bra, shoving it out of the way. He sucked his breath in sharply when she slid his zipper down and slipped a hand inside his boxers, curling around his cock. He was so close to the edge that he had to push her back.

"Tess..." he gasped. "I'm so close. Don't push me too fast."

Tess looked up at him, her ginger eyes bright in the dim light of the boat cabin. She stepped back, stroking a hand down his chest as she did, pushing him gently against the wall, his back to the windows they'd just been looking out. Holding his gaze, Tess used her other hand to free his swollen cock from his boxers. She knelt in front of him. Never breaking her gaze, she slowly licked her lips and leaned forward.

Licking her lips, she spoke. "Don't tell me what I can and can't do tonight. I missed you and we have all night."

Nathan attempted to catch his breath to reply. The only sound that came out was a long groan followed by, "Oh my god," when Tess stroked her tongue up his shaft and then closed her warm, wet lips around him. His head fell back against the window as she took him fully into her mouth, sucking and stroking. She cupped his balls lightly in one hand, curling the other around his cock to follow the rhythm of her mouth which moved in an alternating pace, slow then fast, fast then slow. The heat, the moisture, the suction and Tess's talented tongue pushed Nathan to the brink. Just as he thought he would burst, Tess pulled her mouth free. Nathan opened his eyes to meet hers, dazed out of his mind.

She kept stroking his cock with her hand, the tip just above her breasts, her nipples taut. "How about now?" she said, leaning forward one more time, bringing him fully into her mouth with a deep suction. As she dragged her mouth back up the length of his cock, Nathan couldn't hold back, liquid heat pouring into her warm mouth. Tess smiled, a wicked gleam in her eyes. With a last stroke, she stood and held her hand out. "Now you can tell me to pace myself," she said, grasping one of his hands and tugging him away from the wall.

Nathan turned her and pushed her back against the wall. "Now it's *my* turn." Pressing her against the wall, he laved one of her nipples, pinching the other and alternating between them. With his free hand, he slipped his hand inside her jeans, into her silk panties, past her curls and sank two fingers into her drenched channel. This time, it was Tess who gasped, her head falling back against the window.

He stilled his hand, his thumb resting just above her clit, the barest pressure against it. He could feel her pulse around his fingers and against his thumb. She opened her eyes and met his. His lips quirked. "I might just make you beg," he said.

Her chest rose and fell rapidly. "Okay," she replied softly.

Nathan just looked at her for a long moment, taking in the cloudy passion in her eyes, her swollen lips, her lush breasts, nipples at attention and glistening from his kisses. Leaning forward, he pressed his forehead against hers. "So glad you're here," he said, his lips moving against hers.

"Me too," she said in a soft pant. He pushed away, pulling her with him to the small master bedroom in the boat. It was utilitarian, but the bed was spacious and comfortable. They tugged off what was left of their clothes. Tess crawled onto the bed in front of him. He turned from kicking his jeans out of the way to be greeted with a view of her delicious bottom, her hips curving in an almost perfect heart shape. "Don't move."

She paused where she was and glanced over her shoulder. Nathan reached forward and tugged her hips back, lining her up with the tip of his cock. Without further delay, he parted her and sank into her heat.

Tess gasped and pressed her hips back into him. "Oh Nathan…Oh god."

He began to move, slowly plunging into her and sliding out, her warm, tight channel clenching around him. He was relieved he'd already had his first release because he had a semblance of control now, though barely. He reached a hand around, dipping into her curls to bring his thumb to her clit. With the barest of touches, she cried out, her orgasm rippling around him. Pulling out, he turned her and pushed her back onto the bed. In another second, he'd plunged into her again. As he leaned over her, the feel of her nipples against his chest almost made him lose himself again. He fought for control.

Tess lifted her knees and curled her feet around his back. Nathan grasped her hands and tugged them up beyond her head, holding each of her hands in his. "Tess…look at me."

She opened her eyes, meeting his. Her chest rose and fell, her breath coming in uneven gasps. "Missed you…so much…" she said.

Nathan leaned closer, bringing his lips to hers. "Me too…" he said, pulling back to plunge deeply into her. Between her drenched heat and the lingering pulses from her orgasm, he thought he might explode, but this time he wanted her with him. He leaned over and nipped one of her nipples, sucking sharply for a moment. Tess arced against him, crying out as she tumbled over the edge again. He followed in a burst, falling against her as his orgasm reverberated through him.

Shifting to her side to keep his weight off of her, Nathan lay still, trying to catch his breath. When he opened his eyes, he saw a lone tear slide down Tess's cheek. He wiped it away. "Hey, you okay?"

She opened her eyes and turned to him, nodding. "That was a happy tear."

He chuckled. "Just checking."

Her eyes sobered. "We haven't had much of a chance to talk, but let me just say this now. I'm here to be with you. I just want to make sure you know that's exactly why I'm here." She took a shaky breath. "I wasn't expecting *this*..." she gestured between them "...but I love you. So I decided to follow that feeling."

"I'll follow you if you'll follow me," Nathan replied. "Damn glad you're here to be with me because I love you too. Just wasn't sure how long I'd have to wait."

EPILOGUE

ess walked up the steps to the house and fumbled with the kitchen door, losing hold of one of the too many grocery bags she held. "Dammit," she said when several oranges tumbled out of the bag, bouncing down the steps into the grass. As she leaned over trying to collect what was left of the broken bag of groceries, the door opened.

"Nice to see you too," Nathan said.

Tess turned to look up over her shoulder from where she knelt on the steps to find herself being greeted with Nathan's dangerous dimples and those navy blue eyes filled with laughter. She shifted from kneeling to sit on the steps, laughing as she did.

"Overestimated how much I could carry," she said with a sigh and a shake of her head. Brushing her curls out of her eyes, she watched as Nathan stepped past her, quickly gathering the escaped oranges. In another few moments, he'd carried all of the groceries inside. Tess followed him in and helped get the groceries put away. When Nathan took a phone call, she stepped onto the back deck, which faced the bay. It was late May—her first spring in Alaska. In the past few weeks, she had been startled to see how the barren ground after winter exploded with growth. The days were already long and the extra sunlight gave anything green a burst of power growth. The yard was covered in thick grass with wildflowers already in bloom in some parts of the field beyond the grass.

The air was cool, much cooler than it would be in North Carolina this time of year. Shivering, she scanned the view, boats dotting the bay, some moving in and out of Otter Cove Harbor. The mountains were still snow-tipped, but their lower flanks were rich green now. Tess glanced over her shoulder when she heard the door open. Nathan came to her side, slipping an arm over her shoulders.

"That was Simon," he said. "They're about to board the plane from Anchorage. We should head to the airport in Homer to pick them up in about an hour. You ready?"

Tess giggled and shrugged, a bubble of anxiety rising. "Guess I'd better be."

Nathan turned her to face him, searching her eyes. "Are you having second thoughts? 'Cause it's a little late for that," he said, his serious gaze tempered with a teasing glint.

Tess shook her head firmly, her curls bouncing in the crisp breeze. "No. No second thoughts. Just a little nervous though."

Nathan leaned forward and gave her a thorough kiss before tugging her inside. Her parents, along with Simon, Jordan and a few close friends from North Carolina were flying in for their wedding tomorrow. This would be in addition to Nathan's parents who had just arrived yesterday. Despite her mother's plea to arrive sooner, Tess had held firm to having them show up no sooner than the day before the ceremony. She simply didn't think she could tolerate the whirlwind of planning that would ensue if her mother, Deanna and the Diamond Creek contingent had time to plan together. In return, she and Nathan were planning a brief Alaskan honeymoon in a secluded cabin in Tutka Bay before returning for her family's extended month-long visit. Nathan had suggested they plan a second tropical honeymoon next winter, to which Tess had readily agreed. While she'd thoroughly enjoyed her first winter in Alaska, she could easily see how much she would *love* a tropical vacation when the days were darkest and coldest.

Jared had decreed that she and Nathan would live in the house that all three brothers had once shared. Although Tess had hesitated, Jared had merely given her one of his no-nonsense looks and proceeded to pack up and move out into a small rental home just down the road. He'd declared it ridiculous for him to stay in the large house on his own. For the next few days, their home would be bursting at the seams with guests and activity.

MOONLIGHT REFLECTED on the water in the bay. Tess leaned against the boat railing, her wedding dress rustling in the soft ocean breeze. The wedding and reception were over, and she felt nothing but relief, joy and a thrumming anticipation. They were spending the night on Iris before taking the smaller boat to Tutka Bay to stay in what Nathan promised her was a luxurious, private cabin, complete with a hot tub beside a glacier fed pond. She took a swallow of champagne. Turning at the sound of footsteps, she took in the view of Nathan as he walked toward her. He'd discarded his navy suit jacket, his shirt was unbuttoned and untucked, his muscled chest in view and just delectable, as always. He held a glass of champagne and raised it to hers, stopping just in front of her. "To you, for being the most amazing woman I ever met. I'd have followed you anywhere, but thank *you* for following me here. If there's one thing I figured out, it's that I can't live without you, so..." he paused and swallowed. Tess clinked her glass against him and tugged on his shirt to bring him close enough for a kiss.

"Thank *you* for not letting me get away," she said, her lips curving in a smile against his.

"Oh, you brought out the persistent in me," he replied.

Tess leaned back, taking another sip of champagne, before turning in Nathan's arms to look out over the water. They'd planned their wedding for a full moon and the weather had fulfilled its promise. The sky was crystal clear, stars winking above the mountains, and the moon round and full over the bay. The air was cool and salty with a hint of the warmth to come. They turned in unison at a sound of something surfacing in the water. Between the moon and the harbor lights, they could see a seal's head bobbing in the water alongside the boat. Whether or not it was possible, Tess thought it must have been the seal that followed her along the beach last summer after her first kiss with Nathan.

"Do you think...?" Tess asked.

Her curls shifted against the shrug of Nathan's shoulders and soft rumble of laughter in his chest. She closed her eyes with a sigh, savoring the pulse of desire that leapt when his lips came against the back of her neck in a soft kiss.

* * *

Thank you for reading Follow Love - I hope you loved Tess & Nathan's story!

For more steamy, small town romance, Trey & Emma's story is next in Love Unbroken. Emma comes to Alaska, hoping to leave her past in the dust. Trey is a widowed father, most definitely not looking for love. Desire burns like wildfire between them, while the ghosts of Emma's past chase her. Don't miss Trey & Emma's story!

Keep reading for a sneak peek!

Be sure to sign up for my newsletter for the latest news, teasers & more! Click here to sign up: http://jhcroixauthor.com/subscribe/

Chapter 1

*E*mma closed the back of her truck after putting a cooler inside and leaned against the side. It was just past five in the morning, and she was waiting for her friend Susie to meet her. She glanced at her tiny cabin for a long moment. Just looking at it made her smile. It was tiny and whimsical – a cedar sided A-frame with a bright green roof and purple trim, complete with a purple star at the point of the A-frame. It sat in a small open area amongst spruce and alder. The hill tumbled down behind it, offering a wide-open view of Kachemak Bay. She'd been in Diamond Creek, Alaska for almost three years.

The sun was rising behind the mountains across the bay, streaks of gold and pink reaching into the sky and filtering through the wispy clouds that sat above the mountains this morning. The air was cool and crisp, typical for an Alaskan summer morning. When the sun was high, the chill would dissipate. A faded blue Subaru pulled into the driveway. Susie climbed out of her car, grabbed some fishing gear and walked to Emma's truck.

"Morning! Sorry I'm late," Susie said. Emma reached over and took a fishing rod out of Susie's hands.

Susie was her sister's best friend and had become a dear friend to Emma. Emma couldn't help but smile at Susie. She was a petite bundle of energy and enthusiasm. Susie's head almost reached Emma's shoulder as she barely topped five feet, and Emma was just shy of six feet. Susie had warm brown eyes and unruly brown curls, which were pulled back into a ponytail this morning.

Emma lifted the window to the back of her truck and placed Susie's gear in the back. "You're not late. We said sometime before five fifteen. How's it going?" Emma asked.

Susie tossed her bag in the truck and looked over with a grin. "I'm ready to catch some fish! Promise we can get coffee at Red Truck on the way by though."

Emma nodded. "Of course. How could we not?"

* * *

"OKAY, so why are we going to Homer to fish when we could just as easily fish in Diamond Creek?" Emma asked from the backseat. She and Susie had met her sister Hannah at the harbor parking lot for the drive to Homer. Emma took a sip of her coffee, savoring the rich flavor.

"Because Homer has the Fishing Hole," Susie said as if that explained everything.

"What's the big deal with the Fishing Hole?" Emma asked in return.

Hannah turned to look over her shoulder from the passenger seat. "It's a man-made fishing hole that's stocked with kings, pinks and silvers. It's a fishing dream if you want to stock up on salmon. That's why we're going. It's not quite as fun as dipnetting, but it's close."

Emma nodded, thinking for a moment. She'd quickly learned that the words king, pink, red and silver related primarily to salmon in Alaska. Though she'd been in Alaska several years now, she'd yet to enjoy every possible fishing or outdoor activity because the options were extensive. "So how come every town doesn't have a fishing hole?"

Susie and Hannah shrugged in unison. "Who knows? Maybe because Homer has an ideal spot. The Homer Spit is an easy place to do what they did. It sticks so far out into the bay. There's nothing like it anywhere else in Alaska. So when we want to get a jumpstart on salmon, we go to Homer. Dipnetting fills the rest of the freezer after that."

As Susie drove and kept chatting with Hannah, Emma watched the landscape roll by. Homer was roughly an hour south of Diamond Creek. Homer was another tourist draw in Alaska, dubbed the Halibut Capital of the World. Emma was accustomed to the jaw-dropping views in Alaska, but had yet to lose her amazement. The highway hugged the coastline with view after view of mountains, a few glaciers and beautiful ocean vistas. Occasionally, an eagle or moose would make an appearance. Today, they'd already driven by a mother moose and her calf nibbling on alders by the road.

Not much later, Emma lugged a cooler in one hand with a fishing pole in the other. While she'd become proficient at fishing, she was by no means an expert. She hadn't even had to buy her own equipment because Hannah's husband and his two brothers ran a guide business. They geared her up the first summer she arrived. The Fishing Hole on the Homer Spit was a sight to behold. For starters, the Homer Spit was a narrow 'spit' of land that jutted four and a half miles into Kachemak Bay. The road on the Homer Spit was the longest road into ocean waters in the world. Driving out onto the Spit felt like driving on a bridge, except that it was a narrow expanse of land. Arriving at the Fishing Hole, Emma was startled at how busy it was. Parking was a competitive sport. Every inch of shoreline that surrounded the Fishing Hole was filled with people.

Emma had no idea how they'd manage to find a place to fish, but she gamely followed Susie and Hannah. As they approached the shoreline, Emma discovered that space was to be had among the constant shifting of the crowd. In minutes, she geared up in her waders and dropped a lure in the water. The next hour passed in a blur. According to Susie and Hannah, silver salmon were their goal for today and between them, they caught two apiece in short order.

Emma lifted her fishing rod to cast again and felt a tug on the line. She froze.

"Hey! That's my hat!"

Emma turned, scanning the cluster nearby to find the source of the voice. Her eyes landed on a small boy with stick straight brown hair, holding a baseball hat that appeared to be attached to her fishing lure. She was relieved to see that he was laughing and looking up at a man beside him, so she assumed he wasn't hurt. She walked over, carrying her fishing pole.

"Hey there, I think I may be the one that caught your hat," Emma said with a smile.

The little boy tilted his head back to look up at her. Emma looked down into his eyes, a rich brown with gold flecks.

"Dad, she caught my hat!" the boy said, almost gleefully. He seemed overjoyed at the accident. Emma was just relieved he hadn't been hurt.

The man the boy spoke to had his back to them when Emma walked over. He turned, and Emma's heart leapt. The boy's father was tall with dark hair flecked with silver and had the same chocolate brown eyes as his son. When he looked down at his son, a grin flashed across his face. When he saw Emma, his gaze shifted quickly to a more serious, almost austere look. His features were strong and sharp, his eyes intelligent and probing. Emma wished for his smile to return. With those eyes and that smile, all she felt was a primal pull. Her stomach fluttering and pulse skittering, she didn't speak.

Befuddled, it took Emma a moment to realize that she was staring and hadn't said a word. The man, whose mere presence had reached into the center of her and grabbed hold, walked closer and held out his hand. "Hello there, I'm Trey."

Emma's hand moved of its own accord. She thought for sure anyone nearby would see the sparks that struck when he clasped her hand, but no one appeared to notice. "I'm Emma," she replied.

Trey gave her hand a firm shake, holding on perhaps a moment too long, his eyes questioning. "Looks like you caught Stuart's hat," he said when she didn't say anything else.

Emma finally brought her attention to the moment though her heart was beating so hard she worried he might be able to hear it. "I guess I did. I'm sorry. I was trying to cast carefully."

Stuart looked up from fiddling with the fishing hook caught in his baseball hat. "There's way lots of people!"

Trey's smile returned. Emma realized she finally understood what it meant to swoon because she feared she might just do that. She had to pull herself together and *now*.

Trey glanced down at Stuart. "How about you hand me that hat? Don't want you catching your fingers on the hook," he said.

Stuart handed the hat over, immediately looking back up at Emma. "Have you ever caught a hat before?" he asked, his smile made more endearing by the missing tooth in front.

"Not that I know of. I'm just glad your hat is all I caught."

"No harm done. I'd bet something that's not a fish gets hooked here every day. It's so crowded," Trey said. He glanced up as he finished working the hook out of the hat. "There you go," he said, handing the lure back to Emma.

His fingers brushed hers, the barest touch eliciting another jolt within Emma. She felt hot all over, a blush heating her as it bloomed on her neck and face.

She didn't want to walk away and had no idea what to say. For a second, she thought she saw an answering flare in Trey's eyes, but he shuttered it quickly, that serious look returning.

"Thank you," Emma finally said.

Silence lengthened between them, broken by Stuart's enthusiastic voice. "Dad, can I catch one more fish before we go?" he asked. He walked to the small cooler nearby and peered into it.

Trey held Emma's gaze for another moment before finally breaking away, glancing over his shoulder toward Stuart. "One more and that's it," he replied.

Turning back to Emma, his lips quirked in an almost smile. "Stuart loves to fish. He'd stay here all day every day if I let him."

Emma nodded politely, the wheels of her mind turning, wondering who Stuart's mother was, wanting desperately to know more about Trey and realizing she needed to get a grip. She looked back up into Trey's eyes. Her blush just wouldn't quit. She forced herself to speak. "Well, nice to meet you. Glad Stuart's hat is okay." Lifting her hand in a polite wave, she started to walk away.

Trey's voice halted her steps. "Nice to meet you too."

Emma turned back, that flare she thought she'd seen in Trey's eyes definitely there this time, his eyes darker and brighter. Flustered, her words stumbled. "Oh...okay." She turned away, almost running back to where Susie and Hannah were fishing.

Her face still flushed, Emma quickly got her line back in the water, appreciating the bustle around her.

"So you hooked Stuart Holden's hat, huh?" Susie asked. Susie was situated on the shore between Emma and Hannah.

"Sure did. It was an accident—obviously," Emma replied.

"Stuart's dad is one of the best pilots around. He runs a wilderness flightseeing business and also has a law practice on the side," Susie said with a wink.

"Oh god, no. He's a lawyer?"

Susie gave her an odd look. "Yeah, not sure why that's a bad thing. They moved to Diamond Creek about a year after you did. I don't know Trey well, just as an acquaintance. Even though they've lived in Diamond Creek for a while now, he's not out and about much."

"I'm glad my hook only landed in Stuart's hat," Emma said, her blush returning just thinking about Trey.

Emma felt Susie look toward her. She hoped Susie didn't notice how flushed she was.

"Wow, you are blushing. What does that mean?" Susie asked slyly.

Emma tried and failed to un-blush, which only flustered her more.

"I think you might have noticed that Trey's a bit handsome. Trust me, you're not the only one. He's widowed and has his share of women drooling over him. I mean, he's hot, he's a pilot, and he's prime marrying age at forty. Rumor is that he moved to Diamond Creek to start his flightseeing tours because he's a single dad now and needed more time with his son. I guess he used to be pretty busy doing the lawyer thing in Anchorage. The only reason you haven't heard about him is that he's not seen in public enough to blip on the gossip radar," Susie said with a chuckle.

Emma heard only that Trey was widowed and her mind was off to the races, prodded by the undeniable pull she felt toward him. She didn't even notice she hadn't bothered to respond to Susie.

"Hannah, your sister's gone gaga over Trey Holden," Susie said, leaning in front of Emma to catch Hannah's attention.

Hannah was busy reeling in another silver salmon and glanced over with a wide smile. "You don't say?"

"Oh my god, Susie. I met the man for maybe three minutes. I will admit he's handsome, but I'm not gaga," Emma retorted.

"Coulda fooled me. As soon as I told you he was widowed, you were in fantasyland over there."

Emma's blush deepened. After a moment, she gave in and laughed. "Think whatever you want," she remarked.

Susie's curls shook with her laughter. Hannah glanced over to Emma as she placed the silver salmon she'd caught in their cooler. "Good luck. Once Susie's on the scent, she's hard to shake. If you want her to stay out of your business, you'd better play your cards close."

Emma shrugged. "It's okay. I can deal with nosy friends. Just don't go and embarrass me in front of him," she warned.

"Fat chance of that. Like I said, he's not around much. If you do have the hots for him, you have your work cut out for you," Susie replied. Her gaze sobered. "I don't think I've ever seen Trey without Stuart at his side. I don't know for sure, but I heard his wife died from some heart problem. He doesn't seem too interested in a relationship."

Emma absorbed the information Susie provided and looked over to where Trey and Stuart were standing. He was bending over to help Stuart untangle his fishing line. Susie let her off the hook from further teasing, and Emma found herself strangely disappointed because she didn't get to hear more about Trey.

Within the hour, they were jostling for space at the

cleaning tables. Before they headed home to Diamond Creek, she got one more view of Trey when she saw him walking with Stuart, Stuart's small hand clasped in one of his hands and a cooler in the other. The sparks he elicited were so strong she couldn't ignore them. She wondered if she'd completely lost her mind. At thirty-four, she'd written off any chance of a relationship after her first marriage ended, which had been nothing short of a disaster. She hadn't counted on anyone making her second guess herself.

AVAILABLE NOW!
Love Unbroken

GO HERE to sign up for information on new releases: http://jhcroixauthor.com/subscribe/

<u>Stay With Me</u>

<u>When We Fall</u>

<u>Hold Me Close</u>

<u>Crazy For You</u>

Into The Fire Series

Burn For Me

Slow Burn

Burn So Bad

Hot Mess

Burn So Good

Sweet Fire

Play With Fire

Melt With You

Burn For You

Crash & Burn

Swoon Series

This Crazy Love

Wait For Me

Break My Fall

Brit Boys Sports Romance

<u>The Play</u>

<u>Big Win</u>

<u>Out Of Bounds</u>

<u>Play Me</u>

<u>Naughty Wish</u>

Shameless Southern Nights (with Ali Parker)

Down & Dirty #1

Down & Dirty #2

Down & Dirty #3

ACKNOWLEDGMENTS

It's safe to say this book would never have been written without the unconditional support of my husband. A hero who stole my heart, he also comes up with catchy names in each book. I'll leave it to my readers to see if they can discover his contributions. My mother gets extra kudos for helping with all things tech and so much more. This book was taken to the next level with excellent editing by Laura Kingsley. She pushed me to make this story the best it could be.

I remain honored to receive such amazing and kind support from readers. Last but not least, a bow to Alaska – a wild and lovely place. My decade-plus there was phenomenal. Alaska will always hold a piece of my heart.

xoxo

J.H. Croix

ABOUT THE AUTHOR

USA Today Bestselling Author J. H. Croix lives in a small town in the historical farmlands of Maine with her husband and two spoiled dogs. Croix writes contemporary romance with sassy women and rugged alpha men who aren't afraid to show some emotion. Her love for quirky small-towns and the characters that inhabit them shines through in her writing. Take a walk on the wild side of romance with her bestselling novels!

Places you can find me:
jhcroix.com
jhcroix@jhcroix.com

www.ingramcontent.com/pod-product-compliance
Lightning Source LLC
Chambersburg PA
CBHW032106180726
48284CB00002B/477